TOYING WITH CHILDHOOD

This book studies the dialectic relationship between the image of the child and the toy in literary depictions of childhood in 19th- and 20th-century Anglo-American fiction. Drawing from the psychoanalytic theories of Sigmund Freud, Anna Freud, D. W. Winnicott, and Sudhir Kakar, it analyses themes such as the heterogeneity of childhood and the construction of the ideals of childhood. It explores the linkages between the ideals of childhood in Britain and its travel to America and further dissemination in British India. It discusses the established tropes of childhood such as innocence, a formative period, the centrality of play, and the presence of a toy to argue that the mores of childhood are culturally constructed and lead to the reification of a child into an image of perfection. The author problematises the notion of essential innocence and discusses the repercussions of such stereotypes about childhood. The work also highlights parallels between the ideals of childhood established in 19th-century Britain and the portrayals of postcolonial Indian childhoods in 20th-century Indian English literature.

Toying with Childhood will be useful for students and researchers of education, childhood studies, psychology, sociology, literature, gender studies, and development studies. It will also appeal to general readers interested in cultural perceptions of childhood, literary depictions of children, and the works of Sigmund Freud.

Usha Mudiganti teaches English at Ambedkar University, Delhi, India. She has designed and taught courses in children's literature, British and American literature, and literatures of the Indian subcontinent at the undergraduate, postgraduate, and research levels. Her research interests include the study of childhoods in literature, gender studies, psychoanalytic theory, and popular culture studies. Her interest in the study of childhood began during her master's degree in English at the University of Hyderabad, India. In her MPhil dissertation at the University of Hyderabad, she highlighted the lack of substantial depictions of girlhood even in *bildungsroman* novels with girl protagonists in late Victorian and Early Edwardian England. She obtained her Ph D in 2007 from the Department of Humanities and Social Sciences, Indian Institute of Technology, Delhi, for her thesis on the reification of childhood in Anglo-American literature of the late 19th and 20th centuries. Her latest publications include 'Through the Lens of Childhood: Kipling's Claim to India' in *Kipling in India: India in Kipling* (2021), Eds. Harish Trivedi and Janet Montefiore, 'Virangana', in *Keywords for India* (2020), Eds. Rukmini Bhaya Nair and Peter Ronald deSouza, and '"Et tu, Brute?":' The Child Soldier and the Child Victim in Shobasakthi's *Traitor*' in *Childhood Traumas: Narrative and Representations* (2020), Eds. Kamayani Kumar and Angelie Multani.

TOYING WITH CHILDHOOD

Tracing the Child–Toy Bond from
Britain and America to India

Usha Mudiganti

Routledge
Taylor & Francis Group

LONDON AND NEW YORK

First published 2022
by Routledge
2 Park Square, Milton Park, Abingdon, Oxon OX14 4RN

and by Routledge
605 Third Avenue, New York, NY 10158

Routledge is an imprint of the Taylor & Francis Group, an informa business

© 2022 Usha Mudiganti

British Library Cataloguing-in-Publication Data
A catalogue record for this book is available from the British Library

Library of Congress Cataloging-in-Publication Data
Names: Mudiganti, Usha, author.
Title: Toying with childhood : tracing the child-toy bond from Britain and America to India / Usha Mudiganti.
Description: Abingdon, Oxon ; New York : Routledge, 2022. |
Includes bibliographical references and index. |
Identifiers: LCCN 2021043164 (print) | LCCN 2021043165 (ebook) |
ISBN 9780367480875 (hardback) | ISBN 9781003093275 (ebook)
Subjects: LCSH: English literature--19th century--History and criticism. |
English literature--20th century--History and criticism. | Indic literature (English)--19th century--History and criticism. | Indic literature (English)--20th century--History and criticism. | American literature--19th century--History and criticism. | American literature--20th century--History and criticism. | Children's literature, English--History and criticism. | Children's literature, Indic (English)--History and criticism. | Children's literature, American--History and criticism. | Children in literature. | Toys in literature.
Classification: LCC PR468.C5 M83 2022 (print) | LCC PR468.C5 (ebook) |
DDC 823.009/3523--dc23/eng/20211129
LC record available at https://lccn.loc.gov/2021043164
LC ebook record available at https://lccn.loc.gov/2021043165

ISBN: 978-0-367-48087-5 (hbk)
ISBN: 978-0-367-55389-0 (pbk)
ISBN: 978-1-003-09327-5 (ebk)

DOI: 10.4324/9781003093275

Typeset in Sabon
by Deanta Global Publishing Services, Chennai, India

For

Baba, Amma, Sudhir, and Purnayya

because they believe in the efficacies of talking

CONTENTS

PREFACE

I embarked upon an academic exploration into childhood when I was a young adult. Over more than two decades of sustained engagement with childhood studies, I have learnt much about the slipperiness of definitions and categorisations of human phases and conditions. I have come to realise that all that can be said with any certitude about childhood is that laws set the ages when a child ceases to legally be a child in different societies during different epochs. Everything else concerned with childhood is practised and gets codified in consonance with the changes in perceptions of childhood in cultures.

During the final work on this book, I was acutely aware of the changes happening to childhoods in contemporary times when global resources are focused on battling the virulence of a virus. While writing the final drafts of this book during a long summer of 'lockdown' in a corner house of an urban upper-middle-class residential society in the national capital of India, I took sporadic breaks by walking on the attached terrace. During these walks I would wonder how the children of the neighbourhood were coping with being cooped inside urban apartments. I wondered what they were playing at or playing with, probably without playmates, sometimes without siblings, and most disconcertingly – how come I barely heard the voices of the many children in my neighbourhood. The lives and the childhoods of children in seemingly normal, presumably well-provided families were silently changing during these times of staying indoors for many months. Would I dare to allow my thoughts to move to the social inequities that children too experience, and would I be able to think deeply about the various challenges faced by children who do not have immediate access to food, shelter, personal safety, and health or live in families that cannot or do not provide these basic requirements of life? What about the children who have lost their primary caregivers during this global pandemic? While there would be a reasonable expectation of global interventions by nation states to provide some basic requirements to ensure that children who have suffered grave personal losses have a healthy childhood and hope to have a life of dignity, the immediate work at hand for all those who work with children would be to try to comprehend the changes children are experiencing in the norms of childhood. Under such circumstances that demand a renewed gaze at children and childhoods, it would not be out of place to remind ourselves that the mores of childhood are constructed by cultures. The changes in the ways of childhood become immediately evident in institutions like families and are incorporated within schools and other spaces developed with a pedagogical intent to civilise the child.

During the course of my research in childhood studies, I have realised that the belief in the 'innocence' of children and the perception of childhood as a formative stage of human life have remained constant from the 17th century onwards in Western civilisations. In India, the 'recognition' of these two constants of childhood is seen in the late 19th century but it cannot be traced to have originated within the culture during a particular epoch due to many unique aspects of Indian civilisation. Along with the antiquity of Indian civilisation and its having been an oral culture – in which transmission of knowledge happened through *sruti* and *smriti* for aeons and carrying within it the inherent acceptance of orality's multiple moments of incursions, inflexions, and interpretations – contemporary Indian society holds centuries of multiculturalism and multilingualism in its expressions of postcolonialism. Therefore, it cannot be confidently said that childhood in India was ever perceived to be a monolithic, homogenous experience across regions, social groups, and genders. However, the two notions about children – that they are innocent and in need of training to integrate them into civilised society – are widely prevalent even in contemporary Indian culture, literature, practices, and policies that are connected with children and childhood. The final chapter of this work attempts to understand the presence of these 'Western' ideas of childhood in contemporary India through an examination of the origins of these notions and their iterations through Anglo-American literature of the specific period when legislations for Indians, including children, were formulated in Britain.

In the early stages of the research that finally led to this book, it was observed that the depiction of childhood in literature and other cultural texts usually associates play and plaything(s) with childhood. Therefore, the first exploration was to examine the deep bond between the child and the toy in order to understand adult perceptions of the essentials of the experience of childhood. While conducting this exploration, it was noticed that there were significant differences between the portrayals of childhood in the literary texts written for adults and those written for children even when the protagonists of these texts were children and/or the narrative was focused on childhood. Considering that both the varieties of literary texts about childhoods were constructing and disseminating portrayals of childhood and that my research was largely focusing on the literary genre of fiction, the two varieties were placed under a larger category labelled as the Fiction of Childhood.

This work proceeds by foregrounding the child–toy link, focusing on those works in the Fiction of Childhood in which there is the presence of an object that is treated as a toy in the story. Furthermore, connections are made with the reification of the child into an image of perfection and the role of the child established during the Victorian age, as an adorable, simpering, protected being, whose task was to add warmth to the private world of the Home. This move draws attention to the similarity between the child–toy relationship and the parent–child relationship in Anglo-American literature of the late 19th and early 20th centuries and later literature as far afield as India, which came to be influenced by Victorian stereotypes of childhood. It is hoped that this work will add to the studies of childhood that will look at childhood more from the perspective of the child rather than that of adults, thereby increasing sensitivity towards childhood.

During the two decades of research that formed this book, I have been helped by many people in various ways and I take this opportunity to thank the people whose help was crucial for this book to take shape.

The kernel of this work was formed and much research for it was conducted during my years as a doctoral scholar at the Department of Humanities and Social Sciences of the Indian Institute of Technology, Delhi, under the supervision of Professor Rukmini Bhaya Nair. I am very grateful to Professor Nair for the enthusiastic discussions through which we realised that we never imagine a childhood without a toy or playtime and for her incisive guidance that shaped my early arguments on the child–toy link in literature.

I wish to express my immense gratitude to Professor Sudhakar Marathe, who set me off on the path of academic explorations of childhood with his thorough guidance during the research and writing of my MPhil dissertation at the Department of English, University of Hyderabad and for quoting Shakespeare to me when I shared my early thoughts that eventually became the crux of this work.

My first attempts at reading Sigmund Freud's *Interpretation of Dreams* were noticed by Dr Shiva Kumar Srinivasan who not only was kind enough to point out the standard editions that are used for an academic engagement with Freud's work but also guided my early forays into understanding Freud's theories. I am extremely thankful to him for initiating me into the study of Freud which became the basis for my analysis of depictions of children in literature. More recently, I gained more knowledge about Freud's work from informal conversations, class discussions, and public lectures by the following colleagues from the School of Human Studies of Ambedkar University, Delhi, whom I wish to thank: Professor Ashok Nagpal, Professor Honey Oberoi Vahali, and Professor Anup Dhar.

My colleagues and a few former colleagues from Ambedkar University, Delhi, continuously encouraged me to persevere with this work. I wish to particularly thank Professor Alok Bhalla, Professor Suchitra Balasubhramanyam, and Dr Diamond Oberoi Vahali for some stimulating conversations about this research and wish to express my gratitude to my colleagues, current and former, among the English faculty of the School of Letters and the School of Undergraduate Studies, Ambedkar University, Delhi, for making kind enquiries on the progress of this work.

I also wish to thank my research scholars and many batches of students of my MA course, Literatures of Childhood, and my BA course, Written for Children and Young Adults, for invigorating discussions that continuously refresh my academic engagement with childhood studies.

This research would not have been possible without the support of the staff of the following libraries: the central libraries of Ambedkar University, Delhi, and the Indian Institute of Technology, Delhi; Indira Gandhi Memorial Library of University of Hyderabad; the library of the Osmania University Center for International Programmes, Hyderabad, which granted me a summer fellowship in June 2002 when it was the American Studies Research Center, Osmania University and immensely facilitated the early research for this work; the Goethe Institut Library, Delhi; Sahitya Akademi Library, Delhi; the British Library, Delhi; and the American Library, Delhi.

This book would not have seen the light of day if it were not for Ms Lubna Irfan, Ms Anvitaa Bajaj, and the editorial team at Routledge India who steered this work through the unpredictability of a global pandemic. I am truly thankful for their patient professionalism.

I am immensely thankful to my friends – Bidisha Fouzdar, G. Sampath, Nilesh Jahagirdar, Rakesh Chaudhary, and Shanti Nanisetti – each of whom spared the time to thoroughly read and give honest comments on the respective chapter I requested them to review, thereby giving me the confidence to complete this work.

I am deeply thankful for the constant support and encouragement I receive for all my academic endeavours from my family: Shri M. V. Krishna Rao, Dr M. Ramadevi, M. Sudhir Rao, and M. Purnayya Rao.

1

INTRODUCTION

A *living doll*. These young women were born to be trophies, fully accessorized Oscar-Barbies.

Salman Rushdie. *Fury*. 2001. 72

Childhood is a complex and engaging phenomenon that every adult has experienced, but many of those experiences are mostly forgotten in the course of growing up. In their interactions with children, even as writers for children, adults usually treat childhood as a formative period of human life instead of accepting it as just a phase of human life. This reductive approach towards childhood allows for adults to access the experientially inaccessible realm for them to have seemingly meaningful interactions with children. One of the significant repercussions of this approach towards childhood is that it simplifies the complexities of childhood for those adults who set out to deeply examine childhood. Many adults, including those engaged in childhood studies, tend to create comforting 'fictions' about the phenomenon of childhood. Every serious bit of writing about childhood, in the form of fiction or a record of a study of childhood, therefore, generates a few more 'notions' about childhood. These 'notions' of childhood not only help adults in coming to terms with the forgotten phenomenon of childhood but also helps them in creating childhoods. These 'notions', on gaining acceptance and currency in societies turn into the 'norms' of childhood for that society in those times.

The changes in the imagery of childhood from its 'discovery' in the Western world in the middle of the 16th century to the present time suggest that perceptions of childhood are formed anew in each epoch. This cultural construction of childhood is significantly influenced by the dominant ideas of the period and is informed by the specificities of the culture within which it is being formed. Children, being in a position of dependence due to reasons of biology, economics, and cultural practices, among others, cannot remain oblivious to the 'notions' adults have about them. A significant aspect of civilising the child into society has involved leading the child into

DOI: 10.4324/9781003093275-1

1

performing the 'norms' of childhood. Fiction, poetry, songs, games, and toys, which have a dialogic relationship with literature and culture, help in disseminating these 'norms' of childhood. There are some serious repercussions to the perpetuation of a set of 'norms' that seemingly comprise childhood. One of the first outcomes of widespread dissemination of such norms is that a sense of a homogeneity of the experience of childhood gains traction. Once the idea of homogeneity of childhood is more or less accepted in a culture, much of the work done by many social institutions, such as families, schools, and governments, gets geared towards nurturing and educating children into bringing up every child into an ideal being composed of all the 'norms' of childhood. The creation of an ideal of childhood leads to a harmful homogenisation of childhood, which makes it difficult for adults who work with children to remain cognizant of the uniqueness of each childhood. Not only does every aspect of childhood get measured through set metrics; it is also expected that nearly every child is trained to attain the ideal of perfection. Chris Jenks suggests that: "[b]eing a child, having been a child, having children and having to relate to children are all experiences which contrive to make the category available as 'normal' and 'natural'" (1982, 12) and posits that this awareness is "organized around the single most compelling metaphor of contemporary culture, that of 'growth'" (12). Further he argues that "the physical signs of anatomical development are taken to be indications of a social transition, so that the realms of the social and the natural tend to be conflated" (12). Jenks arguments indicate that the conflation of the social and the natural leads to a homogenisation of the experiences of childhood. An entrenched belief in uniformity of childhood experiences across cultures and epochs facilitates the emergence of the myth of a perfect ideal of a universally acceptable image of a perfect childhood and a perfect child. Jo-Ann Wallace argues that English colonial imperialism in the 19th century and much of the resistance to it in the 20th century became "thinkable" (171) due to their common "investment in the figure of 'the child' and [in] an idea of 'the child'" (1994, 171), suggesting that a universalisation of childhood allows for the treatment of children "as human raw material" (180), which Wallace reiterates is "the necessary precondition of colonialist imperialism" (180), thereby indicating that the figure of the universal child was a potent trope of colonisation. Wallace goes on to conclude that the "site of 'childhood'" (180) becomes a space to return to for postcolonial scholars due to its "explanatory and an emancipatory potential" (180), therefore, suggesting that 'the child' and 'the site of childhood' could become discursive spaces for postcoloniality.

This work, however, attempts to focus on the impact of the construction of the universal child and the depictions thereof in literature and culture to foreground the eventual reification of children into a perfect image. The thesis of the reification of the child into a representation of perfection will be explicated through an examination of a few works of fiction that were influential portrayals of some 'notions' of childhood. These literary works depicted – or examined – the creation and perpetuation of ideals of childhood in the 19th century in Britain. Most of these British ideals of childhood travelled in that period to the United States of America and India through literature, cultural practices, and educational policies, influencing the mores of childhood in these three societies.

A significant aspect of childhood shared by these societies, from the 19th century onwards, is the presence of a bond between childhood and toys. By examining this crucial bond between the child and the toy in fictional depictions of childhood, this work establishes that 19th-century British ideals of childhood lead to a conflation of the ideal of the child with the depiction of the ideal as a toy. It is hoped that the study will be relevant in understanding the formation of the dominant 'myths' of girlhood and boyhood in the Victorian age and the effect of these myths on 20th-century girlhood and boyhood in India. This was the period during which the British Empire had colonies around the world. By the middle of the 19th century, Britain had large colonial holdings in the Indian subcontinent through the British East India Company. These parts of British India were being governed by laws that were passed in the British parliament for execution on the people of colonial India, without centring the cultural practices of the land during the decision-making process. With the transfer of power from the East India Company to the British crown after the failed Indian rebellion of 1857, law and governance for the newly consolidated colony of British India were handled by the imperial government without the mediation of a trading company. This led to a greater dissemination of 19th-century British notions of conduct through the enactment of laws pertaining to education, marriage, inheritance, and many other civil and criminal matters throughout British India. Most of these matters were earlier conducted through conventions and traditions of different communities within the large and culturally diverse subcontinent. These legislations lead to a homogenisation of conduct across sociocultural categories. They were also instrumental in perpetuating notions of ideals of another culture in a society with a completely different cultural history. However, as will be demonstrated later in this work, the effects of large-scale colonisation could be seen in changes in the cultures of the colonising as well as the colonised. While British laws affected many changes in the lives of Indian children of the 19th century, the ideals of childhood in Britain were far from unaffected by the new kinds of knowledge developing in Britain. Some of these changes in British cultural mores could be ascribed to Britain's engagement with the various cultures in its colonies.

In Britain too, the 19th century was a period of unprecedented social and familial change. The reign of Queen Victoria coincided with the aftereffects of the Industrial Revolution. The latter had become a driving force of sociocultural changes in Britain and its colonies across the globe. The effects of the Industrial Revolution were spreading through most of the European and American continents too. Large-scale and rapid production of goods was a significant factor in the virulent expansionist endeavours of many European nations, leading to multiple territorial wars among European nations in continents such as Africa, Asia, and South America, with the dual purpose of procuring raw materials for their factories and markets for the sale of the finished products of their factories. English society was restructuring itself to adjust to the changes brought about by the Industrial Revolution and the expansion of British colonial holdings to all the continents of the world. These changes in the fortunes of the British Empire affected every stratum of society. The landed gentry became richer after having invested in new kinds of trade, including in British holdings in the English colonies in Africa, America, and Asia. The landless poor started doing various kinds of work that was different from what they were used to before large-scale industrialisation. During these times of transition from an agrarian economy to an industrial one, a newly emerging class of society started being recognised as the middle class. The middle class mostly comprised the newly emerging salaried people in the new urban areas of England. Simultaneously, the expansion in trade and increase in income was enhancing the standard of living among a large part of the population of England. Many English people from the upper classes could afford to abstain from working for a living. Thorstein Veblen called this the 'Leisure Class' in *Theory of the Leisure Class* (1899). This leisure class was chiefly involved in the development of the newly emerging disciplines like sociology, anthropology, and psychology. They were also making new discoveries in the natural and physical sciences. Moreover, the expansion of the English Empire contributed to – as well as generated – the need for new kinds of knowledge. The Victorian people had to come to terms with significant changes in their lives and also had to comprehend the knowledge arising from discoveries in the natural, physical, and social sciences. For instance, Victorians witnessed an intense theological debate that arose after Charles Darwin published the *Origin of Species* in 1859.

Coming to terms with the changing worldview was in itself quite a daunting task for the Victorians. Along with comprehending the changing worldview, Victorians also had to bring about serious changes in their households to work efficiently in the new economy. In an agrarian economy, people mostly worked on their own farms and/or households, and some of them also worked on other people's farms or in other households. The practice of many people gathering in one place for the mass production of one kind of product was thus historically new. Moreover, people had to structure their lives around the timings of the factory. People also had to come to terms with the urbanisation of large parts of England. Large-scale migration to these towns was also witnessed. In an agrarian economy, trade intermingled with family life, as almost all members of the family participated in it, whereas this was not possible, in most families, after the Industrial

Revolution. After large-scale industrialisation in England, the economic structure in many families changed in such ways that it increasingly became the practice that the men worked outside the home to earn a living while the women and children did not work towards making money. The world of trade and commerce, which was largely incomprehensible to most of these people, was considered a cruel and stressful world. As a result, the Victorians found it necessary to create a private space that was not 'corrupted' by the world of commerce. Jose Harris suggests that recent studies by historians and sociologists debate on the centrality of the family and wonders whether the family was "an emotional power-base whose support enabled individuals to cope with traumatic social change" (61) or whether it was a "forcing ground for psychic tensions and disorder" (61–62). The family gained a new kind of importance for the Victorians, and the changes in familial structures affected the personal and professional life of the people of those times. Raymond Chapman pointed out in *Forms of Speech in Victorian Fiction* that the "sexes were segregated for much of the time, from schooldays to the withdrawal of women at an agreed point in a dinner party" (140) even as late as the last decade of the 19th century, while there were growing public discussions on women's right to vote. He states that influential public intellectuals, such as John Stuart Mill and Benjamin Disraeli, supported women's right to vote, while Victorian fiction continued to present women "as uninformed about public affairs, accepting their ignorance and receiving with docility the expressed views of men" (141). Furthermore, he argues that the speech of women and children in the fiction written during that period reiterated their perceived roles in the family as upholders of purity, spirituality, and innocence.

A nostalgic longing for 'innocence' was seen in the literature of the period, and many social endeavours tried to preserve this 'innocence' wherever they could do that. 'Home' became a private sphere where the 'cruel' world of commerce had not made its way, and women and children became its guardians. In *The Victorian Girl and the Feminine Ideal* (1982), Deborah Gorham has described this phenomenon as the "cult of domesticity, an idealised vision of home and family, a vision that perceived the family as both enfolding its members and excluding the outside world" (4). The role of the woman in the new middle-class household became that of an upholder of tradition and a preserver of the 'innocence' that the Victorians increasingly felt the loss of in their contemporary times. In *Silent Sisterhood: Middle-Class Women in the Victorian Home* (1975), Patricia Branca says, "[t]he middle-class woman in the Victorian period was a new phenomenon, in a sense the first modernised woman (1)". Branca elaborates:

> Disparaging images besiege [the middle class woman]. She is often depicted as the "*doll-like*, bread and butter miss swooning on a

sofa", the frivolous, irrational, irresponsible creature of whim, the devotee of fashion, and of course, "the virgin-in-the-drawing-room", the strait-laced, thin-lipped prude, who blushed at such suggestive words as "legs". With these stereotypes predominating, her life has been dismissed as a "mass of trifles".

(6, Emphasis added)

Branca has further argued in her book that these women's lives were not the "mass of trifles" they were believed to be, but that they had empowered themselves in their new roles and brought about a significant change in Victorian households. However, Jane Lewis in *Women in England: 1870–1950* (1984) has argued that the "cult of domesticity" made the middle-class woman less empowered than the working-class woman. Lewis states:

> Lydia Becker, a leading Victorian feminist, compared the position of middle class women unfavourably with that of working class women: 'What I most desire, is to see married women of the *middle class* stand on the same terms of equality as prevail in the working classes and the highest aristocracy. A *great lady* or a *factory woman* are independent persons – personages – the women of the middle classes are nobodies, and if they act for themselves they lose caste!'... Becker was rebelling primarily against the idea that the middle class woman should be 'kept', if not by a husband then by a father, brother, or other male relative.

(75)

Britain's imperial enterprise affected its women in other ways, too. Many young men went to work in the British colonies, and women outnumbered men in Britain, leading to a marked increase in the number of single women. Claudia Nelson notes that the 1851 census "listed more than 1.7 million spinsters and nearly 800,000 widows, over half of the adult female population of Britain" (2007, 15). These circumstances also led to discussions on the role of women in the Victorian social structure. Towards the end of the 19th century, the 'Woman Question' was intensely debated in the cultural press in Britain and in North America. These engaged discussions on the 'Woman Question' involved finding a suitable role for women within the new structure of their society, training large numbers of women to fit into their roles, and finding a role for the women who could not adjust in this redefined role due to circumstances or choice.

Along with women, children too were supposed to make the 'Home' a pleasant haven for the Victorian Man, who would return home after battling the cruel world of commerce. Gorham remarks,

[b]oth male and female children were of importance in idealisations of family life, but daughters had a special significance. Sons would help to determine the middle-class family's place in the world, but daughters could offer the family a particular sort of tenderness and spirituality.

(5)

These emerging roles for children within many Victorian families led to a new focus on childhood in 19th-century British society.

Many sociocultural changes during those times too brought about changes in the way childhood was perceived. Children had traditionally helped in farming and other home-based work, but the Industrial Revolution brought drastic changes in children's contribution to work. With the industry becoming the mainstay of the economy of Europe, there was a shift from marking time by observing the movement of the sun to clock-time. People started following 'industrial time' in most places of work and in most cases, much of the day's work was done in factories. This eventually led to a change in the perception of children's presence in work spaces. Undoubtedly, working away from home was more strenuous for children than working in familiar surroundings. Prior to clock-time, the work hours were rather flexible. This was not the case after standardised working hours were adopted by all factory owners. Additionally, most of the new work spaces engaged children in new kinds of work that were perceived to be hazardous. Due to such reasons, among others, children's presence in the workforce was seen to be problematic by many sections of the British intelligentsia. Given the conditions of work, it was in the interest of children to ban their involvement in monetised work, which started being called 'child labour'. In the second half of the 19th century in Britain, child labour was reduced drastically after a multi-pronged struggle involving thinkers, writers, researchers, and activists to highlight the plight of children in the new workforce. The consequences of this reduction were complex. While the laws ensured that children no longer actively and seriously contributed to economic activities, this change also made children completely economically dependent. Although it is true that children of some strata of society were more or less completely economically dependent on their guardians for a few centuries prior to these socioeconomic changes in the nation, most children in British society before the Industrial Revolution earned some money as workers or helped the family in earning money through trade. During the reign of Queen Victoria, most British children were firmly moved, through the passing of a series of Factory Acts and Education Acts, from the bracket of producers to that of consumers.

While the child seems to have gained spotlight in 19th-century British society as a family resource that needed to be nurtured and trained to fulfil designated roles within families, it was definitely not the first epoch to intensely discuss the child as a member of society. There were many works discussing the presence of the child in European and American society, from the middle of the 17th century onwards. Philippe Aries in *Centuries of Childhood* (1960; English trans. 1962) posits that childhood as a separate phenomenon of human existence was first recognised among the upper classes of French society in the 17th century. This 'discovery' of childhood in the West in the 17th century has also been heavily contested among scholars of childhood studies. Nevertheless, Aries's work remains important on account of his thesis that the child gained prominence as an entity meriting notice by adults for the first time among the upper classes of 16th-century French society. Aries mentions family correspondence among the upper classes of France in the middle of the 16th century, in which the child is being discussed as a being to be cherished and trained into the ways of adult societies in spite of the lurking threat of high infant mortality. Towards the end of the 17th century, the child was seen to be a *tabula rasa*[1] that could be trained to fit into social roles determined by adults, due to John Locke's influential work *An Essay Concerning Human Understanding* (1690). By the 18th century, the child seems to have become the subject of much attention in Europe and North America, in religious literature, social debates on policy and governance, and literary works. In France, Jean Jacques Rousseau published *Emile*, a treatise on education, in 1762, in which he laid out the processes to be used to educate the child for integration into civilised societies without losing the innate goodness children were believed to be born with. With the publication of the *Lyrical Ballads* (1798) and the *Preface to the Lyrical Ballads* (1800 and 1802), the influential Romantic Movement in English literature started and led to the creation of the Romantic Child who was deemed to be the 'father of man' by Wordsworth (1802). By the middle of the 19th century, the work of 'civilising' the child into the cultural mores of human societies was in full swing in the West. Towards the beginning of the 20th century, in a huge stratum of society in Britain and North America, the child became a well-fed and much-pampered person with little autonomy. The reification of the child into an adorable, innocent, cherubic being had reached such proportions in Britain that growing up into adulthood was seen as a fall into a world of sin.[2] During the first half of the 20th century, the impact of the theories of Sigmund Freud on the significance of childhood in the emotional lives of adults brought about significant changes in the by-then established perceptions of childhood in the Western world.

The history of childhood, which will be delineated in greater detail in the second chapter, shows that one of the chief reasons for interest in childhood was the belief that it was a formative stage of human life. However, there are at least some studies of childhood that recognise it as a phenomenon that generates intellectual interest independent of it being 'a formative period'. Also, there are studies of childhood that do not generate comforting 'myths' about this phenomenon. For instance, John Holt's *Escape from Childhood: The Needs and Rights of Children* (1975) is an attempt at observing children without any preconceived 'notions' about childhood. Each of these varied studies of childhood ultimately affects children in various societies and brings about changes in the perception of adults towards children, thereby forming and transforming the phenomenon of childhood. At the same time, the now widespread recognition that most kinds of childhoods are essentially different from most kinds of adult experience also led to a 'cult of the child'. This cult of the child, a phrase coined by Leslie Fiedler in 1958 to describe the focus on the child in contemporary societies, introduces some more 'norms' of childhood. An almost universally accepted 'norm' that has remained an important 'marker' of childhood from the late 18th century onwards is that the child is innately an innocent creature. Childhood, therefore, is believed to be an idyllic stage of life. This dominant comforting myth about childhood has had such a serious impact on Western thought that the literature about childhood written in the 19th century more often than not reflects this belief. A period of bliss is usually believed to be one where there are no serious difficulties, whereas any significant depiction of childhood in literature, or any careful study of childhood in society, shows that children do face many challenges on a regular basis. This is the conflict at the heart of much of the significant fiction about childhood written in the 19th century, as this work will try to show.

The much-used descriptor used for childhood, as mentioned above, is that it embodies innocence. The term 'innocent' draws immediate associations with law and religion. One is deemed innocent if one has not transgressed the barriers set by law or religion. In most societies of the present times, children do not have to deal with the law of the State, except in a few exceptional circumstances. However, children have to be extremely careful to not transgress the laws set by their parents. In many depictions of childhood, one comes across children struggling with the 'laws' imposed on them by their families. For instance, Ernest in Samuel Butler's *The Way of All Flesh* (1903) finds it extremely difficult to meet the very demanding standards set by his parents. On the other hand, literature written for children usually depicts children breaking rules and emerging as winners. One of the chief attractions of children's literature for child readers is the ease with which the child characters in some of these novels transgress the set rules without doing themselves any serious harm. If one were talking of 'innocence' as antonymous to 'law-breaking' in terms of the rules of conduct set for children to follow, then one can safely say that no child is or can be absolutely innocent. However, the term 'innocence' as used in the context of childhood in Western thought crucially signifies sexual innocence. Up to the early years of the 20th century, much of Western literature and culture persistently represented the child as an asexual being. As a symbolic representation of the prelapsarian man, the child was representative of the 'purity', 'innocence' and 'immortality' that man had lost before being driven out of the Garden of Eden, having 'fallen' from grace into disgrace. While William Wordsworth's *Ode on Intimations of Immortality from Recollections of Early Childhood* (1806) was one of the most influential literary documents expressing this particular perception of childhood in the early 19th century, William Blake had already covered the spectrum of these representations of childhood as 'innocence' before the 'fall' into the evils of the world and remarked on society's intervention in ruining this perceived innocence through the poems in *Songs of Innocence and of Experience* (1794).[3] On Wordsworth's influential poem, Peter Coveney states in *Poor Monkey: The Child in Literature* (1957) that, "[t]he Ode became undoubtedly one of the central references for the whole nineteenth century in its attitude to the child. It is indeed of the utmost significance that the most intense emotion of the poem is one of regretful loss" (41). Adults, who believed that they had 'lost' this 'innocence' wanted to preserve it in children. With the publication of Sigmund Freud's 'Three Essays on the Theory of Sexuality' in 1905, this belief in the 'innocence' of children was shaken. Freud's theories on infantile sexuality were not at all well received, except within a small group of medical practitioners. Even his group of followers were not prepared to accept the implications of having to consider the child as a sexual being.

Along with making a significant dent in the notion of the innate innocence of the child, Freud's work also foregrounded the uniqueness of each individual's experience of life. Although Freud's theories emerged from Hellenic knowledge systems and he worked with literary and cultural tropes of 19th-century Europe to treat his patients, mostly upper-class Europeans, Freud posited a theory of mind that overturned the basis of Western rational discourse. Through his theories on human sexuality, Freud displaced the centrality of *cogito ergo sum* in the formation of cultural knowledge anchored in a rational framework to foreground the irrational realm of feeling as significant for the formation of the self that engages with social norms. His work on human sexuality radically highlighted that each individual reacts in unique ways to seemingly similar life events. This recognition of plurality in the outcomes of life experiences not only increases the scope to challenge engagements with childhood through set parameters of norms, metrics, and measures but is also useful to foreground the heterogeneity of childhood. However, Freud's theories retain traces of established Western beliefs on femininity and feminine behaviour. Although Freud's theories on infantile sexuality and femininity will be detailed in the next chapter, it is important to note here that he worked to understand female sexuality for close to four decades. In his multiple attempts to understand female sexuality, at least two of Freud's discussions of the development of female sexuality revolve around a girl's interaction with her doll.[4] Apart from the fact that the girl–doll relationship has created industries that generate millions, one of the most important thinkers of Europe seems to have unquestioningly accepted this link between a girl and her doll to conflate one with the other in his study of femininity.

10

Many people who work closely with children – or in the domain of childhood studies – view the toy as a useful prop to enter the forgotten existential terrain of childhood in their diverse intellectual and cultural engagements with childhood. Although biological childhood is a universal phenomenon, few adults appear to retain detailed and specific memories about the emotions and experiences of childhood. Therefore, while engaging seriously with childhood, an adult feels the need for a tool to enter the realm of childhood. The ubiquitous presence of the toy in the literature of childhood facilitates the use of a toy as a peg to study the territory of childhood. Toys are used as a tool or key to enter the area of childhood with the belief that all children, irrespective of socioeconomic barriers, possess, create, and play with toys. In addition to this belief, it can also be said that the toy is such a powerful prop holding up the 'ideology of childhood' that the toy often becomes a signifier of childhood. Brian Sutton-Smith, who clearly states at the beginning of his work, *Toys as Culture* (1986), that it is his intention to "make it clear that toys are matters of considerable cultural importance, not just something that children play with" (12), does not define the toy. However, he begins his work by summarising the various passionate reactions parents and other people who care for children have to the commercialisation of toys and the promotion of toys that are supposed to be harmful to the cultural development of children. Sutton-Smith declares that toys play an essential role in the acculturation of children and refers to Roland Barthes's dismay, in 'Toys' (1957), at the world of toys replicating material possessions of adults and leading the child into identifying itself as an owner and not as a user. He also bemoans the lack of serious studies connecting the toy with play in the study of childhood. For the purpose of this work, any object used as a plaything or created by the child or an adult with the purpose of playing is considered a toy; especially on account of the observation that apart from the toys given to children by adults, many children create toys of their own from everyday objects available in their surroundings. Considering that one of the most powerful tools to keep up the illusion of childhood as a blissful period of human life is the toy, it is possible to draw an analogy between the child–toy interaction and adult–child relationship within the fiction of childhood. The child's play with the toy gives the toy a personality, at least for the child.[5] There are many representations of the relationship of love and care the child has for a plaything or a toy; however, one rarely comes across depictions of this relationship that suggest that the child consistently thinks of a toy as an autonomous object.[6] However, the toy almost ceases to be a toy when there is no child to play with it. It might become a display object, but if no one plays with it, the object cannot really be described as a toy. The toy, the child, and the idea of play are so inextricably linked that it is as difficult to think of a childhood without a toy as it would be to think of a childhood without playtime. Media reports often record that toys are sent with food and clothes in disaster-struck areas. This shows that the toy is considered absolutely *essential* for childhood in contemporary times.

In addition to the toy, which is also called a plaything, play is also considered a marker of childhood in most cultures. In fact, play is seen to belong to the realm of childhood to such an extent that any extended display of playful activities by adults is often negatively connoted as 'childish' behaviour. Although one of the most important philosophical explorations of the element of play in culture by Johan H. Huizinga titled *Homo Ludens* (1944, English translation 1949) begins with the declaration in the foreword: "For many years the conviction has grown upon me that civilization arises and unfolds in and as play" (n. p.) and goes on to call play "a distinct and highly important factor in the world's life and doings" (n. p.) and posits that, "play is to be understood ... as a cultural phenomenon" (n. p.), the playful continues to be perceived to belong to the realm of childhood. Even this exploration that aims to "integrate the concept of play into that of culture" (n. p.), associates play with childhood in its examples of play and the playful. Sutton-Smith, positing the centrality of play to the experience of childhood, sets out to define play and states:

> In sum we metaphorize play as bathos, and we define it as primitive and paradoxical communication, schematic expression, and a succession of disequilibrial bipolar states, with their own rules, sequences and climaxes.
>
> (141)

Scholars of childhood studies in areas such as education and psychology have gainfully linked play with childhood and toys, to understand this stage of human experience.[7] Sutton-Smith suggests that the "expression in play relies much more on the communication of internal states than upon the appreciation of external representations" (139) and sums it up with:

> the main business of play is to be a *paradoxical* form of communication and expression. Playing house is not meant to be real housekeeping. A toy car signifies that it means a real car, but certainly not what a real car means. One can pretend to be driving a car, but one can hardly get inside the toy car and take it to the market.
>
> (139–140)

Furthermore, Sutton-Smith points out the "ambivalent relationship between play and life" (140) and suggests that the process of play "constantly generates conflicts within its boundaries" (140). While Sutton-Smith goes on to theorise that play generates a structural equilibrium, the significance of

Sutton-Smith's theorisation on play for this work is that it recognises the child's awareness that play is pretence. Lois R Kuznets summarised Jean Piaget's theory on play as exploration in the process of cognitive development in *When Toys Come Alive* (1994). Kuznets notes, "of special significance seem [Piaget's] observations of how a child first 'plays' itself in pretend games, then projects its behaviour (or that of others) onto toys or other objects, and finally pretends to be other human beings" (37). Kuznets interprets Sutton-Smith's argument about play as "paradoxical communication" as play is "exciting and fake dangerous because it tests the limits without meaning to break through them—although, by accident, it sometimes does" (42). She goes on to suggest that:

> Sutton-Smith's definition of play also puts it for me in the area of liminal behaviour discussed by anthropologists like Victor Turner, who point out that many older societies provide times and places for 'carnival' at which an individual may cross the usual societal boundaries—sexual and otherwise—without danger of being cast out. Such behaviour does not involve exploratory learning or problem solving, nor even the use of the individual imagination. All these activities—for which children and adults use those objects called toys—Sutton-Smith calls a "primitive form of symbolization of underlying motivations".
>
> (43)

Although Sutton-Smith and Kuznets use Jean Piaget's work to theorise on play and this work attempts to deliberately separate the use of play for observing child development from the significance of play for childhood, the theorisations on play by Piaget, Sutton-Smith, and Kuznets are crucial for the current work. The work of these people clarifies that: play is central to childhood; toys are an important presence in play; "imaginative play" (Kuznets, 1994, 46) is regularly observed among children; play can be a means of acculturation; and play can be carnivalesque in transcending social rules without causing significant damage to children. All these observations regarding play are the entry point for this work to explore the intricate linkages between childhood, play, and the toy.

While summarising the practices of childhood in various cultures across the globe, the two things James Marten (2018) identifies as constant markers of childhood from prehistoric to contemporary times in most cultures are toys and depictions of children at play. Not only does he mention a rubric from the 1300s which identifies the first phase of life as "the age of toys" (3) but also notes that the evidence of children being buried with toys in prehistoric cemeteries is an indicator of parental affection for the child during those times. Furthermore, he states:

Finally, one of the constants in the lives of children everywhere and in all eras, quite simply, is that they played. Archaelogists have found clay and stone balls from the Neolithic period in China, while toy-carts and animal-shaped whistles dating back to at least 1500 *bce* have been found in archaeological digs in the Indus Valley. Egyptian tomb paintings and Greek urns show children playing with toys or one another, while Plato recommended play as a way to socialize and educate children (although only under a teacher's supervision). Tuareg children in the North African desert, Wampanoag children in New England woodlands, Manchu children in northern China, and youngsters living in the teeming cities of medieval Europe, in the early-twentieth-century United States and in twenty-first century Asia all played versions of tag and hide-and-seek, as well as games involving running, jumping, throwing and tackling. The games all had their own names and the rules, such as they were, often differed. But from the beginning of human communities they have lightened days burdened by work or hardship, expended pent up energy, and nurtured competition and leadership.

(6)

Although Marten ends with a caveat that this commonality in the experience of childhood should not lead to a universal reduction of the perception of childhood, across cultures and epochs, as a romantic and innocent phase of life, he also declares that, "it does remind us that children have been children since the beginning of time" (6). Not only does this contradict his stated position that childhood has always been a social construct, thereby always heterogeneous; but Marten also presents three 'constants' of childhood – toys, play, and education – as recurring motifs of childhood across centuries and cultures.

Much of child development theory and practice bases itself on the importance of play in the life of children. Play, quite often with toys, is an important tool to measure growth parameters by psychologists, and child therapists often use toys and play to communicate with children. While acknowledging that play is definitely an important aspect of childhood and that children often use toys to play, this study makes careful use of the concept of play and the concept of the toy to highlight the ways these essential tropes of childhood work in literary depictions of childhood. The aim of this work is to argue that the ideal of childhood in literary representations of the child reduces the child to images of perfection that can easily be mistaken for symbols of perfection, like dolls. Therefore, scholastic work in the area of child development that uses concepts of toys and play to mark growth patterns of children is deliberately not included in this work. The drawing of parameters to track child development also works with a model of childhood that

14

comes across as being homogeneous across cultures. However, there are many studies of childhood by historians, sociologists, anthropologists, and practitioners of various forms of psychology that indicate that childhood is heterogeneous and that each experience of childhood is unique.

Nevertheless, as stated in the beginning, the truism that every child has a toy of some sort to play with is fully accepted in this study. Not only has the toy become a signifier of childhood in many cultures; it also has become one of the many tools used to 'civilise' children. Although the first record of toys in any human civilisation shows that all children played with similar toys irrespective of their sex, many studies show that, by the late 19th and early 20th centuries in Britain and North America, children, by and large, played with gender-specific toys. In fact, one of the 'uses' the toy was put to was 'engendering' the child. Writing during the middle of the 20th century on French social mores, Roland Barthes remarks in *Mythologies* (1957) that French toys are designed in a way that naturalises the adult world for the child and prepares the child to unquestioningly accept set gender roles through play with gender-specific toys (1970, 53). A brief look at the history of toys also reveals the scale of the project of training children into their gender roles as adults in their contemporary societies. Dolls as toys were available only in the later period of the Egyptian civilisation and the Greek and Roman civilisations. According to Karlewald Fritzsch and Manfred Bachmann in *An Illustrated History of German Toys* (1978), during the early days of civilisation, doll-like figures were used for religious purposes. But Fritzsch and Bachmann also agree that a "child's initiation into human society is reached through a true affection for her dolls". Doll houses were used as a means of providing domestic instruction to girls in the 17th and 18th centuries in Europe. In *Toys and Dolls for Collectors* (1973), Eileen King noted that, by the 19th century, thousands of toy-making firms were established in Europe and America, increasing the mass production of toys. King also records that the Great Exhibition of 1851 in London had a children's section that was focused towards improving the learning skills of children. One of the popular toys being exhibited for the first time in that exhibition was a sewing machine.

This civilising project and perpetuation of stereotypes of childhood through toys continues in contemporary literature and cultural practices. There are countless examples in literature and in the life of a disgruntled girl being told that she should play with a doll because that is the 'right' toy for her. Undoubtedly many girls enjoy playing with dolls but that does not necessarily make it the inevitable toy for a girl. However, the doll is so firmly linked to girlhood that almost everybody who engages with childhood in any way has to encounter this linking of girlhood with dolls. Penny Colman records the birth of the first girl born to English parents in Roanoke Island in Virginia in 1587 (2000, 27). Colman mentions that the girl was named Virginia Dare and also includes a detail of a water-colour painting made in 1585 by Virginia's grandfather, John White, in which a sparsely clad Native

American child is depicted holding a doll that looks like a miniature English lady in her hands. This detail could be an imaginative projection of a colonial endeavour or a faithful representation of an early settler's observation of an actual instance of play. In any case, it is a depiction of an intermingling of cultures through a child's play and the linking of a girl's play with a representation of an adult figure of a woman as early as the late 16th century.

During the course of this exploration of the link between the child and the toy, many novels written about childhood, primarily for adults and those especially written for children, were read. Although there are marked differences in both the style and the content of the novels written for these two different sets of readers, they are linked by their focus on childhood. Therefore, throughout this study, all such writing is broadly categorised as the 'fiction of childhood'. Despite this deliberate move to include two kinds of fiction within one category, the essential differences between literature written *for* children and that written *about* childhood were not overlooked. The need for the study of narratives focusing on childhood, irrespective of the target readers, was felt due to the distinct differences in the ways in which both subgenres contributed towards the construction of childhood. Nevertheless, both these subgenres were equally crucial in the reiteration of the norms of childhood in that specific period. Literature written for adults not only informs but also reflects the perception of childhood in the period. Literature written for children reflects the perception of the childhood of the writers of this subgenre of fiction and also works as a tool to 'civilise' children who are the target group of this subgenre. Additionally, both the subgenres perpetuate the notions of childhood that make it easier for adults to interact with children. However, the often detrimental impact of these notions on the lives of children is largely ignored. In the late 19th and early 20th centuries in Britain and the United States of America, girls were treated as animated dolls or had to 'dollify' themselves to be accepted as 'good' girls. The reverberations of this powerful construction of gender are witnessed in the fiction written in English in India by women writers even towards the end of the 20th century. The last three chapters of this work deal with these aspects in greater detail.

The girl–doll link is not specific to Britain and America. The Norwegian playwright, Henrik Ibsen, through his play *A Doll's House* (1869), exposed this girl–doll link as a strong cultural norm that distorts the lives of women. There is evidence of it in 20th-century literature in English in India too. In Attia Hosain's *Sunlight on a Broken Column* (1961), Laila is given a doll by a carpenter whom she had requested for a bullock cart. While Laila is gently pushed towards mainstream ideas of girlhood through a gender-specific toy in Hosain's novel, in Kamala Das's short story titled 'A Doll for a Child-Prostitute' (1977), the childhood of the girl prostitute is supposedly 'recovered' through the gift of a doll by her client. Not only does one see many contemporary children's books with doll-stories written by Indian writers but also innumerable books of doll-stories by Enid Blyton are available in bookstores and libraries in India. In fact, a strong implication of this ubiquitous presence of Enid Blyton's books in India would be that a large number of children in India read her work and are influenced by the cultural stereotypes in her books. Moreover, Indian children have been regularly seeing illustrations of blond-haired, blue-eyed dolls, and have also been receiving such dolls as gifts for many decades now. It is unlikely that children in India would often come across people with a combination of blond hair and blue eyes; yet, the image of the perfect 'doll-girl' in India seems to have remained frozen in colonial times and culture. The recent plethora of novels about girlhood in India reveals, among many other things, that the 'proper' girl was an Indian version of the Victorian 'angel in the house' until the middle of the 20th century in India. The last chapter of this book will trace some of these links.

As one cannot consider the large body of stories written about the child–toy relationship across cultures, this study confines itself to some works of fiction written in English in Britain, the United States of America, and India during the late 19th to late 20th centuries. The late 19th century saw an unprecedented amount of writing for children in Britain and in America. In Britain, the period from 1895 to 1915 was later dubbed the Golden Age of Children's Literature.[8] Publishing for children in Britain and in America was very closely linked in this period. During the Golden Age of Children's Literature, not only were the books published for children in Britain transported across the Atlantic but the thematic trends in writing in both the countries too overlapped. While this was true of the two major English-speaking countries, this was also the period when India was under British colonial rule and educational policies and school syllabi for Indian children were formulated in Britain, discussed in the British parliament, and implemented in India.[9] The legislative policies for India were passed in the British parliament by elected representatives of the people, presumably reflecting the needs and desires of the majority in Britain. The dominant ideas that formed British society in that period were reflected in these policies. Moreover, Indians associating with the British, as employees of the British government or as businessmen, desired to imitate the ruling class. Along with many other kinds of long-lasting sociocultural influences, literature in India was seriously influenced by the dominant ideas in Britain. At the same time, British society too underwent many changes due to its global empire. As argued by Gauri Viswanathan, English studies in Britain is an 'aftereffect' (2015, xii) of its emergence as a necessary part of the school curriculum in the British colonies in Africa and Asia. With school curriculum being standardised through the establishment of a school board in Britain in the middle of the 19th century, it became easier to homogenise childhood experiences across classes in schools. The training of boys in public schools also promoted an ideal of British masculinity that would eventually be carried by them to the British colonies through the imperial services. Commenting on the close coordination between the public schools and the imperial services in late 19th-century Britain, Asa Briggs states:

Reform in the public schools and reform in the civil service had always been closely associated; in both competitive examination played its part, but in both the ideal of the gentleman remained predominant. Reform of the school, it was believed, would lead to reform of the service, and reform of the service would lead to reform of the school.

(168)

While Asa Briggs was specifically elaborating on Thomas Hughes *Tom Brown's Schooldays* (1965), much of 19th-century fiction of childhood also propagated ideas of ideal masculine and feminine behaviour through diverse narratives of the child at school as well as the child in school. In the next few chapters, this work will examine the formation and perpetuation of ideals of gendered childhoods and its repercussions on childhoods in Britain, North America, and India in the late 19th and early 20th centuries.

Notes

1 Although Locke himself did not use the phrase to describe the state of an untrained mind, the phrase gained currency through many discussions of Locke's ideas on education.

2 This idea recurs in many works focused on children and young adults throughout 20th-century Anglo-American literature from Peter Pan's escape from growing up into adulthood in J. M. Barrie's *Peter Pan* (1904) to Holden Caulfield's cynical dismissal of worldly ways and persistent attempts to perpetually preserve children in a state of 'innocence' in J. D. Salinger's *The Catcher in the Rye* (1951).

3 The compiling of the two books together places the songs of innocence and experience in a seemingly chronological manner and lends the poems to a study of the chimney sweeper's rapid movement from innocence to experience on account of the exploitative and hazardous work a child did for sustenance.

4 The play of a girl with a doll and Freud's interpretation of the child's activity did not undergo much change between his 1931 essay titled 'Female Sexuality' and his essay on 'Femaleness' in the *Introductory Lecture on Psychoanalysis: New Series* (1933).

5 This phenomenon is noticed in many early 20th-century British books for children such as A. A. Milne's series of books involving the relationship between Christopher Robin and his stuffed toys, especially Winnie-the-Pooh. It frequently recurs in the ever popular series of children's books by Enid Blyton making this interaction one of the most well-known aspects of childhood among adults in large parts of the English-speaking world.

6 An exception to this is the popular American cartoon series *Calvin and Hobbes* by Bill Waterson in which Calvin seems to deeply believe that he does not fully know or comprehend various aspects of his stuffed tiger Hobbes's life. However, Hobbes is depicted as an inanimate stuffed toy in frames where there are adult characters, even in instances where Calvin is ostensibly playing with Hobbes, suggesting the idea that toys come alive only for the child who plays with them.

7 The toy is used quite frequently to measure development metrics by developmental psychologists who work with children. Child psychotherapists also often use the toy and a child's play with it to reach the child's unexpressed emotions.

18

8 The term was first used by Roger Lancelyn Greene in a 1962 essay with that title to describe the peak of publishing for children in Britain from 1895 to 1915. Greene's use of the phrase 'The Golden Age' is also a tribute to Kenneth Grahame's 1895 novel with that title.

9 While the Charter Act of 1813 initiated policy-level interventions by the British in the education of Indians and Macaulay's Minutes started the process to introduce English as the medium of instruction in schools in India, the Indian Education Policy Report of 1913 gives details such as allocation of funds to schools that solely used English as the medium of instruction; the moral education of children, teaching ethics, and developing the personality of the student; and the development of pedagogical material to be used in the schools funded by the British government in India.

2

CONSTRUCTING CHILDHOOD

In its origin, the doll was not a thing in itself but a representation.
Salman Rushdie. *Fury*. 2001. 73

Childhood as a distinctive state of human existence is recognised in every sphere of contemporary cultural productions. However, it is believed that its recognition as a distinct phase of sociocultural life in the Western world was first made in European societies only in the middle of the 17th century. In his influential work on childhood, *Centuries of Childhood* (1960), Philippe Aries delineates the manner in which the distinction between adults and children crystallised in the middle of the 17th century. Aries notes that faint traces of the awareness of the difference between a child and an adult can be noticed from the 13th century and that from the 14th century onwards a tendency to express the special nature of childhood in art, iconography, and religion is evident. However, Aries notes that before the middle of the 17th century, one of the important markers to announce the end of childhood was to dress the child in miniature versions of adult clothing as soon the child was considered too big for swaddling clothes. Aries argues that soon after this change in attire, the child was also integrated into the ways of the world of adults. He records that boys from the upper classes of French society were the first ones to be recognised as different from adults, at least in the sartorial sense. It was noticed that the costume meant for upper-class boys in the 17th century differed from that meant for adult men. They wore costumes that were similar to the ones worn by adult men in the 16th century, whereas girls from the same stratum of society dressed in miniature versions of costumes meant for adult women in their contemporary society. Aries interprets this difference in dress as recognition of the difference between an adult male and a male child. While the male child was recognised as being different from an adult, the female child was not. Aries further states that boys started going to school as far back as the late 16th century, while girls were trained for adult life by older women in their households. Because of this,

20

DOI: 10.4324/9781003093275-2

the girls were confused with women at an early age just as the boys had formerly been confused with men, and nobody thought of giving visible form, by means of dress, to a distinction which was beginning to exist in reality for the boys but still remained futile for girls.

(58)

However, Aries also refers to personal correspondence between women in the upper segments of French society during the middle of the 16th century and suggests that some of their correspondence includes a new way of looking at girls and boys within their family. These women note behavioural traits that are distinctly different from adults. He quotes from a letter Mme de Sevigne wrote to her daughter in which she expresses her delight at playing with the latter's daughter and expressly records that she does not want the child to die. Aries analyses this expression as a newfound awareness of children's behaviour being entertainingly different from that of adults while carrying the residues of an attitude towards children that indicated "a certain indifference that was traditional" (127). He had earlier on argued that in the 17th century the traditional belief that infants are not to be counted as part of the family persisted because of high rates of child mortality. He quotes a conversation between brothers discussing the plans one of them had for his daughter, in Molière's *Le Malade Imaginaire*, where one of them says, 'How is it, Brother, that rich as you are and having only one daughter, *for I don't count the little one*, you can talk of putting her in a convent?' (125). Aries emphasised that "[t]he little one did not count because she could disappear" (125). He concluded the first part of his monumental work by stating that the upper segments of French society overcame the 'indifference' towards children to start accepting that there was some pleasure in 'coddling' children. This pleasure in the unique ways of childhood, Aries argues, eventually led to the recognition that children need to be treated in special ways for a brief period and also be given training to be integrated into the adult world. He states that by the early 18th century, "[e]verything to do with children and family life [had] become a matter worthy of attention" (130).

Many critics have questioned the Aries paradigm. Lloyd deMause's study, *The History of Childhood* (1974), based on archival records dealing with children and childhood in many countries of Europe, was amongst the earliest works to challenge Philippe Aries's 'discovery' of childhood in the upper echelons of the early 17th-century French society. deMause questions the veracity of one of Aries's primary sources for his study of childhood in 17th-century France. This text was the journal of Jean Heroard who was the chief doctor of the king of France and of the dauphin Louis XIII. Heroard recorded the life and health of Louis XIII from his birth onwards. While this six-volume journal became a comprehensive record of the childhood of a future king in early 17th-century France, it cannot be considered to be representative of childhood in any class of French society in that period. deMause strongly suggests that the journal might not have been a totally neutral record of observations. He indicates that there were many contradictions in the representation of the dauphin. deMause observes:

> The diary opens with the dauphin's birth in 1601. Immediately, his adult qualities appear .... Since he was a dauphin, one skips over these first projections of adult qualities as simple pride in a new king, but soon images begin piling up, and the double image of his being both an adult and a voracious child grows .... The image of the week-old dauphin as alternately an infant Hercules ... and a Gargantua ... is totally at odds with the actual sickly, weak, swaddled infant who emerges from Heroard's record.
>
> (22)

However, neither does Aries base his thesis on the 'discovery' of childhood on Heroard's journal nor is the interpretation of Heroard's journal deMause's main disagreement with Aries's work. deMause states:

> Aries's central thesis is the opposite of mine: he argues that while the traditional child was happy because he was free to mix with many classes and ages, a special condition known as childhood was 'invented' in the early modern periods, resulting in a tyrannical concept of the family which destroyed friendship and sociability and deprived children of freedom, inflecting upon them for the first time the birch and the prison cell.
>
> (5)

deMause's chief objection seems to be the 'invention' of the mores of childhood in the period Aries indicates and the role of the family in training the child into adult society. For deMause begins his work with the statement: "[t]he history of childhood is a nightmare ... the further back in history one goes, the lower the level of child care, and the more likely children are to be killed, abandoned, beaten, terrorized and sexually abused" (1). deMause cites records of the treatment meted out to children in ancient Greece and Rome, to pre-Renaissance Europe to contemporary Europe and North America to substantiate his "psychogenic theory of history" (3). His study of the history of childhood begins with the hypothesis that: "the central force for change in history is neither technology nor economics, but the 'psychogenic' changes in personality occurring because of successive generations of parent-child interactions" (3). Furthermore, deMause lists many child-rearing practices in much of Europe and most of the Anglo-Saxon world from antiquity to as late as the middle of the 19th century that can only be termed as child abuse from 20th-century perspectives of childhood and child-rearing. He lists practices such as swaddling, 'hardening' the child through exposure to extreme weather, whipping, infanticide (mostly of girls but also of illegitimate children of both sexes), abandonment of girls and illegitimate children, rampant sexual abuse, sale of children into slavery, and child labour that was prevalent in many of these cultures. Although deMause's work emerges from sources that have noted children as a category that is different from adults, the difficulties this category of humans faced in their contemporary societies reveals that they received just as bad a treatment, if not worse, as did many adults in those epochs.

While Aries states that the isolation of childhood as a unique phase of human life was the beginning of 'coddling' children and training them for integration into adult societies, deMause establishes that children were treated badly for centuries until recent studies of childhood increased sensitivity towards the needs of children. However, both seem to agree that it was only after the middle of the 17th century that there are some recorded instances of empathy towards experiences of childhood. Therefore, the middle of the 17th century does seem to have been a moment of shift in the perception of childhood in Anglo-Saxon cultures. Ross W. Beale, Jr. argues that "the idea of 'miniature adulthood' must be seen, not as a description of social reality, but as a minor chapter in the history of social thought" (1985, 24). He quotes the work of David E. Stannard, amongst other historians, to substantiate his argument that while it could have been true that children were treated as miniature adults in France until the middle of the 17th century, this was not the case in colonial New England. Beale shows that the church, at least, recognised the difference between child and adult. He has shown that there is evidence of separate provisions for catechising children in the churches of Dorchester and Norwich in the 17th century. In the same vein, Keith Thomas, in 'Children in Early Modern England' (Avery and Briggs, 1989, 45–77) has shown through a study of the toys available for children, the games played by them and the ways in which they were disciplined, that there were not many changes in child-rearing practices from the Tudor period to the 20th century in England.

More recently, Daniel T. Kline has challenged 'the Aries effect' (2012, 21) and states that it led to many scholars ignoring "the widespread appearance of children and childhood in Middle English texts" (22). Furthermore, he argues that not only was there a reasonable presence of children in texts from 1200 to 1500 but these show that children were actively discussed by these societies. Kline states,

> these Middle English texts examine the place and function of children in the broader society and the threatened, violated child presents a discursive opportunity to rearticulate the practices, and thus

reproduce the values, of the prevailing culture. The appearance of pedagogical texts in Middle English literature conveys the ideological importance of even rudimentary childhood education

(22)

Kline establishes that not only was childhood recognised but a need was also felt to prepare the child for an adult world much before the moment of 'discovery' marked by Aries.

James Marten points out in his work titled *The History of Childhood: A Very Short Introduction* (2018) that "[a]s early as the seventh century, the scholar Isidore of Seville distinguished two different phases of childhood each lasting seven years" (2). Furthermore, he gives brief summaries of child-rearing practices in various cultures across the world. Marten's notations on childhood and child-rearing in the cultures he mentions seem to arise from advice given to parents and guardians in a large variety of literature ranging from religious literature, to conduct books, to medico-legal literature. Marten's work reiterates that childhood as being distinct from adulthood seems to have always been present in the recorded history of most cultures of the world. Moreover, Marten also states that many societies recognised that boys in particular,

> would experience a period during which young people on the cusp between dependence and independence—later epochs would call then "youth" or "adolescents"—would test the limits of family and community rules. Their elders did not necessarily approve, or even understand, such behaviour, but they came to expect it and to hold the youth committing disobedience, petty crimes, and unruliness to a somewhat lower standard than adults.

(28)

However, he goes on to argue that social and religious changes in the 15th and 16th centuries in Europe also brought about changes in the perception of childhood, which led to the creation of, "an even greater gulf between childhood in Europe and that in the rest of the world" (29–30). He identifies the Renaissance and Protestant Reformism as two influential moments in opening up education for many and for making family life central for the religious life of people, leading to a sharper focus on the child within the family. He mentions that "[a]lthough Protestants were strongly attached to the notion of original sin, they nevertheless saw children as educable, and thus they developed ideas about parental authority and strict discipline that would shape children into responsible and moral adults" (30–31). Furthermore, he posits that the importance placed on controlling emotions by the Calvinistic wing of Reformation could have had some direct effects

24

on child-rearing. Marten suggests that one of these could be that "[it] may have led many families to 'put out' their children with other families, where they could work as servants or laborers or as apprentices—and be disciplined by parental figures less likely to be ambivalent about mixing severity with love" (31). Although Marten suggests that most cultures always acknowledged the uniqueness of childhood, he marks the 15th and 16th centuries as the moments that brought the child into focus in European society as a member of the family who could be trained into the religious and cultural practices of communities.

Although the accurate date of the isolation of the phenomenon is debatable, serious thought and writing about childhood is seen in Europe in the late 17th and 18th centuries. During this period, many books on educating gentlemen were published. Among these, John Locke's *Some Thoughts Concerning Education* (1693) and Jean-Jacques Rousseau's treatise on education, *Emile, or On Education* (1762) have significantly influenced Western pedagogical theories and practices. In *Corruption in Paradise: The Child in Western Literature* (1982), Reinhard Kuhn has quoted Rousseau's statement: "Nature requires that children be children before being men". Kuhn adds, "Rousseau's originality lies in his recognition of the fact that the childhood world is an autonomous one, different not only in degree but in kind from the adult one" (113). Unlike Locke's work, which was intended for the education of English gentlemen, Rousseau's *Emile* was a treatise on educating the child. Rousseau's thoughts in *Emile* influenced many of his contemporaries. Educating the 'noble savage' became an important preoccupation after his work gained prominence in European societies. Rousseau recognised childhood as a special phenomenon and pointed out the grave consequences of treating children as adults but unfortunately this knowledge eventually started a cult of romanticising and glorifying childhood. In the 'Eye of Innocence' (1971), Leslie Fiedler calls Rousseau the 'prophet' (474) of the shift to, "a belief that the same original disposition once called, 'sin' was more properly labelled 'innocence'" (474). This imbuing of the child with innocence intensified considerably after the publication of William Wordsworth's 'Ode on Intimations of Immortality' in the mid 19th century.

A palpable consequence of the conception of childhood as a period of innocence was that a need to nurture this innocence was strongly felt, giving rise to an enormous amount of didactic writing for children. The rise of writing for children and education of children run parallel with the child becoming central to the family, and a significant presence in society, in the West. Fiedler declares that

Child-worship may begin as one of those pieces of literary hypocrisy (like the courtly adulation of woman), a purely theoretical gesture of compensation by those who, in real life, neither spared the

25

rod nor spoiled the child (and felt a little guilty about it somehow); but it ends in a child-centered society, where the parent not merely serves but emulates his immature offspring.

(473–474)

However, Fiedler's critique of the innate innocence of childhood and the repercussions of the widespread dissemination of this trope through literary and cultural works stems from the sustained presence of the trope of Wordsworth's Romantic Child as a universally accepted image of childhood for more than a century in the Anglo-American world. The image of the Romantic Child suggests that children from all social segments, economic classes, and genders are innocent, blissful beings. Additionally, children were believed to be closer to nature than adults and that children have the power to bring adults closer to nature. This led to a homogenisation of childhood into a period where children coming from various kinds of socioeconomic backgrounds were expected to behave in simple and innocent ways; therefore, children were to 'perform' childhood in a prescribed manner. Childhood, as will be often reiterated in this study, can hardly be treated as a homogenous experience across classes or cultures. As is evident from the fiction of childhood and diverse kinds of studies of childhood, children are as conscious about the social class their families belong to as the adults around them are. A child's everyday experience makes her conscious of her class.

On the one hand, there is significant evidence in 19th-century literature of childhood being romanticised and children being seen as innocent but spiritual creatures; on the other hand, there are sufficient records in the form of laws and legislations to show that enormous numbers of children joined the workforce during the industrial revolution in England. With the industrial revolution the work sphere became firmly demarcated. While in an agrarian economy most of the work took place within the home or around the homestead, with the establishment of factories during the industrial revolution most money-making activities took place outside the home. Children too worked in factories and other commercial establishments. Prior to the change in monetised work with the industrial revolution, children had helped in the farms and had done some of the household chores in an agrarian economy. Children working in mines and factories had to lead the regimented lives of workers and had to follow industrial norms such as fixed timings and rigid distribution of work. Therefore, child-labour became conspicuous and a pertinent issue for agitation.[1] The need for a better childhood for children from working-class families was felt by a large number of people. The involvement of many writers, thinkers, and activists of the period in this issue led to the passing of legislations to ensure that children across class barriers get an education. Meanwhile, children of the landed gentry and children from well-to-do families were being moulded into becoming innocent and blissful people who would make the home a particularly pleasant place. Children from the two social classes led distinctly different kinds of lives. However, in many ways, the lives of both the working-class child and the upper-class child were influenced by the then contemporary notions about childhood.

Although legislations curtailing child labour made the working-class child's life more bearable they also threatened the child's economic independence and left children vulnerable and dependent on parents who were in some cases economically unstable. While the working child lost the little independence she had, the upper-class child had no independence whatsoever. Amongst the upper and the upwardly mobile middle classes, children were taught to be delightful and charming little creatures who would be brought down by nurses or governesses to the dining room for their accomplishments to be displayed to visitors. Quite often, in such families the child's role was to be pleasant to a tired father who would have come back from work and wanted the home to provide him some relaxation. The beginnings of the reification of children as objects that please adults can be seen in this 'role' of the child in many Victorian households.

Upon gaining recognition as a distinct phenomenon, childhood, in Europe, started being treated as a preparatory stage to adulthood. In the middle of the 19th century, various legislations ensured that almost all British children went to school, for a few hours each week. Although they went to different kinds of schools depending on their family's socioeconomic status, by the end of the 19th century, most children from all social spheres firmly moved out of the workforce or nurseries to school rooms. In *Guardians and Angels—Parents and Children in Nineteenth Century Literature* (1978), David Grylls points out that the perception of childhood underwent a major shift in the 19th century. He says that the bond between parents and children shifted from an economic one to an emotional one (16). However, Grylls recognises that the treatment of children had not substantially changed with this shift in the filial bond. He invokes Lloyd deMause's *The History of Childhood* (1974) to the effect that "children have not been treated worse since the rise of school education: they had always been treated abominably" (18). Although Grylls goes on to reassure that the treatment of children has steadily improved with increasing comprehension of childhood, perceiving childhood as a preparatory stage of adulthood persisted even in the 20th century. Emile Durkheim, in his 1979 collection—*Essays on Morals and Education*, traced the etymology of the word *infant* and thereby that of childhood to the Latin phrase *infans* which means 'not speaking'. He then defined it as "the period of *growth*, that is to say, the period in which the individual, in both the physical and moral sense, does not yet exist, the period in which he is made, develops and is formed" (Jenks, 1982, 146–147). As late as in 1979, the human child was still being talked about as if she were a chrysalis. Yet one can see that there has been a serious and consistent engagement with the phenomenon of child-hood from the late 18th century to the present, especially in the West.

Leslie Fiedler posits in 'The Eye of Innocence' (1971) that this serious engagement with childhood grew into a 'Cult of Childhood' (471) and remarks:

> There is something both ambiguous and unprecedented about the Cult of Childhood; indeed, the notion that a mere falling short of adulthood is a guarantee of insight and even innocence is a sophis-ticated view, a latter-day Pastoralism, which finds a Golden Age not in history but at the beginning of each lifetime. The invention of special clothing, special books, a special role in literature for children belongs to a late, a perhaps decadent phase of our culture.
>
> (471)

This engagement with childhood from the 18th century to the present in the Anglo-American world has one common streak – the reification of the child into an asexual being, arising out of an attempt to understand the phenom-enon of childhood. With the publication of Sigmund Freud's 'Three Essays on the Theory of Sexuality' (1905), the notion of children being asexual received a jolt in the early 20th century. This essay and the others delineat-ing Sigmund Freud's theories on human sexuality not only changed the per-ception of childhood as a phase in human development but also sharpened the gaze on childhood as an extremely important period of human life.

In the introductory chapter of this study, it was pointed out that Europe in the 19th century had become increasingly involved in a variety of new disciplines like sociology, anthropology, and psychology. One of the disci-plines that evolved from the old psychology was the new psychoanalysis. The discipline of psychoanalysis emerged from Sigmund Freud's work with women suffering from hysterical symptoms in the final decade of the 20th century. Through his clinical experience as an assistant, and a junior doctor, he developed his theory of psychoanalysis at the turn of the 20th century. In the late 20th century, Freud, who was a trained medical practitioner, was working in the laboratory of Jean Martin Charcot and saw the latter hyp-notise some women to cure them of somatic symptoms. After working in Charcot's clinic for a brief period, Freud joined Josef Breuer's clinic to learn the new methods that were being developed to provide relief to women of the upper classes of European society when they could not be 'cured' by the then prevalent medical treatments. While working in Breuer's clinic, Freud took up some cases in which he used hypnosis to cure patients with somatic problems. Along with Breuer, he recorded a few case histories of women suf-fering from hysteria and they jointly published these as *Studies of Hysteria* in 1895. The study of hysteria by these two doctors led to the knowledge that there is more than one mental 'grouping', independent of and unaware of other 'groupings' in the same individual. The part an individual is aware of is called the 'conscious' and the part that the individual is not aware of is called the 'unconscious'. From his studies of treatment using hypnosis, Freud realised that the unconscious has a hold on the conscious state. Later, Freud faced some difficulties with the hypnotic method and posited a new theory arising from his difficulties with getting a patient hypnotised. When he began working on his own, Freud gave up hypnosis and tried to make his patients remember their thoughts while they were in a conscious state. This technique was later called 'free association'.

Breuer had earlier used hypnosis to treat his patients. He narrated the details of the illness and treatment of a young woman to Freud; this was included in *Studies of Hysteria* (1895) as the case of Anna O. Freud, subsequently, explained this case in detail as an introductory illustration to psychoanalytic cure in his famous Clark lectures. Freud laid out the blueprint of psychoanalysis in these lectures. These five lectures were delivered to a solely medical audience in 1909 at the Clark University in New York. Through the first four of the five Clark lectures, Freud established that all men have lives of fantasy, as reality is generally found unsatisfying. In the fifth lecture, he proposed that energetic and successful men turn their world of fantasies into reality. Sometimes, some men fail in this endeavour and withdraw into their world of fantasy. The contents of this world constitute their symptoms if they fall ill. Some others, under favourable circumstances, regress into an infantile, and therefore more satisfactory, state of sexuality rather than falling ill. The last two sorts of people need to 'regain contact with reality' (81) to function successfully as adult human beings in a civilised world. These are the kinds of people a psychoanalyst would treat.

Freud introduced psychoanalysis as a process that a person goes through with help from a qualified analyst to come to terms with the reality that she has been escaping. The term 'reality' is not used in the usually accepted sense of a social reality but in this context it is the reality of the psychic life of the person of which her social reality might also be one manifestation. Tracing the origin of this technique to his joint endeavours, with Breuer, at treating women with hysterical symptoms, Freud describes Anna O's case. She was a 21-year-old, intelligent, young woman who was suffering from rigid paralysis of the right side of her body accompanied by various other problems such as moments of loss of memory; instances of inability to speak in her mother tongue, German (while she could speak fluently in English); an inability to drink water in spite of extreme thirst; and '*absence*', which Freud defined as: "altered personality accompanied by confusion" (35). Her vital internal organs were functioning properly and she was diagnosed to be suffering from hysteria. In this case, Breuer inferred that the symptoms are caused by "the convergence of several traumas, and often by the repetition of a great number of similar ones" (37) and therefore it was essential to go in a sequence of the latest-one-first to reach the earliest and most powerful one. Patients of hysteria not only remember painful experiences from the past but also tend to cling to them. They neglect the present in their attachment to the past. He says: "this fixation of mental life to pathogenic traumas is one of the most significant and practically important characteristics of neurosis" (40). This happens when a powerful emotion has to be suppressed due to some circumstances rather than allowed expression through appropriate emotions, words, or actions. These emotions remain a burden in the patient's mental life and sometimes manifest in the form of somatic symptoms. In Anna O's case, it was found that she used to utter fragmented sentences while in 'absence'. On being hypnotised, she could recollect her thoughts during and about these utterances. After every such episode, she felt some relief from her symptoms. Therefore, she named this treatment the 'talking cure' and jokingly referred to it as 'chimney-sweeping'.

When Freud started practising on his own he realised that hypnosis has limited and temporary gains. He gave it up and encouraged patients to talk about their dreams or symptoms. Freud discovered that there were a number of obstacles in the process, i.e., many patients could not recollect in spite of his constant urging. He hypothesised that the patient's memories were forced to remain unconscious due to *resistance*. He extended this hypothesis into the logical inference that these resisting thoughts must have been relegated to the unconscious by a similar force, which he called *repression*. Freud says resistance has to be engaged with to relieve the symptoms. He also states that the discovery of repression is, in a sense, the beginning of psychoanalysis. He says hypnosis conceals resistance and hence repressions and resistances can be observed only when the patient is conscious. Repression happens because the desire that is repressed is incompatible with the subject's personality. But this desire is in the patient and is on the lookout for an outlet. If it does not find one, it manifests itself in the form of a disguised *substitute* which Freud calls the *symptom*. A psychoanalyst can assist the patient in recognising the repressed thought that is being manifested in the symptom and in dealing with it. This thought can get sublimated into a higher and unobjectionable aim or get accepted completely in conscious thoughts as a wish or get rejected after realising that the course of action is unjustifiable or get controlled consciously.

Freud then found out that there were many failures in the 'free association' method too. He stated that patients rejected his suggestion that their 'free association' was linked to their symptoms. The patients felt that thoughts occurring during free association were often too dissimilar to the symptom to be connected with it. Freud says that the "idea occurring to the patient must be in the nature of an *allusion* to the repressed element, like a representation of it in indirect speech" (56) and declares: "nothing can occur to [the patient] which is not in an indirect fashion dependent on the complex we are in search of" (58). He then shows three paths to the unconscious: free association; jokes, forgetfulness, errors, and other such unplanned occurrences in everyday life; and dreams. While elaborating on his technique of interpreting dreams to unearth the unconscious, Freud declares that every dream is a wish fulfilment. This can be seen quite clearly, sometimes, in the dreams of small children but is usually not accepted about adults' dreams. This is not obvious in adults' dreams due to the distortion that takes place in dreams. This dream distortion is similar to the process that takes place during the formation of hysterical symptoms. Freud states: "In dream-life the child that is in man pursues its existence … and retains all its characteristics and wishful impulses, even such as have become unserviceable in later life" (63).

Having formed a link between childhood and adult life in his work on interpretation of dreams, Freud further strengthened the link between traumatic symptoms and childhood experiences in the fourth lecture in the Clark series. He asserts: "Psychoanalytic research traces back the symptoms of patient's illness with really surprising regularity to impressions from their *erotic life*" (69). He then declares that a child has sexual instincts and activities from the beginning and it was erroneously believed that these instincts develop during puberty. He goes on to state that at least three others working in the same field observed this and had written about it. Explaining people's disbelief of this phenomenon as resistance, Freud proceeds to explain that he uses the term 'sexuality' not just pertaining to reproduction but in a wider sense of bodily pleasure. He says there are many erotic zones in infants but at puberty the genital zone dominates over the other zones.

The infant's chief source of sexual pleasure is through *auto-eroticism*, which he defines as "the appropriate excitation of certain parts of the body that are especially susceptible to stimulus" (73). Along with this, children have libidinal components that necessitate the presence of an extraneous person as object. The choice of the object narrows down to one of the child's parents. Usually the child chooses the parent of the opposite sex. The child would then like to replace the parent it has not chosen. Freud says the complex that is formed in this process is doomed to an early repression but has a lasting impact on the unconscious. He calls this, along with other complications arising from it, "the *nuclear complex* of every neurosis" (77–78). He mentions the myth of Oedipus as an example of this and states that this complex is "later opposed and repudiated by the *barrier against incest*" (78).

The child forms many infantile sexual theories to fulfil its curiosity but almost always fails in its investigation. Freud states that "the fact of this childish research itself, as well as the different infantile sexual theories that it brings to light, remain of importance in determining the formation of the child's character and the content of any later neurotic illness" (78). He declares that if the child's libido remains fixated on her/his first object of desire, the parent, it will hamper her/his growth into a socially fit person. He concludes with: "You can, if you like, regard psycho-analytic treatment as no more than a prolongation of education for the purpose of overcoming the residues of childhood" (79).

Freud observed that during the course of psychoanalytic treatment every patient experiences *transference*. He explains this occurrence as the patient directing

> towards the physician a degree of affectionate feeling (mingled, often enough, with hostility) which is based on no real relation between them and which—as is shown by every detail of its emergence—can only be traced back to old wishful phantasies of the patient's which have become unconscious.
>
> (82)

Freud believes: "It is everywhere the true vehicle of therapeutic influence" (83). Through transference the patient enacts her/his trauma and unconscious thoughts gain entry into the conscious. Freud believes it is easier to deal with them as conscious thoughts and to transform them into healthy thoughts. The chief purpose of the Clark lectures was to introduce the principal concepts of this new science of psychoanalysis to other physicians. Moreover, by showing his goals for treatment as sublimation, conscious rejection, conscious acceptance and control of wishes, Freud has acknowledged the important role played by civilisation even in the psychic life of an individual.

Freud periodically reviewed and revised his theories until the very end of his long career. He introduced new concepts and discarded old ones quite often. Seventeen years after the Clark lectures, in 'The Question of Lay Analysis' (1926), Freud tried to convince his audience that one need not be a qualified physician to practice psychoanalysis successfully. Having made the pronouncement that a trained analyst is most likely to succeed even if he is not a doctor, Freud clinches his argument against exclusively reserving the practice of analysis to medical professionals with three very clear and cogently placed objections. He points out: the patient is totally indifferent to the distinction between a medical professional and a layperson as long as he finds his analyst trustworthy and efficient; medical professionals do not benefit monetarily by studying for one more year and then spending many years in training when they could be earning as medical practitioners; and if it is restricted to medical professionals the science will get narrowed down to just another way of treating mental illness. Freud also believed psychoanalysis could contribute to greater knowledge of other cultural aspects of human civilisations. He declared that "[a]s a 'depth-psychology', a theory of the mental unconscious, it can become indispensable to all the sciences which are concerned with the evolution of human civilization and its major institutions such as art, religion, and the social order" (168). He also states that knowledge of psychoanalysis can be used in bringing up children. He ends with the speculation: "The use of analysis for the treatment of the neuroses is only one of its applications; the future will perhaps show that it is not the most important one" (168). With this Freud attempts to argue that the ban on non-physicians from practising analysis is detrimental to psychoanalysis rather than fulfilling the lawmakers' presumed motive of 'protecting' it from 'quacks'. Freud has shown in many of his later writings that psychoanalytic theories can be applied in various other fields.

Freud's endeavour to make psychoanalytic practice available to people who were not trained physicians led to an increase in the practice of psychoanalysis by 'lay' analysts. One such lay analyst was Freud's youngest daughter – Anna Freud. Anna Freud was trained to be a school teacher and was working as a teacher when she read her father's works. Anna had also undergone analysis by Freud. There were a few instances of close relatives entering into a relationship of analyst and analysand in the early years of psychoanalysis, which was discontinued after psychoanalysis evolved. Peter Gay notes that Anna's first patients were her late sister, Sophie's two sons – Ernstl and Heinele. Freud, though, had actually never practised child analysis in the orthodox sense of the term. The only very young child Freud analysed, Little Hans, was through reports by the boy's father. Hans's father spoke to Hans and reported to Freud about his 'sessions' with Hans. Freud's disciples, though, soon branched into child analysis. One such disciple of Freud who branched into child analysis is Anna Freud. As mentioned above, Anna Freud started her career as a child analyst by analysing her nephews who had lost their mother to the Spanish flu and were being brought up in the Freud household. She wrote various essays about her experiences from 1926 onwards. A compilation of some of her essays, edited by her and translated into English under her supervision was published by the Hogarth Press in 1974. Anna Freud introduced the methods, experiences, and debates in the analysis of children in this edition titled *Introduction to Psychoanalysis*. Divided into three parts, the first and third parts of this edition are addressed to fellow analysts, researchers, and academics, while the second one is addressed to teachers and parents. Anna Freud differentiated between analysis for adults and analysis for children at the very beginning of the work.

The first part 'Four Lectures on Child Analysis' was presented at the International Psychoanalytic Congress in Vienna in 1926. This was the year Melanie Klein migrated to London and Freud presented psychoanalysis to the layman in 'The Question of Lay-Analysis'. Neither Anna Freud nor Melanie Klein was qualified to practice medicine, but both had some experience in the analysis of children by the time Freud presented his case for allowing non-medical practitioners to practice psychoanalysis. Anna Freud believed that analysis as practised on adults was rather ineffectual with children. From these lectures one can perceive that she was an orthodox Freudian in her views about analysis on adults. But she thought that practising analysis on children called for some changes from the orthodox Freudian method. She believed that adults were usually more mature and independent than children. Therefore, Anna Freud suggested that there should be some modifications from the prescribed practice in analysis for adults and a few more precautions need to be taken while practising with children. In fact, she even warned, "what is necessary for the adult may be risky for the child" (5). While adults go into analysis due to social or emotional discomfort that directs them towards analysis, children are brought to the analyst mostly by parents/guardians who feel that the child is a misfit. In many cases, the child might not even be suffering due to the symptoms that her family found intolerable in the child. The child is almost never asked for her consent before beginning the process of analysis.

The willingness to undergo analysis being a crucial requirement of Freudian psychoanalysis, Anna Freud states that the child should first be made willing. She calls this process making the patient 'analyzable'. To do this, she "induced in the child insight into his disturbance, imparted confidence in the analyst, and turned the decision for analysis from one taken by others into his own" (7). This process of making the child analysable takes some time. Anna Freud calls this the period of preparation for analysis. She seems to imply that the greater the suffering of the child, the more readily does the child become analysable. The analyst needs various kinds of skills to make the patient analysable. Anna Freud says the way to do it is to first befriend the child by playing with her/him, indulging the child, and behaving according to the child's mood. Then the analyst should make herself useful to the child in small ways. The last and crucial step is to point out the practical advantages of analysis to the child. In return for all this, the analyst can 'buy' the child's trust to "surrender ... all his previously guarded secrets ... with which the real analysis [can] finally begin" (13–14).

Delineating the similarities and differences in the analysis of adults and children, Anna Freud says:

> It would be more appropriate to say that in the technique of adult analysis we find vestiges of all the procedures which prove necessary with children. The extent to which we use them will depend upon the degree to which the adult patient with whom we are dealing is still an immature and dependent being and in this respect is closer to a child.
>
> (23)

However, there are many differences in the way analysis is conducted on children and adults. While in the case of adults, analysts refrain from gathering information about the illness from the family of the patient, in the case of children the family is the basic source of information for the history of illness of the child. Analysts also have to use different 'tools' for treatment in these two different analytic situations. According to Anna Freud, the child "refuses to do free association" (32). Therefore, the analyst has to find some other method of reaching the child's unconscious. She says children readily narrate their daydreams as opposed to adults who do not like to reveal them. Some children compose daydreams that are continuations of previous ones. She explains:

> with children who compose such 'serial story' daydreams it is often very easy to get on such terms that even in the earliest part of the analysis they will daily recount a new instalment. These day-by-day continuations can then be used to reconstruct the current inner situation of the child.
>
> (29)

Anna Freud states that another important aspect of analysis of children is that the child does not form transference neurosis. Her explanation for this is that the child's parents still play a very influential role in his everyday life. She says:

> [T]he analyst enters this situation as a new person, and will probably share with the parents the child's love or hate. But there is no necessity for the child to put the analyst fully in the parents' place, since compared to them he has not the same advantages which the adult finds when he can exchange his fantasy objects for a real person.
>
> (44–45)

From this lack of transference neurosis, Anna Freud infers, "the outer world affects the mechanism of the infantile neurosis and the analysis more deeply than is the case in adults" (54). In adults, there is a neater division between the inner and outer worlds of the patients. She says the demands made by the outer world on the adult, i.e., his moral obligations are represented by his superego. The superego stands in for the person's first and most important love objects, usually the parents. In children, since the parents still play a very important role in their lives, this substitution has not been achieved. Therefore, the superego is not rigidly formed. While in adult patients the superego can usually handle the instinctual impulses arising from analysis, in children the analyst has to work towards supporting the superego too.

Another important issue in analysis of children is the post-analysis period. The child goes back to an environment that had contributed in making him ill or troubled. Anna Freud presents a rather bleak picture of this period by stating that the child either becomes neurotic once more or becomes rebellious. She then adds that from a therapeutic angle rebellion is an improvement. She believes that if the parents are supportive of the analyst and the analysis, it is easier for the child to resume normal life as a healthy child after termination of the analysis. But if the home environment is not supportive, it becomes really difficult. She ends this discussion with the rather startling declaration: "Today I would no longer undertake the analysis of a child if the personalities of the parents, or their analytic understanding, did not provide a guarantee against such an outcome" (61). Considering the fact that the parents pay for the analysis and thereby have the power to terminate it at any time – a difficulty discussed in one of her early lectures by Anna Freud – analysing children without complete support by their parents seems a futile effort. At the same time, she points out the advantages of analysing children. They are: major changes of character are possible in children after analysis as compared to adults, it is easier to moderate the severity of the superego in children, and the analyst has more influence on the child's environment too and can therefore ensure that the child has minimal difficulty in adapting to life after analysis. Furthermore, she makes a sharp distinction between child care and the education of a child. She states: "The rearing of the child consists of the fulfillment of his bodily needs .... The child is given all he needs without anything being asked in return. Education, in contrast, always demands something of the child" (94). Education tries to make the child as similar to a grown-up person as can be possible. Anna Freud believes "adults have never taken an objective attitude to children's characteristics" (95–96). Instead they have zealously tried to restrain the child from gratifying her impulses. Anna Freud posits that the child should be led away from indulging in such gratification but this should not be done by coercion. She believed that neurotic inhibition as well as delinquency may be due to either excessive interference by authoritative figures or lack of all restraints in the child's life. She states: "The task of upbringing based on analytic understanding is to find a middle road between these extremes—that is to say, to find for each stage in the child's life the right proportion between drive gratification and drive control" (128). In her framework, the analyst seems to have partly taken on the role of a guardian too. While discussing the superego of the child, Anna Freud says that the superego of a child is in the process of being formed by her parent's influence. The parents educate the child into the ways of the world, i.e., they help in forming the superego that will help the child grow into a socially healthy adult. The analyst joins hands with the parents in this endeavour along with helping the child to overcome her neurosis.

While Anna Freud used the daydreams of children as a substitute for free association, other analysts tried different methods. Hermine Hug-Hellmuth tried to play with the child and conduct analysis in settings familiar to the child, like the child's home, to understand the child's environment. Melanie Klein also used the play-technique. Anna Freud is not totally against Klein's play-technique but she thinks that it is carried too far. She feels it is wrong to equate it with free association. In adults, free association takes place while the adult is aware that she is in analysis. Free association, therefore, has a goal. A child's play might not necessarily have been motivated by a similar goal of facilitating analysis. "Instead of being invariably invested with a symbolic meaning, it may sometimes admit of harmless explanations" (38). It is worth pointing out, however, that according to Sigmund Freud, whom Anna Freud closely follows, there are no harmless explanations for any actions.

Melanie Klein became interested in psychoanalysis after reading Freud's works and was in analysis with two followers of Freud: first with Sandor Ferenczi and later with Karl Abraham. She went to Britain on Ernest Jones's invitation in 1925. Jones had heard her paper 'The Psychological Principles of Early Analysis' at the Psycho-analytic Congress in Salzburg in 1925. Klein thereafter moved away from the orthodox Freudian framework by positing that the superego exists in the pre-genital stage too. In the second phase of her work, she formulated that the fundamental structure and strength of the ego is determined in the early months of a child's life and this then determines the way in which the genital Oedipus complex will be experienced. She introduced the concept of *position* as against Freud's term *phases* to describe the various stages of infantile sexuality. A position comprises the state of the ego, the object-relation of the child, the anxieties prevailing in the child and its defences. The positions identified by Klein are paranoid–schizoid and depressive.

In 1946, Klein wrote 'Notes on Some Schizoid Mechanisms' which proposes a new psychoanalytical theory of development based on concepts like anxiety and the evolution of object relations. According to this theory, anxiety arises in the ego right from birth due to the perception of death instinct. This death instinct is deflected into the primary object – the breast of the mother – and then is diffused throughout life into various objects. Similarly, the life instinct present in the infant gives rise to loving relationships with objects. In this way, there are many *ideal objects* and *bad objects* in a person's life. These objects are internal as well as external. An infant develops defence mechanisms to steer through the states of bliss and frustration. Some such mechanisms are denial, control, and projective identification. In projective identification, some parts of the infant's personality are projected onto the object. Melanie Klein labels this mechanism as that used by an immature psyche and states that it precedes repression. Klein believed that since the child's natural form of expression is through play, she could make contact with a child's inner world through observing a child's play. She thought of the child's play as a symbolic language. She provided her child analysands with simple play material and toys that could lend themselves to imaginative use and left them free to play with them. The aim of analysis was to help the child strengthen her 'good' internal objects.

D. W. Winnicott from the British School of Object-Relations also highlighted the importance of the toy in the psychic life of a child. For Winnicott, spontaneity characterised the aliveness of a person. If a person did not show spontaneity, Winnicott would consider her ill. He says this happened if the person did not experience a good enough mother as an infant. Adam Phillips remarks: "It was to be part of the contribution of what became known as the British School of Object-relations theorists, to translate psychoanalysis from a theory of sexual desire into a theory of emotional nurture" (10). Winnicott posits that the environment around a child is very important in determining the health of the child. The mother, as the first environment, adapts herself to the needs of the infant. The child has a right to use the mother to recognise as well as gratify his developmental requirements. It is the mother's job to introduce the world in small doses to the infant. According to Winnicott, the trauma lies in not being able to make sense of the world and not in the inability to experience it. To the infant, the mother is an arbiter between the world and its own needs. If the infant's first relationship is that of reciprocity rather than conflict or submission, all will be well. But if the mother is unable to provide this reciprocal relationship due to reasons of her own, the child will have to comply with her wishes. To elaborate this further, Phillips says, "[t]o manage the demands of the mother, and to protect the True Self of personal need and preoccupation, the child would construct what Winnicott called a False Self" (4). During analysis, the False Self gets eroded and the True Self comes out. For this to happen, the patient should feel that the environment the analyst maintains is reliable. Phillips says: "For Winnicott a capacity to be spontaneous can only come out of an early experience of reliability. Only with a backdrop of continuity, one might say, can the patient re-find his own developmental lines" (64). In fact, Winnicott says that the child tests her parent's reliability too. She needs to be assured that they will remain good parents despite all the hurtful or annoying things she might do. They should be able to withstand all that the child does to them without rejecting her. The mother's 'sensitive adaptation' to the infant's need is its route to reality. Winnicott says, "Fantasy is more primary than reality, and the enrichment of fantasy with the world's riches depends on the experience of illusion" (84). He explains illusion as the infant's belief that she has created the object that fulfils her desire. Winnicott explains this with the example of the mother's breast, which is readily available when the child had just conjured it upon desiring it. When this happens the child believes that she has 'created' the breast. If the child experiences fulfilment of its desire, i.e., the object of its desire is readily there, it can learn to wait for it and also to long for it. Phillips says that according to Winnicott,

> only then does the child's inner world find an incentive for contact with the external world. Because his desire has been met and satisfied he has had the primitive experience of a match between inner and outer reality .... At the very beginning fantasy is not a substitute for reality but the first method of finding it.
>
> (84)

When the external environment fails the infant, it will develop a fantasy of self-sufficiency in which the mind will displace the mother's care. The infant gradually acknowledges the mother as the object of its desire and becomes concerned for her welfare. The infant goes through a 'benign circle' comprising four parts in this stage of concern. If the mother can survive the first stage – instinctual experience – and is there to receive the last stage – "restitutive gesture" – the

> infant becomes able to imagine and so to connect the object of desire—what Winnicott calls the Object Mother—with the object of more general care—the environment Mother. And by the same process he will connect himself as a desiring person with the more quiescent and comfortable person he is between feeds.
>
> (108)

Winnicott suggests that once the infant is assured of a good-enough early environment, and has primary creativity and a capacity for illusionment, it reaches a stage where it needs to achieve relative independence. This is done through its use of its "first Not-Me object, which Winnicott called the transitional object" (118). The child finds continuity between the mutually exclusive positions of: subjectivity or objectivity, unity with the mother and separateness, invention and discovery, due to the Transitional Object. Phillips defines the Transitional Object as: "always a combination, but one that provides, by virtue of being more than the sum of its parts, a new, third alternative. And it is never a substitute for something else" (114). This object gets added to an already existing pattern. The qualities of this object must overlap with that of the mother. This object thus helps the child into tiding over the changes taking place in its environment. Winnicott gives the example of some children's need to carry a particular toy or some such tangible and familiar thing to bed. The Transitional Object is crucial for the child not only to execute the shift from one state to another but also to achieve a sense of reality.

The work of Anna Freud, Melanie Klien, Winnicott, and others not only led to an enrichment of and diversified usage of psychoanalytic theory but also paved the way for developmental psychology. Jean Piaget, Erik Erikson, and Bruno Bettelheim have used psychoanalytic theories in varied but related fields of knowledge. In fact, Jean Piaget and Erik Erikson not only wrote on the significance of toys in the life of children but also conducted many empirical studies to observe children's plays through their developing years. Many child psychologists and scholars in the field of childhood studies use the techniques evolved by Piaget and Erikson to study child development. One of the early instances of a study of children playing with dolls was conducted by Freud's contemporaries, A. C. Ellis and G. S. Hall. William Kessen has presented extracts of a paper based on this study and titled 'A Study of Dolls" – written by Ellis and Hall and published first in the *Pedagogical Seminary* (1896) – in *The Child* (1965). This paper was later abridged and reprinted by G. S. Hall and some of his students in *Aspects of Child Life and Education* (1907). Ellis and Hall claim that theirs is the first such study in the field of "psychogenetics" (152). They studied 845 children between the ages of 3 and 12. They asked the children their preference between dolls and a substitute object that is used as a doll in play. They used a range of dolls made of a variety of material and representing different racial types or professions. Then they asked children specific questions about their interactions with their dolls. Some of their conclusions are that: boys abandon playing with dolls very early because it is considered girlish; pretending while playing is very important and is the most engrossing thing about play; children usually lose interest in dolls by the age of nine; the child's moods and ideals in life come to the forefront in spontaneous play with dolls; and the educational value of dolls is enormous. Kessen remarks that William James, their contemporary, was appalled at the 'raw philistinism' of the project led by Ellis and Hall. James, it is presumed, was aware of the work of Freud as James's sister was undergoing analysis in the late 1890s. This project led by Ellis and Hall was wound up many years before Freud introduced psychoanalysis to the Americans through the Clark University lectures of 1909, which he dedicated to G. S. Hall who had invited him to deliver those lectures.

During the course of his long engagement with finding ways to help people find relief from illness whose origins Freud located in the formation of the person's psyche, Freud not only formulated a theory of the mind but also foregrounded the importance of childhood in the psychic life of an individual. His theories on infantile sexuality, formulated for the first time in 'Three Essays on the Theory of Sexuality' (1905), are central to his theory on the significance of childhood on the development of adult sexuality. He begins this work on infantile sexuality by remarking on the neglect of the study of the sexuality of children. He says the two reasons that could explain this silence is the qualms of the writers on child sexuality due to their upbringing and the well-known fact that no one remembers their childhood quite clearly. He calls this forgetting of one's childhood as infantile amnesia. Freud believes that infantile amnesia does not really signify a total deletion of the memories of childhood, but signifies repression of the memories. He states that infantile amnesia is responsible for the fact that not much importance is attached to childhood in the development of sexual life. Through this work, Freud delineates the importance of the experiences of childhood in adult sexuality. Freud states that there are sexual impulses in a newborn child but these are gradually suppressed. He posits that human sexuality is 'diphasic' (200), i.e., the child is born a sexual being but then around the age of four or five years a period of latency sets in and sexuality is once again awakened during puberty. In the first phase of sexuality, the child moves through three stages which Freud called the oral phase, the anal phase, and the genital phase. At the genital phase, the final act of repression occurs. During the oral phase, the child derives pleasure from sucking. The anal phase sets in once toilet training begins. The child's will clashes with that of his caregiver about toilet training. Freud believes that the child gifts his faeces as a gift of love to his caregiver. Around this time the child would have made a choice of his object of love between his parents. During the anal phase, the child discovers the pleasurable feeling arising from the genital zone. This is the beginning of the genital phase of infantile sexuality. In the genital phase, the child is either admonished for touching his genitals or is seriously discouraged from any form of auto-erotic activity. This and various other factors combine to bring a period of latency. During puberty, the child's sexual impulses are awakened and the choice of love-object is redefined. The process described above is an ideal way in which a human being achieves his/her sexual identity. This ideal is very difficult to achieve. In most cases, many intervening events change the course of this process. Freud states that most 'aberrations' in adult sexuality can be traced back to one or more traumatising event/s during childhood.

Although Freud did not mention the Oedipus complex in the 1905 version of this essay, he says in the summary of the three essays comprising this work: "Children themselves behave from an early age as though their dependence on the people looking after them were in the nature of sexual love" (224). Freud, thus, clearly links childhood with sexual love. In a footnote added in 1920 Freud declared:

> It has justly been said that the Oedipus complex is the nuclear complex of the neuroses, and constitutes the essential part of their content. It represents the peak of infantile sexuality, which, through its after-effects, exercises a decisive influence on the sexuality of adults. Every new arrival on this planet is faced by the task of mastering the Oedipus complex; anyone who fails to do so falls a victim to neurosis.
>
> (226)

This is not the first instance where Freud links the experiences of childhood with neurosis. In fact, Freud consistently points out the similarities between the behaviour of children and neurotics through all the three essays.

Freud first suspected that hysteria's causative factors could be traced back to childhood in the 'Preliminary Communication' (1893) that he published with Josef Breuer. Freud mentions the main characteristics of hysterics as: extreme repression of sexual impulses; an intensification of the 'barriers' against sexual impulses, e.g., feelings like shame, disgust, and moral qualms; and an aversion towards thinking about sexual problems. Due to this, hysterics are mostly quite ignorant about sexual matters. He says that sometimes a seemingly contrary element is also observed – a predominant development of the sexual instinct. He believes this presence of the sexual instinct to be a screen to their hysteria. Freud, then, demonstrates how hysterical amnesia is formed:

> Hysterical amnesia, which occurs at the bidding of repression, is only explicable by the fact that the subject is already in possession of a store of memory-traces which have been withdrawn from conscious disposal, and which are now, by an associative link, attracting to themselves the material which the forces of repression are engaged in repelling from consciousness. It may be said that without infantile amnesia there would be no hysterical amnesia.
>
> (175–176)

 Thus by showing that the hysteria can be directly traced back to memory-traces from childhood, Freud has reiterated the significance of recognising that the child is a sexual being.

 Towards the end of the essay on infantile sexuality in 'Three Essays on the Theory of Sexuality', Freud has described the child as 'polymorphously perverse' (191), i.e., the child can derive pleasure from various auto-erotic zones of the body, whereas the goal is to channelise one's libidinal energies towards attaining genital sexuality. To attain this goal, one has to overcome the castration complex during the Oedipal phase. In the Oedipal phase, the child shows a clear preference for the parent of the opposite sex. The daughter shows more partiality towards the father and the son shows more affection for the mother. The child wishes to replace the parent of the same sex in the affections of the parent of the opposite sex. In the case of boys, Freud posits, the essential threat of castration lies in the child's discovery that women do not have a penis. The child, according to Freud, assumes that the woman has been castrated. Therefore, the possibility of castration becomes a real threat. Furthermore, the child is also, usually, actively discouraged by caregivers from touching its genitals. During this process, all forms of repression of the sexual impulses start developing. The child, temporarily, gives up the desire to replace the father. While the child is overcoming his Oedipal desires, the superego begins to be formed. Once the child has successfully overcome his sexual impulses, the superego is completely formed and the child is ready to be civilised into an adult human being as time passes. When sexuality is reawakened during puberty, the adolescent's choice of object will depend on the course his Oedipal phase would have taken. Freud repeatedly points out that in most cases the transition from one phase of sexuality to another is not smooth. While this model of 'diphasic sexuality' was satisfactorily explained in the case of boys, this framework when applied by Freud on the development of sexuality in girls does not work out sufficiently satisfactorily.

Although Freud's work on human sexuality began with the treatment of women and he treated many women patients throughout his career, he is said to have declared, almost at the very end of his career, that he cannot decipher what women want.[2] Ernest Jones had written in 1955 that:

> There is little doubt that Freud found the psychology of women more enigmatic than that of men. He said once to Marie Bonaparte: "The great question that has never been answered and which I have not yet been able to answer, despite my thirty years of research into the feminine soul is 'What does a woman want?'"
>
> (326)

Freud has written at length and comprehensively on his theories of femininity in the *New Introductory Lectures* (1933) written and published after Hitler had publicly burnt his works. He begins his discussion of femininity by giving a psychological definition of femininity as "giving preference to passive aims" but quickly distinguishes it from passivity by stating that, "to achieve a passive aim may call for a large amount of activity" (149). He says psychoanalysis does not describe what a woman is but enquires into "how she comes into being, how a woman develops out of a child with a bisexual disposition" (149). Then he says that this choosing of femininity happens after a lot of struggle and takes place before puberty. Using the structure of the three phases in infantile sexuality that he had explained in the *Three Essays on the Theory of Sexuality* (1905), Freud posits that

> in the phallic phase of girls the clitoris is the leading erotogenic zone. But it is not, of course, going to remain so. With the change to femininity the clitoris should wholly or in part hand over its sensitivity, and at the same time its importance, to the vagina.
>
> (151–152)

The second change the girl needs to bring about is changing her object of love from her mother to her father. He traces back the turning away from the mother to the castration complex. He states that "it was … a surprise to learn from analyses that girls hold their mother responsible for their lack of a penis and do not forgive her for their being thus put at a disadvantage" (158). The girl regards her 'castration' as an individual "misfortune" (160–161) and later realises that other females, including her mother share this with her. Freud justifies this with a skewed logical explanation:

> her love was directed to her phallic mother; with the discovery that her mother is castrated it becomes possible to drop her as an object, so that the motives for hostility, which have long been

43

accumulating, gain the upper hand. This means, therefore, that as a result of the discovery of women's lack of penis they are debased in value for girls just as they are for boys and later perhaps for men.

(160–161)

Freud does not consider the possibility of empathy and bonding arising from this shared 'lack' in this situation and states that it leads to hostility and debasement. One can believe that other reasons for hostility, such as: weaning, toilet training, disciplining, and in some cases the birth of a sibling, would already have sown the seeds of hostility and it could just get encouraged by an additional disappointment with the mother. However, when the social positions of the sexes are not considered in the study, it is not clear whether the preference of sons and therefore privileged treatment of boys in most cultures is an influential factor in the purported desire of the girl to possess a penis to emulate the father and abandon the mother in the path to sexual development.

However, Freud's delineation of femininity and the route to adult sexuality was repeated in three of his essays on female sexuality from 1925 to 1933.[3] The trajectory he lays out is as follows: On being disappointed with the mother for not giving her a penis, the girl turns to her father with the wish her mother could not fulfil – that of a penis. With this shift to the parent of the opposite sex the girl enters the Oedipus complex. Unlike the path to ideal sexual development amongst boys, in girls the castration complex prepares the way for the Oedipus complex instead of destroying it as it does in boys. He delineates female sexual development in his last essay on this matter in the following way:

> Almost the opposite [from that of a boy] happens with the girl. Instead of destroying the Oedipus complex, the castration complex lays the ground for it; penis envy drives the girl to detach herself from her mother and to seek refuge in the haven of the Oedipus complex. Once the fear of castration has disappeared, so too has the primary motive that forced the boy to overcome the Oedipus complex. The girl remains in it for an indefinite period; she dismantles it only late and then incompletely. In these circumstances, the formation of the Uber-Ich must suffer: it can't achieve the strength and independence that lend it its cultural significance—feminists never like it when we point out the effects of this fact on the average female character.
>
> (1933, 119)

Not only does Freud declare women to be doomed with a supposedly inferior sexual organ and a lifelong state of hopelessly irresolvable love but also asserts that the female character is not satisfactorily formed due to weak superegos. Later, he even asserts that women are perceived to have little sense of justice as envy predominates their mental life.

Earlier in the essay, Freud had declared that the feminine situation is fully established only when the girl's wish for a penis from the father is replaced by the wish for a baby. He then states that the girl wishes for a baby even in her pre-Oedipus phase. This can be seen in her playing with dolls. He says:

> But this playing did not actually express her femaleness: it served her identification with the mother, with the intention of replacing passivity by activity. She played the mother, and *the doll was herself*; now she could do everything to the child that her mother used to do to her. Only once the desire for a penis enters into it does the doll-child become a child of the father—and from then onwards it becomes the strongest female aim and desire.
>
> (Emphasis added, 118)

Furthermore, Freud posits that if the girl does not achieve the transition into femininity she either develops a masculinity complex or regresses into fixations of the pre-Oedipus phases. The former, at its extreme, manifests in the form of homosexuality and the latter keeps occurring throughout some women's lives with alternations between masculine and feminine behaviour therefore displaying symptoms of bisexuality.

Freud then goes on to state that while there is a chance for a man of thirty to be able "to take full advantage of the developmental possibilities that psychoanalysis opens up to him" (124), he has the following to say about a woman of the same age:

> However, a woman of a similar age often shocks up by her psychical rigidity and unchangeability. Her libido has taken its final positions and appears incapable of exchanging them for others. There are no paths open to her for further development: it is as if the whole process had already run its course, as if it remained beyond influence from now on, perhaps even as if the difficult development that leads to femaleness had exhausted all the individual possibilities. As therapists, we lament this state of affairs, even when we manage to end the patient's suffering by overcoming her neurotic conflict.
>
> (124)

Although Freud does not delineate the process through which the "psychical rigidity and unchangeability" (124) of the woman patient is overcome through therapy, it is evident that Freud has not given a logical reason for two significant declarations in his theory of the development of female sexuality.

45

First, Freud does not clarify the reason for the girl's believing that she has the 'inferior' genitals on first observing the anatomical difference between the two sexes. He just states it without giving any theoretical explanation or any evidence from observations or records of cases. Second, he completely overlooks the cultural practices that might contribute in girls perceiving the male gender to wield more power thereby originate her wish to identify with that gender. With the motive to establish the transfer of object-choice from the mother to the father, Freud uses the example of the doll the girl plays with to argue that the doll first stands in for the girl herself, during the stage when the girl's choice is still the mother, and the doll later stands in for the penis-baby the girl wishes her father would give her. This would mean that Freud suggests that the doll the child plays with substitutes for herself and for her desired penis-baby at different points in the development of sexuality of a girl. He posits that in the pre-Oedipus stage the child fantasies that the doll is a substitute for herself and expresses all her desires and transfers all her experiences onto the doll. Later, in the Oedipal stage, if the girl cannot manage to convert the doll into the desired penis-baby, she moves into masculine behaviour or regresses into her former pre-Oedipal behaviour. If the latter happens, the girl goes on substituting herself for the doll. With this declaration Freud is not only affirming the Victorian stereotype of the asexual, doll-like, women but also demonstrating a well-argued procedure for the birth of this 'type' that had gained popularity as the ideal of womanhood in that period. Thus, Freud's theories on femininity validated the existing stereotype by giving it 'scientific credibility'. Since women's sexuality did not fit into his 'scientific' framework, Freud *made* it fit into his paradigm.

Moreover, the conflation of the doll with the girl/woman and vice versa gained the authority of science with a theory of female sexuality that was developed around the confusion of the girl with her doll while the doll-like female was already a prevalent trope in literature and culture of the period. Considering that scientific theories were backing the doll-like passivity of women and girls, it was easy to believe, through the 20th century that the depictions of passivity as the natural feminine state in 19th-century literature and culture stemmed from an innate biological difference between the sexes. Although it is true that Freud goes to great lengths to explain that acquiring this desired passivity requires an immense amount of activity by girls, the pivoting of his theory of sexuality on anatomy facilitates in perpetuating the idea that biology is destiny. Given that a scientific expostulation of human sexuality established that passivity is the ideal feminine condition, any divergence from this 'natural' passivity of the feminine and the opposite as the ideal masculine state could remain largely unchallenged in literature and culture. Not only was this binary of the ideal states perpetuated, any divergence from it could readily be considered unnatural or a subversion from the 'norm'. Freud's theories of the mind and sexuality remain not just relevant but also quite central to make sense of many cultural motifs of

19th-century Europe and Anglo-American literature of the late-19th and early 20th centuries in the two continents.

In the next chapter, we will look at the ways in which the notions of natural passivity of girls and the corollary as the true condition for boys affected the formation of the ideals of childhood in the 19th century. It will also draw linkages between these aspired ideals in a few works of fiction in Anglo-American literature of the turn of the 19th century and its reverberations in the 20th century.

Notes

1 Jane Humphries in *Childhood and Child Labour in the British Industrial Revolution* (2010) states, "[c]hildren and young people comprised between one third and two-thirds of all workers in many textile mills in 1833 and regularly over one quarter in many mines in 1842" (5). However, Humphries also points out that government inquiries were usually confined to the textile and mining industries and cautions that with little hard data across industries and trades the issue of children's work and the extent of child labour during the industrial period remains open to interpretation. Nevertheless, Humphries also states that the autobiographies of working-class men she studied in this work "document astonishing levels of child labour throughout the period of the industrial revolution and throughout the British economy" of that period, extending to the late 19th century (7).

2 In a footnote to "Some Psychical Consequences of the Anatomical Distinction between the Sexes" (1925), the editor of Volume 7 of the Penguin Freud Library, Angela Richards, records Ernest Jones's statement of 1955 but also remarks: "Unfortunately Jones gives no date for this remark". Richards also adds: "Freud himself suggests a part explanation of his difficulty in the last paragraph of Section 1 of this later paper on 'Female Sexuality' (1931 b), where he attributes it to a peculiarity of his transference-relation with women" (326).

3 The three essays are: 'Some Psychical Consequences of the Anatomical Distinction between the Sexes' (1925), 'Female Sexuality' (1931), and 'Femaleness' (1933).

3

SAVING THE CHILD

> She is not even a person to him. He has reified her. She's his
> Oscar-Barbie statuette. His doll.
>
> Salman Rushdie. *Fury*. 2001. 11

In the first chapter of this work, the phrase 'the fiction of childhood' is used for the fiction that deals with childhood, irrespective of its target audience. However, in this chapter and the next one, there will be a differentiation made between writing for children and that for adults with the specific purpose of bringing out the ways in which gendered childhoods are constructed with the help of the toy as a prop for the two different kinds of readers. The two chapters will also examine varied ways in which the child is conflated with the toy in a few works of fiction from the middle of the 19th century to the early decades of the 20th century in the Anglo-American literary landscape.

The fiction of childhood often shows that although it is an accepted fact that the innocence of childhood is a myth, this myth is created and perpetuated more for the benefit of the adults who are interacting with the children than for children. By declaring the child to be innately innocent adults rule out the possibility of a child having any knowledge or awareness of 'sinful' feelings like sexuality.[1] Also, perpetuating the myth of the blissfully innocent and pure child through some works of the fiction of childhood helped in 'saving' the child – i.e., retaining the child in a pre-designated role in the established family structure of a post-industrialised society. In the late 19th and early 20th centuries in Britain and North America, there were set ideals of childhood that the child was expected to perform. This chapter will focus on three works written in the late 19th century in these continents with the objective of examining the way in which this project of 'saving' took place in literature. The repercussions of the reification of childhood by saving these fictional children into designated roles in the set family structure of those times will also be examined in this chapter. The three Anglo-American literary texts which will be closely examined are: *Hard Times* (1854) by

DOI: 10.4324/9781003093275-3

Charles Dickens; *What Maisie Knew* (1897) and *The Turn of the Screw* (1898) both by Henry James. These texts will be read using Freud's work on childhood and development of sexuality. A few other works of fiction from the middle of the Victorian Age to the early 20th century will be briefly glimpsed as instances of the creation and perpetuation of norms of childhood that eventually became entrenched as aspects of childhood in various cultures that were influenced by the dominant ideology of the 19th-century colonial power of Europe.

As established in the previous chapter, the ideals of childhood were formed through a few centuries of awareness of childhood as a distinctive phase of human life, with experiences that are significantly different from that of adults. It was also argued that in the course of recognising childhood, there was a homogenising of childhood in the Western world and that children were taught to aspire to attain a few ideals of perfection of childhood based on their gender and their established roles within the family. Children, as was argued by David Grylls (1978, 16) Carol Dyhouse (1981, 7), and Deborah Gorham (1982, 5) among others, were taught to join women of the family to make the home a pleasant place for the man. From being contributors to the family's economy in a pre-industrialised society, children in the 19th century were to make an emotional contribution to the happiness of the family. Not only were women, who were confined to the domestic sphere of the home, expected to guide children by being exemplars in making the home a comfortable space, Jane Lewis argues that the newly evolving natural sciences during the Victorian times were instrumental in establishing that women and children were less evolved as compared to men, thereby making them equally dependent on the 'provider' of the household (Lewis, 1984, 83).

Although Patricia Branca points out that many studies of Victorian women's writing in the late 20th century have noted the "theme of discontent" on being confined to the domestic sphere among women of the middle to upper classes (1975, 10), she also states that, "[i]n general, historians have viewed the Victorian middle-class woman's role in society as merely ornamental rather than functional or responsible" (6). However, Victorian women of those classes had the important function of training their daughters and pre-school sons into behaviour that was pleasing for the male head of the family and other adult men of the family. Carol Dyhouse in *Girls Growing up in Late Victorian and Edwardian England* (1981) and Deborah Gorham in *The Victorian Girl and the Feminine Ideal* (1982), establish that one of the chief activities of a mother was to guide the children into gendered behaviour by reinforcing the by then established notion of the separation between the home and the world. Dyhouse points out that:

There were many aspects of the organisation in a middle-class household which would have reinforced children's impression of the dignity and separateness of the male world. The existence of a study, for instance, into which fathers might retire in the evenings, a place into which the children did not normally venture .... A mother's time, however, mattered much less—her attention was often freely available to her husband, her children, the servants' needs and demands.

(8)

Furthermore, she argues that children did not learn "sexual division of labour" (9) only by "observing patterns of activity in which adults involved themselves" (9) but that quite early in life "children were recruited into these activities in a way which was often highly sex-specific" (9). She states that even in working-class households in urban areas or in rural households, girls were expected to help their mothers with housework while boys were given to understand that they will have to make contributions to the family's income. However, she also notes that "[s]mall boys in working-class households might be given to understand very early on that they would soon be able to make a more substantial contribution to their family's resources than would their sister" (9). She goes on to argue that "[g]irls were taught that deference towards brothers was part of the natural order of things" (12).

Similarly, Gorham too states that "the theme of brother-sister companionships figures frequently in stories for young children" (45) in the late 19th and early 20th centuries and that in many of these stories, "a brother—usually an older brother acts as a guide for his sister in intellectual and practical matters" (45) and that many such pairs were broken by the boy's "departure for school, while the sister remains at home ... and continues to focus her attention on her brother, even in his absence" (45). Furthermore, Gorham also states:

> To retain her moral authority with her brother, a sister had to retain her sheltered purity. A brother's love, respect and admiration, it was suggested, ought to be enough to cause a girl to adhere strictly to the canons of femininity.
>
> (45–46)

Gorham goes on to declare that "[m]aking the home pleasant for the males who belonged to it was thought to be her highest calling" (46). The mother had a special role in teaching her "daughter how to be truly feminine" (47). Gorham states that "it was generally agreed that a mother should have a special relationship with her daughter" (47). She elaborates that the ideal relationship between the mother and daughter was described in the following way:

The mother-daughter relationship was portrayed as one in which the daughter always confided in her mother who would be, above all other people, her moral, spiritual and practical guide .... The dutiful daughter would always seek and follow her mother's counsel, whether it was about friendships she should form or about spiritual matters or about what books she should read.

(48)

Additionally, Gorham quotes a Victorian writer, Mrs Roe in *A Woman's Thoughts on the Education of Girls* (1886), to describe the ways in which the ideal girl could "be both ladylike and useful" (50) with the following quotation from Mrs Roe's work:

My beau-ideal of a young lady is one who is equally in her place in the parlour and in the kitchen; who can converse pleasantly and rationally with her friends, make her voice and fingers 'discourse most eloquent music', use her needle skilfully for the adornment of her own person or in household matters, or go into the kitchen, and prepare a dinner.

(50)

Gorham also mentions that the "image of the ideal middle-class daughter was that of the sheltered flower" who would "never need to learn how to confront the harsh world outside the home" (50). Gorham goes on to delineate the repercussions of confining women to the domestic sphere but also establishes that girls were actively encouraged to emulate their mothers to eventually attain the ideal of womanhood for those times.

A frequently recurring image of womanhood in early 19th-century British literature was that of the 'Angel in the House'. While the qualities of ideal womanhood encompassed in that phrase were getting consolidated into creating an ideal British womanhood for a few decades before the phrase gained popularity, the image gained rapid circulation through the educated classes in the middle of the 19th century because it was the title of a long poem by Coventry Patmore. The poem delineated qualities that were considered ideal for a Victorian woman of the upper and middle classes of society to possess and display. Among these traits were purity, virtue, docility, meekness, humility, self-effacement, and a host of other such traits that reduced the ideal woman to a state of being in which she had no volition at all but came very close to being "a thing which [the Victorian man] desire(s)" (1856, Book II, Canto VIII. I, 162). This is what Patmore wishes his partner to be:

But let my gentle Mistress be,
In every look, word, deed and thought,

Nothing but sweet and womanly!
Her virtues please my virtuous mood,
But what at all times I admire
Is, not that she is wise or good,
But just the thing which I desire.

(162)

Not surprisingly, there were objections to this complete objectification even in the 19th century. Elizabeth Barrett Browning wrote a scathing counter to it in her *Aurora Leigh* (1856). Although both the books were published in 1856, Patmore's poem had first been published in 1854 and a revised and expanded version was published in 1856. Bina Freiwald mentions the 'fight' between the two poets over their idea of ideal womanhood and also quotes Virginia Crawford who declared in 1901 that "Mr Patmore never gave a thought to the feminine soul save in its relation to a man" (1988, 541). A few other 19th-century women too were questioning the roles assigned to middle- and upper-class women of their contemporary society through their writing. Elaine Showalter quotes one such writer in "Family Secrets and Domestic Subversion: Rebellion in the Novels of the 1860s". This writer, Isa Jane Blagden wrote *Agnes Tremorne* in 1861, in which she revealed:

It must be confessed ... that the so-called happy homes of England belie their name miserably. A family of grown-up daughters ... debarred from freedom of action and freedom of opinion, with miserable little occupations which fritter away, but do not occupy time—often prohibited the healthy exercise which is as necessary to the mind as the body, and systematically leaving the intellect, the heart, the blood, in total stagnation—is it surprising that such women grow old as sickly invalids or confirmed hypochondriacs?
(In Anthony S. Wohl, Ed. *The Victorian Family: Structure and Stresses*. 1978. 106)

While a few women expressly wished to move away from conventionally prescribed roles during the late-Victorian and early-Edwardian period, there was a lack of role models that these women could emulate. Raymond Chapman pointed out in *Forms of Speech in Victorian Fiction* (1994),

[t]here were few role models for women—wife and mother, devoted spinster daughter or aunt, governess or companion. For the working class there was the prospect before marriage of 'service' or manual labour, with the terror of 'the streets' as the final abyss.

(140)

Martha Vicinus states that even in the fiction of the times, single women "were not permitted to be single and happy outside a carefully defined set of family duties" (1985, 11).

Many scholars engaged in tracing a feminist historiography even in the last two decades of the 20th century brought up the image of the 'angel in the house' as one of the chief obstacles faced by 19th-century women writers in their attempts at writing and in creating fictional women characters that did not mirror this ideal. Deborah Gorham describes this ideal in the following way:

> Victorian conceptions of the idealised role of women are epitomised by Coventry Patmore's poem *The Angel in the House*, the title of which captures its essence. The ideal woman was willing to be dependent on men and submissive to them, and she would have a preference for a life restricted to the confines of home. She would be innocent, pure, gentle, and self-sacrificing. Possessing no ambitious strivings, she would be free of any trace of anger or hostility. More emotional than man, she was also more capable of self renunciation.
>
> (4)

Jane Lewis in *Women in England: 1870–1950* (1984) mentions Eric Trudgill's work in 1976 in which he "has drawn a biting picture of the Victorian middle class wife as 'a mental and moral cripple', both angel of the house and idiot" (125). Virginia Woolf has elaborated upon the detrimental effects of this stereotype of the ideal woman in *A Room of One's Own* (1929), in multiple ways, including in her creation of a writer sister of Shakespeare. She argues in this landmark work that women, in the history of English literature and in the then contemporary times, were not part of the canon of celebrated authors because they did not have a private space in their households to think and work on writing. Woolf believes that if women were given access to the kind of education and other opportunities that men had historically received, they would be able to make an indelible mark in the fields of literature and academics. Through this work, Woolf challenged quite a few conventional stereotypes about women. For instance, she argued that the prevalent belief that women's nervous system was not equipped to take the strain of thinking was erroneous. Woolf was among the first writers in the early 20th century to declare that women can write only if they successfully battle the entrenched image of 'angel in the house'. In a paper delivered in 1931 to the Women's Service League, titled 'Professions for Women', Woolf suggested writing as one of the professions that women could and did pursue. She warned her audience that the internalised persona of the 'Angel in the House' would try to thwart every aspiring woman writer's attempts towards addressing serious issues in her writing. Woolf bravely declared, "[k]illing the Angel in their House was part of the occupation of a woman writer" (*Collected Essays*, Vol.2, 1972, 286).

Despite objections by women writers from the very year the eponymous poem that popularised the phrase 'Angel in the House' was published, the phrase and the image it created gained popularity to such an extent that the image of the ideal woman – a close approximation of an angelic persona, the Perfect Lady – as an asexual, vulnerable, dependent person was established as worthy of emulation in most Victorian households. Many scholars researching the lives of Victorian women in the last decades of the 20th century attributed the prevalence of this image of ideal womanhood to socioeconomic reasons. Deborah Gorham (1982) posits that the Victorian response to industrial capitalism was to draw sharp boundaries between the world of work and that of personal life. Gorham calls this "cult of domesticity, an idealised vision of home and family" (4). She goes on to argue that "[t]he creation of a sharp division between the private world of home and the public world of commerce, professional life and politics, had a profound impact on the way in which women were perceived in the Victorian period" (4). While Lorna Duffin called the Victorian Perfect Lady "the perfect symbol of status" (Delamont and Duffin, 1978, 26), a "symbol of conspicuous leisure and the agent of conspicuous consumption" (24) whose status "gave her no purposeful activity but instead rendered her progressively more and more useless" (26), Gorham argues that the ideal woman had a very important role to play in the Victorian family. Elaborating on the division of the Victorian world into "two 'separate spheres'" (4), Gorham states:

> Each of the two spheres was thought to be inextricably connected either with women or with men. The public sphere of business, politics, and professional life was defined as the male sphere. The private sphere of love, the emotions and domesticity was defined as the sphere of women. The public sphere was the male's exclusive domain, whereas the private sphere was seen as presided over by females for the express purpose of providing a place for renewal for men, after their rigorous activities in the harsh, competitive public sphere.
>
> (4)

Furthermore, Gorham describes the roles carved out for members of the "idealised Victorian home" (5) as:

> just as the parental roles were suffused with intense emotional significance, so also was the role of children. Both male and female

children were of importance in idealisations of family life, but daughters had a special significance. Sons would help to determine the middle class family's place in the world, but daughters could offer the family a particular sort of tenderness and spirituality.

(5)

As she goes on to delineate the ways in which girls were trained into a particular performance of femininity, Gorham convincingly argues that the process of projecting innocence onto the girl child was easier on account of established cultural perceptions of the innocence of childhood. She states:

Much more successfully than her mother, a young girl could represent the quintessential angel in the house. Unlike an adult woman, a girl could be perceived as a wholly unambiguous model of feminine dependence, childlike simplicity and sexual purity. While it might be believed that an adult woman should retain a childlike simplicity, clearly a real child could be conceived of as more childlike than could an adult woman.

(7)

The particular role of the girl child in a Victorian household became that of a miniature Perfect Lady – perceived as diminutive women, their mothers became their role models and trainers. Considering that it was expected of mothers and daughters to be close to each other and for the latter to learn her feminine roles from the former, there was much written on the conduct and training of girls. Gorham quotes Marianne Faringham, who wrote an advice book titled *Girlhood* in 1869, in which she states that the daughters of Victorian families should be "sunbeams that make everything glad" (38). Gorham elaborates the traits of the sunbeam as "creatures whose self-forgetfulness, whose willingness to help others, would create a harmonious environment". Furthermore, she states that "[t]he good daughter would always put the claims of home and her obligations to her father first, before any outside concerns" (38) and also declares that "[i]n a happy home, the daughter's obligation towards her father was to be a cheerful, accommodating 'sunbeam'. Should the family situation present difficulties, more arduous duties and qualities were demanded of the ideal daughter" (39). However, Gorham also states that there was an awareness of the ideal being unachievable. She states:

If the image of harmonious domesticity remained a pervasive ideal that shaped both individual and collective consciousness, so also did a sense of uneasiness about that ideal. Out of this uneasiness, this unspoken recognition that the ideal must, by its very nature, remain unattainable, arose a series of parallel images, images that were negative in character ... the image of the perfect daughter had its counterpart. The good daughter was gentle, loving, self-sacrificing and innocent: the bad daughter was vulgar, self-seeking, lazy and sexually impure.

(37)

Gorham also describes a contrast to the "sunbeam". She calls this "image" of girlhood a "hoyden" and clarifies that "[t]he image of the hoyden did not serve precisely the same function as the image of the lazy, vulgar girl of the period" (56) and that "[d]escriptions of hoydenish girls do not imply that they will become husband-hunters, but rather that they will become mannish 'strong-minded' women" (56). Carol Dyhouse, who presents a similar argument regarding the ideals of femininity demanding "service and self-sacrifice as quintessential forms of 'womanly' behaviour" (2) states that:

From early childhood girls were encouraged to suppress (or conceal) ambition, intellectual courage or initiative—any desire for power or independence. The feelings of guilt and/or ambivalence which many strong intelligent women wrestled with in the attempt to reconcile their drives with what they had been taught to perceive as their 'feminine' social identity are a recurrent theme.

(2)

The recurrence of this ideal and the various 'images' of girlhood it generated throughout the 20th century in feminist scholarship in Britain indicates that this image had gained wide popularity through the second half of the 19th century. Indeed, 19th-century British realist fiction has its fair share of 'angels in the house' and this image of ideal womanhood as pure, gentle, self-effacing, unambitious, asexual became a recurring motif not only in British literature but also in American literature almost until the middle of the 20th century. Indian English literature, even until the end of the 20th century, records a marked presence of this image of ideal womanhood.

Many male writers of 19th-century British literature helped in many ways to perpetuate the stereotype, as can be seen in the works of Charles Dickens, William Thackeray, and George Macdonald, all of whose heroines either aim to be or are expected to be the 'angel in the house'. Gilbert and Gubar (1979, 26) call these male writers who created these angel women characters "male angelographers" after having stated that "[t]he ideal woman that male authors dream of generating is always an angel" (20). They also declare that "there is a clear line of literary descent from divine Virgin to domestic angel, passing through (among many others) Dante, Milton and Goethe" (20) thereby, stating that Victorian fiction was reiterating a firmly established fantasy of the asexual woman as the goddess of the domestic hearth. However, they also argue that these fictional depictions that show that "the angel woman manipulates her domestic/mystical sphere in order to ensure the well-being of those entrusted to her care reveal that she can manipulate; she can scheme; she can plot—stories as well as strategies" (26), which proves that these women are more human than angels. They concede that the "Victorian angel's scheming, her mortal fleshiness, and her repressed ... capacity for explosive rage are often subtly acknowledged even in the most glowing texts of male 'angelographers'" (26). Women writers too – including the three Bronte sisters, George Eliot, Elizabeth Gaskell, and Frances Hodgson Burnett, among others – either created their heroines according to the stereotype or made them submit to the stereotype. In some cases of these fictional depictions, the protagonists put up intense resistance or struggle against the stereotype and in a few other instances, they fatally fail in getting transformed into the ideal.

Charles Dickens had a menagerie of 'angels in the house', with varying degrees of 'angelic behaviour' and of different ages, in his corpus of work. Dickens covers the entire range from the sunbeam to the angel, with many variations of the two ideals. Some of these characters are: Nelly Trent in *The Old Curiosity Shop* (1841), Florence Dombey in *Dombey and Son* (1848), Clara Copperfield and Dora Copperfield in *David Copperfield* (1850), Little Dorrit in *Little Dorrit* (1857), and Lucy Manette in *A Tale of Two Cities* (1859). Although Dickens seems to have moved from the image of the 'angel in the house' to that of the 'Victorian helpmeet'[2] with his depiction of David's second wife, Agnes Copperfield in *David Copperfield*, he continued to create variations of the trope in his portrayals of other women characters in his later work too. Despite sketching a sharp caricature of the Perfect Lady in the character of Mrs Gradgrind in *Hard Times* (1854), Dickens promotes the Victorian stereotype of the sunbeam in the same novel through his depiction of Sissy Jupe. Whereas he also does a scathing critique of Utilitarianism, showing it as a harmful system of rearing children to fit into set notions of ideal social behaviour. The project of upbringing delineated in *Hard Times* will be examined in detail later in this chapter.

Women writers, however, seem to present the struggle to attain the ideal much more than the depictions of the ideal of girlhood or womanhood noticed in the work of Dickens. While George Eliot's Eppie in *Silas Marner* (1861) is a perfect 'sunbeam', her Maggie Tulliver in *The Mill on the Floss* (1860) is a perfect 'hoyden'. Maggie's cousin Lucy is the 'angel in the house' whom she is supposed to emulate and fails with fatal consequences. Eliot's rendering of Maggie's travails show that she empathised with Maggie in her inability to conform. In a rare depiction of a girl playing with a doll, in Victorian fiction, Eliot portrays the doll as a projection of her anguished self by Maggie, who retires to her safe space of the attic to express her anger, anguish, frustration, and grief by subjecting the doll to such violence that all that remains of the doll is a trunk with a misshapen head. A post-Freudian reader might note the substitution for herself and the enactment of the treatment she perceives to have received from the mother in Maggie's interaction with her doll. However, Eliot's depiction of the psychic life of Maggie in her struggles to overcome her desire to be more like the Victorian 'hoyden' than the Victorian 'sunbeam' is a rare exception. In *Jane Eyre* (1847), Charlotte Bronte also shows that the transition from childhood to girlhood and further on to womanhood is nothing short of a pyrrhic victory without describing any moment of play or relaxation in Jane's life. Emily Bronte's *Wuthering Heights* (1847) juxtaposes the namesakes Catherine Earnshaw and her daughter Catherine Linton as the perfect 'hoyden' and the perfect 'sunbeam'. Neither Catherine has an easy time of acting out their expected feminine roles within their families in the two isolated houses on an English moor.

The widespread prevalence of the ideal image of womanhood and the reverence with which it is treated in literature through almost two centuries not only makes it the aspirational ideal but it is also frequently presented as a composite of the 'natural' qualities of all women. Despite much scholastic work by women challenging this image, its continuing dissemination through the arts and popular culture makes it a sustaining ideal for all women and for girls to emulate. It was believed, even in the first half of the 20th century, that all the traits deemed to be desirable in women of a certain class in the 19th century were innately present in all women. In the middle of the 20th century, Simone de Beauvoir heralded a new debate in gender studies with "[O]ne is not born, but rather becomes a woman" in *The Second Sex* (1949, Trans and Ed, H. M. Parshley, 1953, 295). Beauvoir's work establishes through a detailed argument that although biology is important, gender is socially constructed. She argues that woman is constructed as the Other by man who believes that man was created in the image of the Absolute, i.e., God. Since woman is seen as the Other when laws are made to safeguard the family and other established social institutions, they are made from the man's perspective. She gives an instance of such an occurrence, "the Roman law limiting the rights of woman cited 'the imbecility, the instability of the sex' just when the weakening of family ties seemed to threaten the interests of male heirs" (22).

Moreover, de Beauvoir's work was path-breaking in positing that gender roles are not innate but are inculcated among children. This argument can be considered as the foundation to understand that gender is performed and that the processes are perpetuated through strong stereotypes and cultural tropes for long periods. Sue Sharpe, who has done an empirical study of girls in 20th-century Britain, shows in *Just Like a Girl* (1976) that perceptions of girlhood are rife with stereotypes even in the last decades of the century. In 1983, Sharpe added a few more chapters to her book and republished it after some more fieldwork. The later edition has data from the Asian quarters of London and reiterates all the stereotypes Sharpe noted in her 1976 study conducted among white middle-class London girls. She observed that the choice of formal education for boys and girls was made by families after considering their prescribed 'roles' in society. Girls were trained in home-making skills, while boys were taught more technical, mathematical, and scientific things. She notes that the outbreak of the war in 1914 brought large numbers of women into the workforce and this changed their position in society. Sharpe observes that despite this large-scale change in women's work, many of the stereotypes established in the 19th century were firmly present even in the 1970s and early 1980s. For instance, it was generally believed that women are more preoccupied with physical beauty and moth-ers in the early 1980s in London were still actively trying to inculcate the importance of an awareness of set standards of beauty in their daughters. Sharpe also noted that gender-based behaviour of various forms was dis-played by most of the people she spoke to; especially so when they were talking about children. With regard to the choosing of toys for children, she says:

> Toy makers, sellers and buyers are all agreed in their assumptions of what is more suitable and enjoyable for boys and girls, and this reflects children's supposed interests, skills and future roles. Boys' toys are more active and technical, and include cars, trains, planes, spacemen, and cricket bats, chemistry sets and miniature microscopes. Girls have a selection of far less active or exciting toys which stimulate a rehearsal of women's traditional role. They have dolls, teddy-bears and other animals, doll's houses and prams, tea-sets, miniature ovens, pots and pans. There is usually some overlap, especially through sharing toys with brothers, but children soon become able to distinguish girls' toys from those of boys.
>
> (78)

It is evident that the ideals of development of femininity and masculinity, which had gained currency in literature and perpetuated through many works of 19th-century writers, developed into established gender roles in societies and were propagated through prevalent cultural practices even in the final decades of the 20th century.

As mentioned earlier in this work, in addition to the perpetuation of a passive, submissive demeanour as the ideal, the Victorian period strongly developed the idea that girls were almost asexual beings. Coupled with the long-standing idea of the sexual innocence of children was the Victorian idea that older girls too were ignorant of sexuality. Gorham describes this notion in the following way:

> In polite Victorian discourse, the idea that a young girl could have any sexual thoughts at all was simply bypassed. It was part of the Victorian belief system that girls were not only innocent of

sexuality, they were ignorant of it: indeed, their ignorance was the main safeguard of their innocence. If a girl lost her ignorance, if she became aware of sexuality, she was in imminent danger of becoming unchaste.

(54)

With such a strong premium on sexual purity not only in actions but also in thoughts, it is understandable that Victorian girls in the fiction written even by women writers struggled to attain the ideals of the 'innocent' 'sunbeam' who would effortlessly grow into the 'asexual' 'Perfect Lady'. One of the most serious repercussions of deeming Victorian girls as asexual was noted by Jane Lewis in *Women in England: 1870–1950* (1984). She states that "[t]he denial of sexuality in children was so complete that the rape of a girl child was considered to be of much less importance than the same crime against an adult" (126). Along with denying the harm a violent sexual encounter could do to a girl, the notion of asexuality of girls even after they faced sexual assault shows the reification of girls into doll-like objects.

The plethora of 'angelic' girls in Charles Dickens's oeuvre and the large number of girl characters who struggled with the dissonance between their desires and societal expectations in the considerable body of work by women writers of the Victorian period is testimony to the widespread propagation of an ideal of womanhood that involved focusing on the development of an asexual, self-effacing, nurturer. Whereas Dickens created a range of 'angelic' daughters and inefficient and ineffectual albeit mostly cherished wives and mothers who were adored as perfect ladies, his starkest sketches of all the four stereotypes of Victorian womanhood and girlhood – the Angel in the House, the Perfect Lady, the sunbeam, and the hoyden – are present in *Hard Times* (1854). In this novel, Dickens uses caricature as a potent tool both in form and content. Coketown, the fictitious industrial town where the novel is set, invokes soot and grime through its very name. The few descriptions of the town depict the smoke-filled chimneys, the unhealthy air, houses designed for functionality, the ditches that serve as homes for runaway children, and the rows of claustrophobic boxes in which the factory 'hands' live. There is hardly any mention of the healthy aspects of the countryside around the town. The countryside, when it is briefly mentioned, is the space where a victim of the industrial structure, Stephen Blackpool, dies. While the setting and description of Stephen's death act as a foil to the rigid dehumanising of the industrial society of Coketown, Dickens also emphasises the societal mores of the industrial township as contributory factors for the almost allegorical characters of the novel. His stark declaration, "[y]ou saw nothing in Coketown but what was severely workful" (19) is the "key-note" (18) of the setting of the novel and also of the philosophy governing the lives of the characters of the novel. The contrast brought into the structures of Coketown is through a traveling circus. Rather than being a welcome addition of colour to the starkness of Coketown, they seem to bring the threat of the unknown and unpredictable into the town by attracting the attention of the townspeople, including children who are strictly brought up in formulaic ways that would guarantee disdain for non-structured activities and ways of life. Shortly after the narrative begins, it is reported by the leading intellectual of Coketown, Thomas Gradgrind, that he caught his oldest son, Tom and oldest daughter, Louisa, committing the 'shameful' act of surreptitiously peeping into the circus tent. Their action is deemed unworthy of their education and upbringing by their father; especially because the circus is the polar opposite of the Utilitarian system of education promoted in his school and rigorously applied even in his household. The contrast of the itinerant lives of the circus people with the fixity of Coketown's chimneys is highlighted through descriptions of the spaces, the people, their actions, and their speech. While the circus people seem to lead a dynamic life in the temporary structures where they live and perform, Gradgrind, the member of parliament for Coketown and its chief capitalist benefactor, Bounderby, not only rigidly hold on to their beliefs but also actively perpetuate it among the denizens of the town. In a unique move that gives an unusual sense of agency to women, the characters whose actions led to the eventual breakdown of these structures are the women in the novel. However, the women are not depicted as overt rebels who would eventually challenge these structures. On the contrary, they are almost perfect products of the belief systems that upheld the chimneys of Coketown. All of them emerged from the post-industrialised Victorian society's value systems that drew a strong demarcation between the home and the world, with clearly defined roles and responsibilities of the two genders in these separate spheres.

In a departure from Dickens's earlier depictions of the 'angelic' women as belonging to the middle class, in this novel the 'Angel in the House' is a working-class woman, Rachel. She is so self-effacing that she chooses to ignore her feelings for Stephen and overlook his love for her. Furthermore, she not only convinces Stephen to stay married to a dissipated woman but also cares for Stephen's wife when the latter is severely unwell. In recognition of her worth to him, Stephen declares, "Thou'rt an Angel; it may be, thou hast saved my soul alive!" While Rachel is among the least empowered persons in the Victorian social structure, being a working-class single woman, she is also the most cherished Victorian trope – The Angel in the House.

However, the character who is seemingly the one with the least agency in the novel is Mrs Gradgrind. She is almost the last of the principal characters to be introduced into the narrative and is described as

a little, thin, white, pink-eyed bundle of shawls, of surpassing feebleness, mental and bodily; who was always taking physic without any effect, and who, whenever she showed a symptom of coming to life, was invariably stunned by some weighty piece of fact tumbling on her.

(13)

D. J. Thorold calls her the "polar opposite of the lively circus women" and opines that she "must be one of the most crushed wives in English fiction" (2000, xx). There are many instances in the narrative which hint at the complete lack of utility of Mrs Gradgrind in the Gradgrind household – multiple instances of her being mentioned as semi-recumbent on a couch in the drawing room performing the role of the invalid; nervous wreck, who does not contribute in any way to the efficient running of the Gradgrind family; seldom has anything to say and is almost never heard when she summons the energy to express coherent thoughts. Even her interactions with her children are either complaints about her ill-health or admonishments that are expressed as, "Go and be somethingological directly" (15) before retiring into an invisibility that is described by the narrator as "she once more died away, and nobody minded her" (15). While Dickens' depiction of Mrs Gradrind is a caricature of the Victorian Perfect Lady, she's rescued from complete uselessness in the scene where she is dying and finally expresses herself to her daughter, Louisa. In a telling depiction of the dysfunctionality of the mother–daughter relationship due to the formulaic ways of the Gradgrind household, the mother expresses her feelings as coherently as she is capable of in the following conversation:

> "Well, my dear," said Mrs. Gradgrind, "and I hope you are going on satisfactorily to yourself. It was all your father's doing. He set his heart upon it. And he ought to know".
>
> "I want to hear of you, mother; not of myself."
>
> "You want to hear of me, my dear? That's something new, I am sure, when anybody wants to hear of me. Not at all well, Louisa. Very faint and giddy."
>
> "Are you in pain, dear mother?"
>
> "I think *there's a pain somewhere in the room*", said Mrs. Gradgrind, "but I couldn't positively say that I have got it".
>
> (Emphasis added, 156)

This becomes a unique death-bed scene among a large number of death-bed scenes in Victorian literature due to the severe difficulties the mother–daughter duo display in articulating their feelings. When Mrs Gradgrind, for the very first time in the narrative, asks her daughter about her emotional well-being, Louisa is unable to share her feelings with her mother. Furthermore, she deflects the anxiety about her emotional well-being by asking her mother about her physical well-being. Not only is Mrs Gradrgind unable to receive this gesture of care without a sharp retort of it being a rare instance but is also completely unable to locate the pain within herself. The conversation would, in post-Freudian times, serve as a good illustration of one between two dissociated beings who suffer the lack within but neither is able to recognise it sufficiently to be able to coherently articulate it to each other.

Nevertheless, Mrs Gradgrind finally proves herself useful for her family, and for the narrative, by articulating her thoughts just before actually disappearing from the narrative through the following words:

> "You must remember, my dear, that whenever I have said anything, on any subject, I have never heard the last of it: and consequently, that I have long left off saying anything."
>
> …
>
> "You learnt a great deal, Louisa, and so did your brother. Ologies of all kinds from morning to night. If there is any Ology left, of any description, that has not been worn to rags in this house, all I can say is, I hope I shall never hear its name."
>
> "I can hear you, mother, when you have strength to go on". This, to keep her from floating away.
>
> "But there is something—not an Ology at all—that your father has missed or forgotten, Louisa. I don't know what it is. I have often sat with Sissy near me, and thought about it. I shall never get its names now. But your father may. It makes me restless. I want to write to him, to find out for God's sake, what it is. Give me a pen, give me a pen".
>
> (156)

Although her death is described by the narrator as "the light that had always been feeble and dim behind the weak transparency, went out" (156), Mrs Gradgrind firmly placed the spotlight on the lack within the Gradgrind system as she faded out of it. She accurately spotted Sissy as the character that carried within her the missing element in the structure created by Gradgrind.

Sissy Jupe, the abandoned daughter of the failing clown from the circus, is taken in as an 'experiment' by Mr Gradgrind. The girl is first brought to his notice as Girl Number 20 in the schoolroom where he is propagating his system of education that works on a reiteration of facts and a discounting of fancy. Sissy lives among the horse-riding people from the circus but cannot accurately give a scientific description of a horse. On discovering that her father has walked out of the circus and her life, with his fanciful belief that her life would improve without the presence of her failing father, Sissy accepts Gradgrind's offer to join his household with a fond hope that she would be fulfilling her father's dream by acquiring an education. Far from turning into the model pupil of the Gradgrind system, Sissy acts as an efficient foil to highlight the lacunae within the said system. She cannot but continue to use terms such as 'fancy' and 'wonder' while being ensconced within the emotionless facts of the Gradgrind school and home. She stubbornly holds on to the hope that her father will come back to find her and towards the end of the narrative, in an interaction where Sissy is trying to save the Gradgrind family from a scandal, she describes herself as "Sissy Jupe, a poor girl ... separated from my father – he was only a stroller – and taken pity on by Mr Gradgrind. I have lived in the house ever since" (184). She is an integral, useful, and indispensable person in the Gradgrind household by this point in the narrative but does not identify with the 'Gradgrindery' prevalent in the family. She continues to identify with the opposite domain of the circus – the world of fancy – and brings in the best aspects of that world into the Gradgrind world when the latter is crumbling. She chooses to see Gradgrind's act of taking her in as an act of pity instead of accepting his clearly stated motive of it being an experiment. Although Gradgrind's experiment with Sissy fails, just as his experiment with his children also fails, Sissy successfully completes the task set out for her in the narrative. Thorold noted that Dickens had given her the label of 'Power of Affection' in his working notes for the novel (x). As the sole representative of the circus people, integrated into the Gradgrind world, Sissy brings in the power of affection into the facts-infested, soot-filled lives of the post-industrialised Gradgrind family. She is the quintessential "sunbeam that makes everything glad"(38), described by Marianne Faringham in 1869 and quoted by Deborah Gorham in 1982 to depict the stereotype of the ideal Victorian girl. Dickens had, in fact, clearly described her as "the beginning of a sunbeam" (5) while contrasting her placement in the schoolroom with the most successful student of the Gradgrind system as seated in such a way that he 'caught the end' of the sunlight. Dickens goes on to describe that the boy's "skin was so unwholesomely deficient in the natural tinge, that he looked as though, if it were cut, he would bleed white" (5).

While Dickens uses a unique shorthand for this novel to suggest that the nurture the students received from nature and from the systems of nurturance they were part of formed them into healthy or seemingly unhealthy individuals in his play of contrast in the physical characteristics of Sissy Jupe and Bitzer, he also seems to indicate, through his label for Sissy in his working notes and the role she plays in the narrative, that Sissy innately and 'naturally' carries the healing aspects of the Victorian 'sunbeam'. The mostly voiceless Mrs Gradgrind had recognised that about Sissy. Eventually, the progenitor of the new system of nurturance based on facts and logic, Mr Gradgrind, also reaches the same conclusion when he witnesses "the pride of his heart and the triumph of his system, lying, an insensible heap, at his feet" (171) in a nervous collapse. Before she collapses, Louisa describes her internal battle between her hopes for herself and the Gradgrindian system's expectation of her with the pithy statement: "In this strife I have almost repulsed and crushed my better angel into a demon" (170). With that declaration, not only does Louisa describe herself as having become the 'hoyden', a foil to Sissy's 'sunbeam', but also suggests that she 'naturally' carries the binary of the angel and the demon within herself. She clearly indicates to him, through the collapse and a declaration of the failure of his system that the 'nurture' she received has failed her and that her father has to find an alternative to his system to save his daughter. Just before fainting, she says:

> I do not know that I am sorry, I do not know that I am ashamed, I do not know that I am degraded in my own esteem. All that I know is your philosophy and your teaching will not save me. Now, father you have brought me to this. Save me by some other means!
>
> (171)

Taking the logically enunciated hint of his daughter, Gradgrind finds the alternative of 'nature' in Sissy Jupe to help his daughter work her way out of the breakdown. He completely hands over the care of the recovering Louisa to Sissy after wrangling with Bounderby to briefly release Louisa from her wifely duties in order to "leave her to her better nature for a while" (189). In spite of Gradgrind's anguished admission to his friend Bounderby that he failed his daughter with his Gradgridian system, Bounderby harshly admonishes him to not make himself "a spectacle of unfairness as well as inconsistency" (189) and declares:

> As to your daughter, whom I made Loo Bounderby, and might have done better by leaving Loo Gradgrind, if she don't come home tomorrow, by twelve o'clock at noon, I shall understand that she prefers to stay away, and I shall send her wearing apparel and so forth over here, and you'll take charge of her for the future. What shall I say to people in general, of the incompatibility that led to my so laying down the law, will be this. I am Josiah Bounderby, and I had my bringing up; she's the daughter of Tom Gradgrind, and she had her bringing up; and the two horses wouldn't pull together.
>
> (191)

In his use of the metaphor of horses and his refusal to accept his legally ordained responsibility of the upkeep of Louisa, Bounderby reveals the cracks in the edifices of education and marriage built upon rational frameworks of facts and laws. In that conversation with Gradgrind, Bounderby not only divests himself of any responsibility for Louisa's collapse but also declares that the entire enterprise of education is a complete waste. In consonance with the myth of the self-made man that he routinely propagates, he chooses to tell Gradgrind what education should be in the following words:

> You have found it out at last, have you? Education! I'll tell you what education is—To be tumbled out of doors, neck and crop, and put upon the shortest allowance of everything except blows. That's what *I* call education.
>
> (188)

Although they seem to take diverging and conflicting paths in their perceptions of their responsibility towards Louisa, Gradgrind and Bounderby reach the same point of discarding 'nurture' and placing their faith in 'nature'. With the many failures of the 'unnatural' during the course of the narrative, the 'natural' is foregrounded as the failsafe principle for the upbringing of children. The system of education described to be in conscious opposition to the 'natural' instincts of children radically fails. Louisa's mother whose 'natural' instincts are overwritten by her authoritarian husband fails in protecting her daughter from getting into a loveless marriage. Louisa, who is made 'unnatural' through her father's system, has a collapse and is, then, gently led by the 'Power of Affection' of the more 'natural' Sissy towards recovering her 'natural' instincts of care and concern for her family. The 'unnatural' actions by Gradgrind and Bounderby are corrected by the 'natural' instincts of the women characters who display their agency through actions that are deemed appropriate for their gender in their social milieu. The subtle foregrounding of the 'natural', through various instances in the narrative, underscores the entrenched 19th-century notion that gender is defined by anatomy.

Moreover, women and girls with a highly developed sense of self are objectified in ways that lead to their becoming 'projects' of experiment and exchange among the men in the narrative. Ironically, the only one who rejects the label of the angel to point out the reality of their situation is the least socially empowered one among the women and girls in the narrative. Rachel, on being called an angel by Stephen, states:

> I am, as I have told thee, Stephen, thy poor friend. Angels are not like me. Between them, and a working woman fu' of faults, there is a deep gulf set. My little sister is among them, but she is changed.
>
> (70)

By invoking her dead sister, whom she identifies as an angel, Rachel is making a clear distinction between disembodied ethereal beings and the struggles of the earthy, living woman who has to behave in angelic ways to uphold Victorian morality. In stark contrast to this assertion of selfhood stands Louisa, who agrees to be given away in marriage at the age of 20 to her father's 50-year-old friend. Her hidden motive for agreeing to a loveless marriage is that it will lubricate her brother's career trajectory while her clearly expressed refrain regarding her life at that moment is: "What does it matter" (79). Neither does her logical acumen allow her to save herself from being moulded into the perfect ideal of her father's system nor does her 'natural' instinct of affection for her brother set her on a path to finding happiness for herself. Despite being one of the main women characters in the narrative, she is the one toyed with and moulded by multiple people to suit their purposes. Her father moulds her to be the perfect model of his education system. Her mother enables the experiment by not articulating her discomfort with the experiment. Her brother indicates that she could facilitate his happiness by marrying their father's friend. Her father's friend hankers after her from the time she is around 15 years old and declares her to be unfit to remain as his wife within a year of their being married, when she is around 21. Her new male friend expresses love for her and proposes that they elope while he is fully aware of the social repercussions of that act. Her education and her knowledge of socio-religious injunctions stop her from accepting the proposal but precipitate a nervous collapse. Sissy acts on her behalf to ensure that her tempter disappears from her life. Louisa spends the rest of her fictional life as an affectionate sister to her younger siblings, the head of her father's household while spending her spare time "watching the fire as in days of yore, though with a gentler and a humbler face" (233). The narrator also depicts all that Louisa might see in the fires of the hearth in her father's living room but will never experience. They are:

> Herself again a wife—a mother—lovingly watchful of her children, ever careful that they should have a childhood of the mind no less than a childhood of the body, as knowing it to be even a more beautiful thing, and a possession, any hoarded scrap of which, is a blessing and happiness to the wisest? Did Louisa see this? Such a thing was never to be.
>
> (234)

The narrative not only robs her of any agency during the course of the narrative but also declares that her future entails a mostly passive act of staring at the fires of life around her without much scope to actively participate in life as a wife or a mother. She is a Victorian girl who is consciously brought up to be a 'hoyden', is steered towards emulating a 'sunbeam' after facing a serious obstacle in the path to selfhood but does not grow into womanhood either as the Perfect Lady of the house or as the Angel in the House. The Victorian social mores that are deemed 'natural' by Dickens fail Louisa just as much as she is failed by the 'unnatural' Utilitarian system that was scathingly attacked by Dickens in this novel. Unlike other heroines in Dickens's fairly large repertoire of women characters, Louisa is not a model for emulation by his contemporary or later readers of his work. She is a warning of the horrors that await any act or experiment of tweaking the 'naturalised' sense of ideal womanhood for the times. Although Louisa has within her access templates of the ideal Victorian types to emulate among the women around her, the dominant presence of the male, her father, in the domestic sphere seemingly ruins the beneficial influences that women can exude within the private sphere. In keeping with the prevalent ideology of the clear demarcation of work spheres for men and women during the middle of the Victorian Age, Dickens seems to castigate Gradgrind for interfering in work which was supposed to be done by his wife – the Victorian mother who was supposed to train her daughter to become the ideal Victorian homemaker. With his critique of the changes the Utilitarian system was ostensibly bringing about in the education and upbringing of children, Dickens reiterates the by then established preference for nature in a struggle between nature and nurture. Furthermore, through his delineations of the fortunes of the four stereotypes of Victorian femininity and indicating ones that are to be considered exemplary by his child–woman protagonist, Dickens suggests that the most laudatory form of femininity is the self-effacing, asexual, chaste person who "would always put the claims of home and her obligations to her father first, before any outside concerns" (Gorham, 38) thereby freezing Louisa into an eternal child-like state of the good daughter to her Victorian father – his favourite child who will remain within his fiefdom for him to "conjure" (168) into action and articulation when required.

The paternalistic control of Louisa's life displayed by Gradgrind resonates with some early accounts of the control early hypnotists had over their subjects of hypnosis during the periods of temporarily induced hypnotic trance in the course of treatment for hysteria. Nina Auerbach notes "an alluring conjunction of women and corpses" (1981, 282) in the imageries of women in the 1890s and goes on to describe "a key tableau of the nineties" (283) as: "three men lean hungrily over three mesmerized and apparently characterless women, whose wills are suspended by those of the magus/masters" (283). Auerbach elaborates:

> The looming men are Svengali, Dracula, and Freud; the lushly helpless women are Trilby O'Ferrall, Lucy Westenra, and (as Freud calls her) "Frau Emmy von N., age 40, from Livonia". It seems as if no men could be more culturally and inherently potent than these, no women more powerless to resist.
>
> (283)

Although Auerbach differentiates between Freud and the two fictional characters, she declares that "in his contribution to *Studies of Hysteria*

(1893–1895), written with Josef Breuer, there is delicious magic in his use of hypnosis, which he had not yet abandoned" (283).

In her introduction to *Studies in Hysteria* (1895), by Josef Breuer and Sigmund Freud, titled "Never Done, Never to Return" (2004), Rachel Bowlby records that in the middle of the 1880s Freud had followed the work of Charcot, a psychiatrist at the Salpetriere Hospital in Paris. Bowlby describes the method in the following words:

> The patients were exhibited before an audience; their illness was seen in the form of a repeatable performance, in the four character-istic 'phases' of a hysterical attack. Charcot used hypnosis to induce hysterical acts and attacks as a means of demonstrating their typical features. The effect was also to suggest that the illness, if it could be stimulated artificially in this way, was not primarily organic or hereditary.
>
> (viii)

Bowlby goes on to point out that Breuer and Freud continued with the method of hypnosis for treatment but removed the spectacular aspect of the treatment by taking it into the private space of their clinic, with the important addition of shifting their focus to the speech of the patient. Bowlby argues that

> the rehearsal of the symptoms is not didactic (for an audience) but therapeutic (for the patient). The theatre … is no longer a real one, in which symptoms are made to appear, but an analogical one in which they spontaneously perform for one last time.
>
> (viii)

While 19th-century fiction depicts an awareness of the suffering of women who were expected to mould themselves into set images of ideal wom-anhood, it is clear that late 19th-century medical treatments for women who reached these clinics as long sufferers of seemingly incurable illnesses became subjects of spectacular experiments by well-meaning men. Although the spectacle of the hypnotised but sick woman commanded by an older and more powerful man to help her become healthier establishes that the illness was neither hereditary nor unnatural, it also reiterates the notion that women can be trained to obey the commands of a more knowledgeable and rational man to overcome their illness. However, as Freud and Breuer noted, the symptoms of the illness did not vanish after a hypnotic session but recurred fairly regularly among many of their patients. This made them change the course of their experiments.

In their introduction to the accounts of the cases treated by them and compiled as *Studies in Hysteria* (1895), which they had earlier published as

"Preliminary Communication" (1893), Breuer and Freud noted that: *hysterics suffer for the most part from reminiscences* (11). They further argue through the cases that the method of hypnosis, which induced a recurrence or remembering of the symptoms had an alleviating effect on the suffering of their women patients. However, Freud soon moved away from sustained faith in the efficacy of hypnosis in the treatment and promoted the method of 'free association', which worked through a process of the patient being fully conscious and communicating through words, and sometimes through silences too, with the analyst, after a relationship of trust is established between the patient (analysand) and the doctor (analyst). Quite often, Freud published the case history of some of his cases with the purpose of sharing the process of treatment and its outcomes for the development of these new methods of treatment. This continuous sharing of his 'findings' over four decades established the new method of psychoanalysis as a science. Additionally, it also created an archive of the changes in Freud's thoughts and theories towards the treatment of people who were finding it difficult to function within accepted norms of their culture.

Although Freud's work deals with helping people negotiate the normal, it emerges from a rather clear definition of socially acceptable norms of behaviour, as was argued in the previous chapter. Freud's investment in 19th-century social mores becomes evident in the ways in which he addressed the question of female sexuality and femininity from 1893 to 1933. One of Freud's important case histories titled 'Fragment of an Analysis of a Case of Hysteria' (1905), which has been the subject of much writing by many scholars who have worked on Freud and femininity, is relevant to this study, too, to showcase Freud's complex engagement with the situation of women in patriarchal households of 19th-century Europe. This case history is not only significant for Freud's own expressed discomfort at the various turns the course of the treatment took and its abrupt termination by the patient but also for the questions it throws up on Freud's acceptance of 19th-century notions of female sexuality. Other than Freud's surprised report of how much Dora, his 18-year-old patient seems to know about adult sexuality, a seriously disturbing element in the case history is Freud's unquestioning acceptance of Dora's father's version of the events that led to Dora being brought for treatment to Freud's clinic. At the age of 17, Dora is caught in the cross-currents of a complicated sexual tangle among the adults in her immediate intimate circle. She refuses to stay on for a family holiday with close friends of her parents after the man of the other family, Herr K, kisses her in a room where there is no one else. This event is a culmination of a series of incidents that lead her to believe that her father and Herr K. seem to have made some unconventional arrangements to facilitate their personal desires. While Freud is wary of most of Dora's reportage, he seems to concur with her seemingly recurring expression of hurt that "she had been handed over to Herr K. as the price of his tolerating the relations between her father and [Herr K's] wife" (34). Although Freud notices that she was very angry with her father for betraying her faith in him as her protector and also observes that she continues to have affectionate feelings towards her father, he goes on to remark: "The two men had of course never made a formal agreement in which she was treated as an object for barter; her father in particular would have been horrified at any such suggestion" (34). Moreover, he speculates that if this hurt felt by his daughter were brought to the attention of Dora's father with suggestions that it could be a harmful arrangement, Dora's father would be able to "evade a dilemma by falsifying their judgement" (34). Furthermore, Freud elaborates upon his speculations of Dora's father's objections to the inappropriateness of their arrangement with the following words:

> If it had been pointed out to him that there might be danger for a growing girl in the constant and unsupervised companionship of a man who had no satisfaction from his own wife, he would have been certain to answer that he could rely upon his daughter, that a man like K. could never be dangerous to her and that his friend was himself incapable of such intentions, or that *Dora was still a child and was treated as a child* by K.
>
> (Emphasis added, 35)

However, as the analyst located outside of the sexual tangle of the two families, Freud states his perspective on the situation as:

> But as a matter of fact things were in a position in which each of the two men avoided drawing any conclusions from the other's behaviour which would have been awkward for his own plans. It was possible for Herr K. to send Dora flowers every day for a whole year while he was in the neighbourhood, to take every opportunity of giving her valuable presents, and to spend all his spare time in her company, without her parents noticing anything in his behaviour that was characteristic of love-making.
>
> (35)

Freud not only points out that the adults continued to condone impropriety, he makes it clear that he does not consider Dora an asexual person. Freud's position with regard to Dora's situation is in consonance with his theory of the development of sexuality in girls. However, in his wonderment at Dora's knowledge of adult sexual behaviour, Freud displays residues of a 19th-century man's unquestioned acceptance of the sexual innocence of 'respectable' women.

In *The Literary Use of the Psychoanalytic Process*, Meredith Skura rephrased Paul Ricouer's observations on Freud as: "his whole intellectual development can be seen as a series of increasingly complex answers to the single and essentially moral question of how we can cope with our uncivilized instincts" (64). This was discussed in some detail in the previous chapter. To reiterate the argument, Freud more or less accepted the then contemporary stereotype of socially acceptable and 'normal' behaviour for children as well as adults. This becomes glaringly obvious in Freud's acceptance of the conventional stereotype of feminine sexuality in his own society. As we have established in the previous chapter, his theories of femininity can be seen as a scientific demonstration of the ways in which feminine sexuality is formed in a patriarchal tradition. Therefore, most of his cases can be read as attempts to 'save' the analysand from falling out of the accepted social paradigm. This project of 'saving' is also evident in the fiction of childhood written during the late 19th and early 20th centuries. However, Freud also states the grave repercussions of obliviousness to children's sexuality and the ensuing guilt-free 'sexual' behaviour of some adults towards children in many of his writings. One such instance is his essay "On the Universal Tendency to Debasement in the Sphere of Love" (1912). In this essay, he says,

> [t]he "affection" shown by the child's parents and those who look after him, which seldom fails to betray its erotic nature ("the child is an erotic plaything"), does a very great deal to raise the contributions made by eroticism to the cathexes of his ego-instincts, and to increase them to an amount which is bound to play a part in his later development, especially when certain other circumstances lend their support.
>
> (parenthesis by Freud, PFL, 7, 249)

As elaborated in the previous chapter, Freud's theories helped in weakening the myth of the sexual innocence of childhood in the early 20th century. By showing that the child was a sexual being, Freud's theories posed a significant challenge to the established stereotype of the sexually innocent, thereby 'pure', child. Apart from the fact that his theories were not very well received, except in a rather small professional circle, the idea of the innocence of childhood was so well-established in the Western tradition of thought that it kept recurring in the work of late 19th-century writers, including in the work of writers who were aware of the various developments in the treatment of women declared to be dysfunctional within the frameworks of the 'norms' of the times in Europe and North America. One such writer is Henry James (1843–1916), whose two novels with child protagonists highlight the discomfort displayed by adults with children who were considered to be privy to sexual knowledge.

In Henry James's *What Maisie Knew* (1897), Maisie is six years old and her parents – Beale and Ida Farange – have ended their marriage with a rather bitter divorce. The result of all the legal wrangling her parents undertake is that Maisie has to live with one parent for one half of the year and spend the other half of the year with the other parent. Both the parents remarry and soon fall out with their new spouses too. From Maisie's perspective, the turn of events introduces more confused adults seeking her attention and showering her with various degrees of affection for variable amounts of time. Soon Maisie learns that the only person she can depend on is the least attractive of these adults. This is Mrs Wix – an old lady her mother employs as her governess – when her more accomplished governess, Miss Overmore, makes it clear that she intends to become the new Mrs Beale Farange. Her mother is married to Sir Claude. A short while after these remarriages take place, the spouses of her parents get interested in each other while her parents go on to seek the company of some other people. At the age of six, Maisie discovers that there are things going on around her that she cannot pass on to her French doll, Lisette, thereby completely discounting an identification with the doll or making it a substitute for a desired love object. In a seemingly precocious choice, Maisie clings to Sir Claude, on account of his being very affectionate towards her. Her attachment to Sir Claude extends to the extent of her always carrying his photograph with her. Towards the end of the story, Maisie makes an astonishing metaphorical leap in time and asks Sir Claude to choose between her and the second Mrs Beale Farange. Sir Claude chooses the latter and Maisie is left to fend for herself and get whatever emotional sustenance she can from Mrs Wix – who has been mourning the death of her seven-year-old daughter for decades. Maisie has to be a substitute for the dead Clara Matilda.

Henry James has himself likened Maisie's situation to that of a shuttle-cock in a badminton game in the preface to the 1907 edition of this work. Maisie is not only tossed around by the elders but also used as a messenger by her parents who frequently send her with hostile messages to each other. Both her stepparents too, individually and in quite different ways, use her as a stepping stone to gain the attention of the parent each is interested in. When Maisie expresses her position in front of the only person in the quartet she comes to trust – her stepfather, Sir Claude – he promptly abandons her. She is to take care of and be 'cared' for by Mrs Wix. All the elders in the story play with Maisie. And not a single one of them is doing it with malicious intent. They seem to be 'innocent' of the harm they are doing to the girl. The intricate web of their relationships is seen as unusual but their treatment of the girl is not seen as unusual by the other characters in the novel. The novelist seems to be the only one who has noted the reification of Maisie into a doll the parents and stepparents toss among themselves.

Maisie's situation has been compared to that of Freud's Dora by Neil Hertz in "Dora's Secrets, Freud's Techniques". Hertz begins his essay by asking a few questions that could apply both to Dora's case and Maisie's story. The reader is led to believe that Hertz is asking pertinent questions about Freud's rendering of his analytical sessions with Dora but Hertz subsequently reveals that he has been paraphrasing James's preface to *What Maise Knew* (1897). Hertz goes on:

> James and Freud alike anticipate being reproached for both the nature of the stories they have to tell and for the manner of the telling. And both meet these imagined reproaches in ways that suggest that the two faults might be one, that they run the risk of being accused of a perverse and distasteful confusion, of not striking the right balance between the child's world and the adult's. There is, to begin with, the possibility that each is gratuitously dragging his heroine into more knowledge, more sordid knowledge, than girls of her age need to come to terms with.
>
> (222)

However, there are two incongruities in Hertz's criticism of Freud and James. Hertz's criticism makes one infer that he believed that there is a limit to the quality and quantity of knowledge that girls of Maisie and Dora's ages can acquire irrespective of their circumstances. Also, it needs to be pointed out that Hertz ignored the fact that Maisie's story begins when she is six years old and thereafter the timescale of the narrative is ambiguous. Dora, however, was brought to Freud's clinic for the first time by her father when she was 16 years old and shared incidents in her life from the time she was 14 to the point where she was brought again to Freud's clinic at the age of 18 for treatment of a persistent cough, which was perceived to be a hysterical symptom by her father. She withdrew from analysis after one year and a very short while after that, even before the case history was published, she married and started a family. Besides, a person's biological age need not necessarily reveal anything significant about her experiences or mental age. Hertz's accusations against James and Freud suggest that he seemed somewhat invested in the culturally entrenched idea of 'innocence' of childhood. However, Hertz also notes that the usually stated reasons for Freud's failure in the Dora case are:

> he was insufficiently alert to his own erotic or paternal or erotic-paternal feelings about Dora; or—to extend this allusion to the counter-transference into a sociological or historical dimension—Freud's attitudes toward young, unmarried, unhappy women shared the blindness and exploitative bent of the prevailing patriarchal culture.
>
> (225)

Hertz suggests that Freud's failure was not just a matter of unrecognised transferences. He hints that the problem lies in Freud being the chief interpreter for Dora and accuses him of sacrificing her to gain scientific legitimacy for the technique which Freud believed would cure hysteria. Both James and Freud are accused of using self-serving ways such as editorialising the language of the subjects of the narrative to better the narrative.

Not only did James insist on knowing and narrating what Maisie knew, he also explicitly mentioned his desire to 'save' this child. In the preface to the 1907 collection of three of his novels, in which *What Maisie Knew* (1897) was included, James has clearly stated that

> the small expanding consciousness [of Maisie] would have to be *saved*, have to become presentable as a register of impressions; and saved by the experience of certain advantages, by some enjoyed profit and some achieved confidence, rather than coarsened, blurred, sterilised, by ignorance and pain.
>
> (Emphasis added, 24)

James repeatedly emphasises that Maisie retains an angelic nature despite having nasty parents. Maisie is indeed treated rather abominably by her parents. Moreover, the attitude of the other adults who are involved in Maisie's upbringing is also quite deplorable. Just as Maisie is an unwanted doll tossed about between her biological parents, she is the doll Sir Claude, Miss Overmore (also after becoming the new Mrs Beale Farange), and Mrs Wix use to further their own interests. By the end of the narrative Maise *knows* that she has to take care of herself and gives up her doll-girl status. By asking Sir Claude to choose between her and Mrs Beale Farange (formerly Miss Overmore), Maise has placed herself in the same position as her former governess. She has moved on from being the stepchild who can be pushed around to a person competing with an adult woman for Sir Claude's affection. With this action, Maisie firmly moves from being a doll-girl to becoming a girl. James fulfils his stated intention by ending the narrative with the description that moment marked the "death of her childhood" (28). James's project was to 'save' the 'innocent', vulnerable, adorably lisping child whom unconventional parents were exposing to bizarre sexual tangles. His heroine's triumph was greater than the framework of James's project could have logically assured. While James had set out to 'save' the 'cherubic' child from turning into anything other than the 'sunbeam' – and eventually the 'angel in the house' – she was expected to be on account of her social class, Maisie grew into an independent, clear-thinking, generous girl who devised a way to outgrow her doll-girl status.

The very next year, after *What Maisie Knew* (1897), James published a 'ghost' story in which the narrator–protagonist of the tale tries to 'save' two children, with dire consequences for the protégés. *The Turn of the Screw* must be among the most discussed ghost stories in Anglo-American fiction.

This tale was published as a serial in *Collier's Weekly* in 1898 and was then brought out as a book with another one of James's stories around Christmas that year. It was reviewed by almost all papers and most of them seemed appalled by the contents of the story. Much research has been done to find out the origin of the tale. Some researchers have attributed its origin to the event of James being told a ghost story involving some children and the ghosts of bad servants by the then Archbishop of Canterbury (A. C. Benson's father), by others to a case history published by the Society for Psychical Research and by a few others to his sister Alice James' hysteria, for which she was undergoing clinical treatment. There has also been a lot of debate about the presence of the two ghosts in the story. Some critics believe that James had successfully written this tale as a ghost story and some others believe that James had cleverly disguised the fact that the governess was hallucinating. Discussing James's intention behind the tale is beyond the scope of this project but the story will be discussed here with the assumption that the governess was psychologically disturbed. One important aspect that will be kept in mind in this particular reading of this tale is that the principal narrator of the story is the governess herself.

In this story, a clergyman's daughter from Yorkshire is interviewed by a rather attractive man in his Harley Street office and is then sent to an out of the way town in Essex to take complete charge of his orphaned nephew and niece. She seems to take her implied promise to her employer – of taking total charge of the children without ever bothering him – a little too seriously. The governess assumes the children are absolutely cherubic and innocent. She seems to truly believe in the tradition of considering the child to be closer to God than an adult and therefore inherently incapable of any act that can be construed as evil. A note from her employer with an unopened letter from the boy's headmaster arrives before the boy arrives for his vacation from school. The governess discovers that the school does not want the boy to come back after the vacations. Without any evidence to support her assumption, she assumes that the boy has been bad at school and has therefore been dismissed. The boy, Miles, does not do anything that can be considered evil to prove her suspicions about him.

Three days after her arrival at the mansion, having been shown around the house and told about its inmates – present as well as former – by the girl, Flora, and having welcomed the boy back from school, the governess goes on an afternoon walk and sees a stranger staring at her. The young governess spots this stranger while she is fantasising about meeting her employer suddenly – *a la* Jane's first encounter with Rochester in Charlotte Bronte's eponymous novel. Upon sighting the stranger she wonders if there is some secret, like a mad relative being kept hidden away in the secluded country mansion, that she was not told about by her employer. Later, on seeing the stranger once again, this time near the house, she discusses this presence with the housekeeper, Mrs Grose. They conclude that the governess has encountered the ghost of Peter Quint – the former valet of the master of the household. The master seems to have had full faith in Quint but Mrs Grose's report of Quint is not very flattering. Mrs Grose seems to have disliked the children's former governess, Miss Jessel too. She completely prejudices the present governess against Miss Jessel by sharing her suspicion of a liaison between Quint and Miss Jessel. To the staid daughter of a country clergyman, a liaison between a governess and a servant of the household is the height of depravity. Soon she sees the 'ghost' of Miss Jessel too. Then she reaches the conclusion that Miles is being influenced by the dead Peter Quint and Flora is being influenced by her dead governess, Miss Jessel. The governess's fears end with Flora pleading to be taken away from her and in the governess scaring Miles to death by coercing him into confessing his association with Quint's ghost.

Despite her good intentions, the governess proves to be inept at efficiently taking charge of the well-being and education of the children. It is evident from the zeal with which she tries to take total charge of her employer's wards and the brief fantasy of accidentally meeting her employer during an afternoon walk that the governess was infatuated with her employer. In this sense, Quint and Miss Jessel are rather clever and convenient 'ghosts' to conjure. By virtue of their positions in the household and the trust they enjoyed with their employer, they were quite influential in the household. These two former employees of her employer had been in positions of trust in the secluded mansion and must have taken many important decisions for Miles and Flora. The governess conjures up the past to justify her inability to take charge of the children. Although she gets literally 'charmed' into her job, it is evident that she is also overwhelmed by the sense of responsibility it brings along. She does not renege on her implied promise to the person she is infatuated with but shows her inability to carry it out by driving herself and one of her charges to illness and the other to death. Again we have an instance of children being treated as objects due to some notions about childhood held by their caregiver. The governess's illness can be seen as a regression to a state where the pretension becomes more real than the reality around.

There was a spate of reviews of James's novel in the early 1900s. Most of the reviewers professed their shock at James's exposing the children in the story to evil. One of the reviewers confessed to being scared by the novel. This reviewer was Virginia Woolf. The review, 'Henry James's Ghosts' was published in the *Times Literary Supplement* on 22 December 1921. Woolf remarks that "Henry James's ghosts have ... their origin within us" (Kimbrough, 179). She says that the readers are not afraid of Peter Quint but "are afraid of something unnamed, of something, perhaps in ourselves" (Kimbrough, 180). Again, in 1923, another reviewer, F. L. Pattee argued the story to be a "triumph of science over romance" (Kimbrough, 180) in "The Record of a Clinic" and describes it as the study of the growth of a suggested infernal *cliché* in the brain of the nurse who alone sees the ghosts, of her final dementia which is pressed to a focus that overwhelms in her mind every other idea, and makes of the children her innocent victims.

(Kimbrough, 180)

Harold C. Goddard did a close reading of the novel, in the early 1920s, to show that the ghosts were the hallucinations of the governess and that the children were aware of her insanity. In 1924, Edna Kenton independently arrived at a conclusion similar to that of Goddard in 'Henry James to the Ruminant Reader: The Turn of the Screw'. In 1934, Edmund Wilson declared the governess to be a sexually repressed person. Others too have convincingly argued that Peter Quint and Miss Jessel were indeed ghosts. Eric Solomon in 'The Return of the Screw' (1964) does some sleuth work, after invoking Sherlock Holmes, to show that James's novel was a murder mystery and the perpetrator of the said crime is Mrs Grose who is murdering anyone who places an obstacle to her having complete control on Flora. In effect, Solomon blames a psychotic Mrs Grose rather than the neurotic governess for the happenings at Bly. However, one way or another, many critical articles on this novel concentrate on the adults in the novel. Peter Coveney in *Poor Monkey: The Child in Literature* (1957) guardedly states: "In treating of childhood in *The Turn of the Screw*, we see how closely, for patently neurotic reasons, he came to complete artistic disaster" (154). From Coveney's perspective in his essay on this novel, James was neurotic. Even Coveney has sacrificed the children in the story to focus on the adult author of the story.

Miles and Flora are ten and eight, respectively. Flora, who is there to welcome her governess, is described as an adorable girl with blue eyes and yellow ringlets of hair. The governess discovers that Miles is 'beautiful' – a term used many times in the narrative to describe Miles's looks. Neither child displays any indiscipline towards anyone in the narrative nor do they trouble the governess in any way. However, they do indulge in some pranks. The chief example of their mischief was the two children conspiring to scare the governess by being away from their respective beds at midnight. That prank provoked the governess into believing that Quint and Miss Jessel are at work again, as harmful supernatural presences. Miles had reason to be slightly nervous because he had been rusticated from school for saying said 'bad' things to his peers. It is hinted by everybody in the narrative, including the narrator, that the things the boy said in school revealed his sexual knowledge. The governess describes the children as: "certainly quite unpunishable. They were like the cherubs of the anecdote, who had—morally, at any rate—nothing to whack!" (31). However, she is also almost obsessively curious about Miles' transgression in school. Since she is sure it is something evil – and therefore somehow related to sex in the mind of this Victorian clergyman's daughter – she believes that the 'ghost' of the purportedly evil Peter Quint influences the 'cherubic' boy.

Additionally, she speculates that Quint's reported partner in 'depravity', Miss Jessel has a hold on the 'angelic' Flora who, is partnering with her brother in acting out evil deeds. Although the narrative does not, at any point, give any evidence of unusual behaviour in the children, there are numerous instances of unusual interpretations of their actions by the governess. When the governess openly accuses each child, individually and at two different times, of communicating with the 'ghosts' of Miss Jessel and Peter Quint, both the children get scared. When Flora is explicitly asked whether she sees the 'ghosts', she bursts out: "I don't know what you mean. I see nobody. I see nothing. I never *have*. I think you're cruel. I don't like you!" (101) and, clutching Mrs Grose, wails, "[t]ake me away, take me away – oh, take me away from her!" (101). Flora's outburst shows that not only is she scared of her governess but also hints at a possibility that Flora has been suspicious about the governess's mental stability for a while. With her declaration, "I never *have*" (101), Flora seems to suggest that the governess has been covertly coercing her into admitting that she has seen the 'ghost' of Miss Jessel for quite a while and that she has been 'rejecting' the suggestion for just as long. Although the narrative makes it clear that the two children do not meet after this outburst by Flora, when the governess later confronts Miles, he asks her if she thinks that the 'ghost' of Miss Jessel is around. The governess tells him that it is not Miss Jessel. The boy then asks her if she meant that Peter Quint was there. On being answered in the affirmative, the boy dies in her arms. The governess's neurosis drives her into projecting her fears on the children and her insecurity about her ability to 'save' these 'cherubic' children from evil influences leads to the nearly complete destruction of one child and the death of the other. The girl is 'saved' from the governess by being taken away by Mrs Grose while the boy dies in the arms of the governess. Once again it is the girl who is 'saved' into 'innocence'. The implications of being 'saved' are unmistakable here. Flora rejects having any kind of 'evil' knowledge and declares, "I see nothing" (101). Although her ability to declare that betrays her lack of innocence, she finally goes back to being a helpless child pleading to be taken away from the person who scares her with incomprehensible accusations.

The governess's firm belief in the innocence of childhood was a catalyst in making her ill. Not only was she supposed to lead a lonely life in the country mansion of the man she had become infatuated with but she also had to protect his 'cherubic' wards from the evil she suspected them to be aware of. The governess's actions revealing that she is projecting the *unheimlich* (Freud (1919), 2003, 124) 'presences' on her *heimlich* wards is a manifestation of her neurosis. Through his reading of a few literary texts, Freud lays down his thesis on the fear of the uncanny in the following manner:

> In the first place, if psychoanalytic theory is right in asserting that every affect arising from an emotional impulse—of whatever kind—is converted into fear by being repressed, it follows that

among those things that are felt to be frightening there must be one group in which it can be shown that the frightening element is something that has been repressed and now returns. This species of the frightening would then constitute the uncanny, and it would be immaterial whether it was itself originally frightening or arose from another affect. In the second place, if this really is the secret nature of the uncanny, we can understand why German usage allows the familiar (das Heimliche, the "homely") to switch to the opposite, the uncanny (das Unheimliche, the "unhomely") (p. 134), for this uncanny element is actually nothing new or strange, but something that was long familiar to the psyche and was estranged from it only through being repressed. The link with repression now illuminates Schelling's definition of the uncanny as "something that should have remained hidden and has come into the open".

(147–148).

Earlier in the essay, Freud had stated that an investigation of the German word *unheimlich* would reveal "that the uncanny is that species of the frightening that goes back to what was once well known and had long been familiar" (124) and goes on to do an etymological investigation of how the familiar acquires the semantic valence of strange and frightening. During the process, Freud notes that:

among the various shades of meaning that are recorded for the word *heimlich* there is one in which it merges with its formal antonym, *unheimlich*, so that what is called *heimlich* becomes *unheimlich*. As witness the passage from Gutzkow: 'We call that *unheimlich*; you call it *heimlich*.' This reminds us that this word *heimlich* is not unambiguous, but belongs to two sets of ideas, which are not mutually contradictory, but very different from each other—the one relating to what is familiar and comfortable, the other to what is concealed and kept hidden. *Unheimlich* is the antonym of *heimlich* only in the latter's first sense, not in its second.

(132)

Furthermore, he refers to a remark by Schelling that reveals that "the term 'uncanny' applies to everything that was intended to remain secret, hidden away, and has come into the open" (132). Finally, he states that "[t]he negative prefix *un*—is the indicator of repression" (151).

Therefore, Freud's exposition reveals that this pair of seemingly anton-ymous words has a complex semantic and etymological relationship in which one might morph into the other under specific circumstances such as a repression of the familiar or an unconscious driven refusal to recognise or confront the familiar. Moreover, a residual but repressed familiarity makes the unfamiliar a frightening presence.

The young governess's projection of sexual knowledge on children who were believed to be innocent – in the sense of ignorant of sexuality and oblivious to sexual feelings – by the social mores of their society, is an instance of her imbuing children who were deemed to be 'asexual' with the knowledge that her contemporary social milieu could not acknowledge as a possibility. Any instance of a child's display of such knowledge or even a suspicion that the child could have sexual knowledge was considered the presence of 'evil' – with a strong focus on the theological connotations of the word to suggest the action of the Devil of ungodly 'presences'. In this instance, the ghosts were believed to be of employees of the household who had been dismissed ostensibly for being involved in a sexual relationship that was considered socially and morally questionable in Victorian times. Additionally, unmarried young girls of the middle and upper classes were expected to be ignorant of sexuality and women who were to take charge of training young girls into growing up into angelic creatures were to lead by example. Therefore, the governess's 'recognition' of sexual knowledge in the two children scares her. It starkly suggests that she can recognise and spot sexual feelings. Moreover, perceiving sexual knowledge in children suggests to her that she is in the presence of ungodly activities. Her fear results in her persistent attempts to enquire about the children's knowledge. Lloyd deMause would have read the governess's dealing with her wards as "use [of] the child as a vehicle for projection of the contents of [her] own unconscious (projective reaction)" (1974, 6). deMause also defines two other reactions that happen "when an adult is face to face with a child who needs something" (6). These are reversal reactions – where the adult "can use the child as a substitute for an adult figure important in his own childhood" (6) and empathic reaction – in which the adult "can empathize with the child's needs and act to satisfy them" (6). deMause goes on to posit that:

> Projective and reversal reactions often occurred simultaneously in parents in the past, producing an effect which I call the "double image", where the child was seen as both full of the adult's projected desires, hostilities, and sexual thoughts, and at the same moment as a mother or father figure. That is *both* bad *and* loving.
>
> (7)

The governess's youth and situation of being in charge of two young children with no positive support, but much negative information from the housekeeper regarding the behaviour of the former governess and butler, the deep influence the latter pair had on the children and the secluded location of the mansion, could have added to the stress of the work the governess seems to have taken on. In addition, the governess's fantasies, signalling an infatuation towards her employer, reveal that the governess is not the asexual person a woman of her station is expected to be. The situation the governess finds herself in leads to her simultaneously manifesting projective and reversal reactions (deMause, 7) on her charges and locating the *unheimlich* in the children. She projects her repressed sexuality onto the children and "conjure[s]" the children to "tell [her] what is the matter" (Dickens, 1854, 168). Moreover, by sighting the ghost of a dead servant and sensing the supernatural influence of a dead peer on the two children she is also displaying a reversal reaction; in which she is hoping for the support of the 'cherubic' children who will eventually reveal their 'natural' purity by confessing that they are 'haunted' by evil. Her inability to form an empathic reaction (deMause, 6) and her heavy-handed attempts at extorting 'confessions' from the children reveal that the governess was approaching the children with set Victorian notions about childhood and pedagogy, which included the reification of children into ideal images of perfection. Her set belief in the 'angelic nature' of children clashed with her perception of 'evil' in the children and she attempted to resolve this clash by forcing the children to perform the 'familiar' asexuality of childhood instead of pushing her towards sightings of the 'unfamiliar' through their behaviour. She tried to coerce the children into accepting that they were the reified cherubs she had hoped to be in charge of to mould them into the predetermined roles of the ideal Victorian public school boy and the ideal 'angel in the house', respectively. However, with her neurotic insistence on getting them to confess, she not only mishandled the children but also displayed her obliviousness of the personalities of the two children. She desperately needed to believe in their innocence to such an extent that she pushed the older and more 'knowing' child into dying of fear and the younger child into a nervous breakdown. The governess destroyed the children in her zeal to 'save' them.

In an earlier Freudian reading of this work titled 'Turning the Freudian Screw' (1966), Mark Spilka argued that Victorians, in trying to protect their homes from the influences of science and commerce, encouraged domestic affection while repressing sexual feelings. He says the conditions "were just about perfect for producing sexual neurosis" (251). According to him:

> The cult of childhood innocence flourished, abetted by writers like Dickens, Eliot, Carroll, Spyri, and Barrie. At Oxford in the 'eighties students invited little girls (as opposed to big ones) to their rooms for tea. Art critic Ruskin, unable to consummate his marriage, worshipped a severely religious girl of fourteen; poet Dawson worshipped one of twelve while at the same time going to prostitutes; bachelor Dodgson doted all his life on little Alices; and bachelor James, always fond of a sister who went mad and a cousin who

died young, wrote a first novel (*Watch and Ward*) in which a young man in his twenties adopts and raises a girl of twelve to be his wife.

(parentheses by Spilka, 251)

Although Spilka lists the adults who had covert or overt sexual feelings for children when they could not come to terms with adult sexuality, he does not accuse the governess of a similar act. He just comments that

> *The Turn of the Screw* can be seen as a step toward that acceptance, a recognition of the impossibility of an adult life which excludes sexuality in the name of ideal innocence, a recognition of the impasse which his own cultural assumptions made inevitable.
>
> (252)

Spilka, who comes the closest to openly recognising the sexual feelings behind the governess's project of 'saving', does not foreground the fact that the governess was *toying* with the children. The governess acting out her hysteria on her wards is analogous to Sara Crewe 'pretending' with her doll in Frances Hodgson Burnett's book for children, *A Little Princess* (1905), which will be examined in detail in the next chapter. The governess's behaviour with the children was similar to that of an 8-year-old playing with her doll but the governess's play has far graver consequences.

Henry James's oeuvre is full of girls of various ages whom someone, either the author or one of the characters in the work, is desperately trying to 'save' and she is seriously refusing to be saved or is spectacularly unsuccessful at getting herself saved. Some of James's girl characters whom he tried to save into acceptable feminine behaviour, through the course of the narratives, with dubious degrees of success, are Nora in *Watch and Ward* (1871), Daisy in *Daisy Miller* (1878), Maisie in *What Maisie Knew* (1897), and Flora in *The Turn of the Screw* (1898).

Nora is Henry James's first young girl character and the only one who achieves the transformation from girlhood to womanhood quite successfully but only after putting up a good deal of resistance. Nora is left an orphan after the violent death of her bankrupt father when she is 12 years old. The father had tried, unsuccessfully, to kill her and then dies by suicide in a hotel room. The child is supported for a few hours by the couple who owned the hotel till Roger Lawrence, a 29-year-old stranger, decides to become her guardian. Although Roger is her guardian for all practical purposes, he does not legally adopt her and encourages her to address him by his given name. Nora treats him as her guardian and becomes immensely fond of him. She is also aware of the fact that she is very indebted to him for a comfortable life. She spends two years under Roger's tutelage and the matronly care of his housekeeper, Lucinda Brown, in his country house. Those are the only two carefree years of Nora's childhood. They end when she is sent to school on the advice of Roger's cousin Hubert. Hubert is a priest and he points out to Roger that the girl is growing up a 'hoyden' and that would never do.

Nora's tenure at school, away from his home, makes Roger realise how central she is to his life. He decides to bring her up to be his wife. She comes back from school as a rather attractive 16-year-old girl. An unscrupulous cousin of hers, George Fenton, finds out about her existence and about her benevolent benefactor. He comes to meet her with the hope of making some monetary gain out of the visit but ends up falling in love with her. Nora is also quite taken in by the idea of having a blood relative. After a rather messy scene, arising from Roger's jealousy and George's mercenary plans, George leaves the household. George's arrival, stay, and the obvious antagonism between the two men contribute to Nora's growing up. Roger takes help from his old friend and former love-interest, Mrs Keith, to come to terms with his emotions towards Nora and to put finishing touches to her education as a lady. Mrs Keith takes her to Europe for a year and brings her back as a very beautiful lady. Meanwhile, Roger falls gravely ill and has to send his cousin Hubert to receive Nora at the port. Hubert finds Nora extremely attractive. Despite being engaged to another woman and fully aware of his cousin's love for Nora, Hubert flirts with her. Nora falls in love with him just as he too does with her. However, he leaves town on being admonished by Mrs Keith the day after declaring his love to Nora. The lovelorn Nora rejects Roger's proposal although she is not completely taken by surprise with the proposal. Despite earlier hints by Roger about his intentions, she is quite traumatised by the actual event of his proposing to her. She finds it improper to live in Roger's house after the turn of events and goes to George Fenton's house. Her cousin turns out to be even more unscrupulous than he had shown himself to be during his first visit. He tries to blackmail Nora and exploit Roger to make some money out of the situation. She flees his place and goes to Hubert's place. Hubert expresses his inability to help her and tells her about his engagement. Nora is again homeless and penniless. Roger Lawrence once again takes her into his household; this time as his wife.

Nora was Henry James's successful attempt at 'saving' a girl into the respectability and protection that late 19th-century patriarchy could offer to young single women but the work itself was not a success. James continued to create girl characters who fail in their attempts at transformation from girlhood to womanhood. Chronologically, the next in line was James's personal favourite – Daisy Miller. Daisy Miller must be one of the most spirited of Henry James's creations. "That is all I want—a little fuss!" (73), she says as a retort to one of Winterbourne's remarks and quite unwittingly reveals the key to her puzzling personality. Winterbourne is one of the protagonists of this novel and one of the many young men with whom Daisy was supposedly flirting in Geneva.

Daisy Miller is a young American girl who is traveling in Europe with her mother and her younger brother. Winterbourne, an American man who has lived in Europe for most of his adult life meets her in the most informal and unusual way. Daisy's brother, Randolph Miller, a ten-year-old boy, strikes a conversation with Winterbourne with a demand for a lump of sugar from the man's tea table. While Randolph's behaviour could be construed as bad manners, his sister, who goes to call Randolph back to their table, manages to puzzle Winterbourne by her behaviour. Daisy not only allows Randolph to introduce her to Winterbourne but also watches in silence when her brother starts reeling out such facts about her that were kept private among acquaintances in their contemporary society. While indiscretion is forgiven in Randolph due to his age, Daisy's being totally oblivious of or indifferent to the rules of propriety among American expatriates in Europe is not forgiven. In an age where no young girl was allowed to move out of home without a chaperone, Daisy Miller is seen talking to young men without being properly introduced to them. Her mother is portrayed as totally incapable of behaving like other matrons who were in charge of young and single girls in that society. Neither does she stop Daisy from breaking cultural norms nor does she show any awareness of the norms. The entire family's complete oblivion to the norms of the social circles of Geneva and other watering places in Europe frequented by the same set of families every year shocks the community of Americans and other regulars in these places.

Daisy wants to be accepted by this society but refuses to follow their rules. When Winterbourne tries to point out the impropriety of her decision to go on an expedition with him without a chaperone, she thinks an unnecessary fuss is being made. She also makes friends with other young men across social barriers such as class, community, and nationality. As a result, she is shunned by the women in her social circle. Although Winterbourne tries to convince them that Daisy's 'transgressions' are unintentional or that she is misguided, he first participates in Daisy's 'scandalous' plans and eventually abandons her. Daisy wants to enter the upper-class social circles of Europe's watering places, but only on her terms. She is invited to their parties due to her beauty and popularity with the young men. Very soon she loses her popularity as the matrons of that society – the self-proclaimed guardians of tradition – discover that Daisy refuses to recognise the established rules of the courtship games played in those circles. Daisy is not oblivious of the rules; she simply refuses to follow them. When Winterbourne pleads with her to stop flirting with a young Italian on the ground that "they don't understand this sort of a thing here .... Not in young unmarried women" (99). Daisy declares, "It seems to me much more proper in young unmarried women than in old married ones" (99). Winterbourne tries to explain the reasons behind the societal disapproval of her friendship with the Italian. He tells her that she might harm herself as flirting is an American custom and is not recognised in Rome, to which she spiritedly retorts, "And if you want very much to know, we are neither of us flirting; we are too good friends for that; we are very intimate friends" (100). To this, Winterbourne suggests that he would not interfere if she were in love with the young man. Daisy Miller blushes at the suggestion and makes it clear that Winterbourne is mistaken and also dismisses the likelihood of such an eventuality. Her reaction shows that she does not consider a match between her and the Italian as viable but she would not let Winterbourne or others teach her 'good conduct'. Daisy's refusal to be guided leads to behaviour that is socially unacceptable to the people she wants to associate with. As they start shunning her, Daisy does more stunning things to get them to pay attention to her. That social acceptance is important for her is very clear from her behaviour, but it is also clear that she will not consider societal norms important enough for her to make changes in her personality. Her inability to resolve this eventually leads to her death. Daisy Miller pays with her life in her project of resisting society's attempt to 'civilise' her. With Daisy's death, James seems to suggest the fate of the girl who puts up a spirited resistance to attempts at 'saving' girls into acceptable social mores.

This 'saving' is another way of stereotyping the child to fit her into the framework of an image created for her by a patriarchal tradition. Louisa Gradgrind, Sissy Jupe, Flora, Maisie, Nora, and Daisy Miller are resisting being 'civilised' into the social roles chalked out for them by others. Daisy has to pay with her life while resisting being 'saved'. While Nora grows into the role chalked out for her, Flora and Maisie surprise us. Flora refuses to be trampled upon and Maisie overshoots her assigned role. These girls resist being 'saved' into the prevalent patriarchal culture. Therefore, resistance to this kind of 'saving' can be seen as a feminist stance. However, these children, including the boys – Miles and Tom Gradgrind – are continuously toyed with due to the entrenched beliefs of the adults in charge of their upbringing. Although these adults are making seemingly well-meaning attempts to civilise them into accepted sociocultural norms of their times, they are unable to form empathic reactions (deMause, 6) to their charges.

In the next chapter, through a close reading of three texts written for children at the turn of the 19th century, we will examine the ways in which children's literature reflected the social acceptance of the toy–child bond.

Notes

1 Lloyd deMause points out that childhood innocence was a notion that entered social discourse through Christianity. He interprets Christ's description of the child to mean that "people should become as 'uncontaminated' as children, pure, without sexual knowledge" (47) but also argues that this meant that "Christians throughout the Middle Ages began to stress the idea that children were totally innocent of all notions of pleasure and pain" (47).

2 Deirdre Beddoe describes this trope as one delineated by John Ruskin in *Sesames and Lilies* (1864) as the role of the woman who was to be "man's complement and helpmeet" (22) and remarks that this meant that "[m]an was the doer of deeds and the great function of woman was to praise" (22).

4

THE CHILD AND TOY BOND

Behind him through the thick, humid air, he could hear his
dolls, alive now and jabbering behind their closed door, each
loudly telling the other his or her "back-story", the tale of how
she or he came to be. The imaginary tale, which he, Solanka,
had made up for each of them.

Salman Rushdie. *Fury*. 2001. 50–51

Children's literature and the criticism of literature for children have been
significant pathways to study perceptions of childhood through the centuries. In *Children's Literature: The Development of Criticism* (1990), Peter
Hunt mentions that before the 18th century there was no specific literature
for children. Children were perceived to be a part of a general audience.
The few children who could read were not stopped, by authoritarian mechanisms, from reading books written for adults. In *Written for Children:
An Outline of English-Language Children's Literature* (1965), John Rowe
Townsend mentions Penelope Mortimer's remark that John Locke "published his *Thoughts Concerning Education* and invented the child" (27).
Although Townsend suggests that Mortimer's remark cannot be taken completely seriously, he also endorses the statement by describing the significance
of Locke's work for the development of writing for children. Locke's work,
published in 1693, started a discussion on the kinds of books to be made
available especially for children and the ways in which reading can be educational as well as entertaining. Although Townsend thinks Locke's work
was path-breaking, he quickly points out that the two books Locke recommended for children, *Aesop's Fables* and *Reynard the Fox*, were published
at least a century before Locke's recommendation. Furthermore, he points
out that three books that were published close to Locke's essay and eventually went on to become children's classics – John Bunyan's *The Pilgrim's
Progress* (1678), Daniel Defoe's *Robinson Crusoe* (1719), and Jonathan
Swift's *Gulliver's Travels* (1726) – were actually written for adults.

DOI: 10.4324/9781003093275-4

Scholars of childhood and children's literature differ on the origin of the category of children's literature and the kinds of texts that comprise it but most of them agree that the origin of this category in the English language cannot be pinned down to a specific time or to a particular person. Townsend guardedly remarks: "The 1740s are commonly regarded as the decade in which both the English novel and the English children's book got under way" (28). He posits that the tale, which he described as "unsophisticated fiction for everybody" (28–29), created a space for children's literature. He substantiates his hypothesis by pointing out that Samuel Richardson's *Pamela* was adapted for young readers shortly after it was first published.

During the early years of publishing for children, the publisher, often, not only published the book but also wrote it. While Townsend notes that Harvey Darton has given John Newbery the honour of being the first publisher of an exclusive book for children in *Children's Books in England* (1932), he points out that there were a few others who published books exclusively for children. For instance:

> As early as 1694 (the year after Locke's *Thoughts*) one "J.G." had published *A Play-book for Children* to "allure them to read as soon as they can speak plain"; and probably in 1702, "T.W." issued *A Little Book for Little Children*, "wherein are set down, in plain and pleasant Way, Direction for Spelling and other remarkable Matters. Adorned with Cuts". But these, and others like them, were directly concerned with teaching children to read and spell. Closer to Newbery in date and approach was Thomas Boreman, who brought out from 1740 onwards a series of tiny books, the size of a snapshot, which he called *Gigantick Histories*. Then there was a Mrs Cooper of Paternoster Row who issued *The Child's New Plaything* (second edition 1743), and there was Mr J. Robinson of Ludgate Street, who sold the *Little Master's Miscellany*, first published in 1743.
>
> (30)

Although Newbery was not the first, he surely was one of the most enterprising of the publishers for children. Newbery sold his first book *A Little Pretty Pocket-Book* (1744) for six pence per copy and offered a "Ball and a Pincushion, the use of which will infallibly make Tommy a good Boy and Polly a good Girl" at the payment of two pence extra (quoted in Townsend, 1983, 30–31). Newbery also used unique methods to advertise his ware. During the New Year season in 1755, he offered to give a copy of one of his books free to any boy who paid him only the binding charges that amounted to two pence for each book. The trend of offering playthings as accessories with books and giving freebies was set way back in the middle of the 18th century.

While the other writers mentioned by Townsend wrote variations of primers or courtesy books, as did Newbery, Sarah Fielding's *The Governess* (1749) was a novel written for children. In *The Oxford Companion to Children's Literature* (1984), Humphrey Carpenter and Mari Prichard confer the "distinction of being the first original work of full-length children's fiction" on this work. This book was also called *The Female Academy* in some editions. J. S. Bratton has given a detailed history of publishing for children in *The Impact of Victorian Children's Fiction* (1981). Bratton directly links publishing for children to the awareness of children as beings who are emotionally different from adults. He argues that the Industrial Revolution produced a general consciousness of the importance of a child as an "instrument of change" (13–14) leading to institutionalisation of education of children. Bratton also establishes, as does Townsend, that the first books written especially for children were primers. Until the beginning of the 19th century, only the children of the upper-class read books. In the 19th century, there were public debates advocating education for the poor. Eventually, this led to an increase in publishing for children as the reading public also increased. Quite a few periodicals were also published for children. As can be perceived from the individual researches undertaken by Townsend and Bratton, the entire project of publishing for children was inspired by a pedantic motive of civilising children through the books written for them.

The project of civilising the child through literature produced especially for the child was also taking place across the Atlantic Ocean. In *Behold the Child: American Children and Their Books 1621–1922* (1994), Gillian Avery traces a link between children's publishing in Britain and America in the 18th and 19th centuries. Avery shows that most of the writing for children in the 18th century in America arose from the belief that children are spiritually nearer to God and can bring erring adults back to the religious path. One can see another form of objectification of the child in this deliberate placing of the child on a spiritual pedestal. Apart from creating ideals that were almost impossible for children to emulate, these works must have created a sense of inadequacy and guilt in the children who read them. In this work, she also highlights very interesting differences in the lifestyles of children in the two countries. From this and other evidences of early writing for children in Britain – detailed in John Rowe Townsend's *Written for Children* (1965) – we can infer that children in Britain, as well as North America, were introduced to the ideals of childhood through literature from the 18th century onwards.

Along with publishing for children, there arose a simultaneous debate about the kind of writing that would be suitable for children. In *Children's Literature: The Development of Criticism* (1990), Peter Hunt discusses

Sarah Fielding's preface to her novel, *The Female Academy* (1749), in which Fielding describes the kind of writing she would consider ' suitable' for children. Hunt has also quoted from Elizabeth Rigby's essay 'Children's Books' in *The Quarterly Review* of 1844, in which she argues that children are not inferior to adults but are different from adults and, therefore, a weakened version of literature for adults is not desirable for children. Although Rigby's sensitivity in recognising childhood as a unique phenomenon, thereby requiring a different kind of writing is admirable, this recognition started a long and widespread project of civilising the child, including through educational writing for children. The recognition of the phenomenon of childhood while being beneficial for the child also reiterated the notion that children are special kinds of creatures, leading to the creation of an Other. Hunt's work also mentions that more than a century-and-a half after Rigby, J. R. R. Tolkien in a lecture 'On Fairy Stories' (1983) warned writers for children against thinking that children are "special kind of creature[s], almost a different race" (22) and asked them to think of children as "normal, if immature, members of a particular family and the human family at large" (22).

Despite warnings against this 'special treatment' of children, much of children's literature talked down to 'civilised' and nurtured children into the prevalent norms of the day. Humphrey Carpenter and Mari Prichard have concisely documented the rise and fall of prescriptive literature for children from the mid-18th century to the late 20th century in *The Oxford Companion to Children's Literature* (1984). One such writer of prescriptive literature was Charlotte Maria Tucker, who wrote under the pseudonym A.L.O.E. – an abbreviation of A Lady of England – between the 1850s and the 1890s. Carpenter and Prichard declare her work "too strict and didactic even by the standards of the times" (19). Another writer of prescriptive books for children was Anna Laetitia Barbauld. She started writing because she did not find books that she thought were suitable to teach her 3-year-old son to read. She then published an entire series from 1778 to the early 1800s called *Lessons for Children*. Carpenter and Prichard state that her work inaugurated a new approach to the teaching of reading but also mention that she suffered notoriety as Charles Lamb disparaged her writing as dull and E. Nesbit noted her as one of the 'unpleasant Book people' in *Wet Magic* (1913). In the early 19th century, writers like Maria Edgeworth and Eleanor Fenn started writing books for young children based on children's experiences rather than adults' notions about appropriate reading material for children. Maria Edgeworth and her father Richard had jointly authored an influential book titled *Practical Education* (1801) to usher an education that focuses on "the education of the heart" (Armstrong, 1987, 15). In the early part of the 19th century, many instructive books were published for children with 'facts' in them. As was discussed in the previous chapter, this zest for inculcating 'facts' in the minds of children was satirised by Charles Dickens in *Hard Times* (1854). However, a large amount of didactic writing was produced as children's literature in Britain and was made available to American children too. Most of these books were reprinted by American publishers, increasing their availability to children across the Atlantic Ocean.

The early Puritans in America had also been actively engaged in writing didactic fiction for children. Cotton Mather is mentioned as the first American-born author to write specifically for child readers by Humphrey Carpenter and Mari Prichard (1984). Cotton Mather was a puritanical preacher who tried, very successfully, to get children and their parents to believe that wicked behaviour could lead to early death. John Rowe Townsend has quoted from Mather's *A Family Well-Ordered. Or An Essay to Render Parents and Children Happy in One Another* (1699) in *Written for Children* (1983). Mather's warning reads:

> The Heavy Curse of God will fall upon those Children that make Light of their Parents ... The Curse of God! The Terrible! The Terriblest Thing that ever was heard of; the First-born of Terribles! ... *Children*, if you break the Fifth Commandment, there is not much likelihood that you will keep the rest .... Undutiful Children soon become horrid Creatures, for Unchastity, for Dishonesty, for Lying, and all manner of Abominations .... And because these undutiful Children are Wicked overmuch, therefore they Dy before their Time ....

Children, if by Undutifullness to your Parents you incur the Curse of God, it won't be long before you go down into Obscure Darkness, even into Utter Darkness: God has reserved for you the Blackness of Darkness for ever.

The debate about such a prescriptive attitude towards writing for children is far from history even now. Most countries have continuous discussions about school syllabi. Apart from educationists, sociologists, anthropologists, psychologists who have influenced studies of childhood, the historical experiences of nations and the politics of the day also influence the syllabi of school children. In countries that have been colonies of other nations, the history of the nation and cultural changes over time become relevant in teaching any form of basic social science and also in the literature taught in schools. At present, in India, debates on education policies and school curricula are going on. Such debates arise from the recognition that 'facts' are based on opinions. The issue of the appropriateness of any kind of writing or knowledge for children is not confined to children's literature alone. Moreover, the zest to incorporate knowledge into children was active from the beginnings of writing for children and continues even in contemporary discussions in children's literature. Carpenter and Prichard have recorded that, in 1908, with the publication of *Children's Encyclopaedia*, a lot of information was made available at one place. In fact, variations of and improvements on the encyclopaedia mentioned above are still to be seen in the bookshelves of many homes, children's section of bookstores, school libraries, and other libraries.

There are other ways too in which children's literature is utilised to socialise children. One such 'use' is the consistent reiteration and perpetuation of gender stereotypes. The first published 'criticism' of children's literature, in Sarah Fielding's Preface to *The Female Academy* (1749), was the harbinger of an entire cult of constructing distinct stereotypes of girlhood and boyhood. In 1879, *The Boy's Own Paper* was started in England. The very next year a magazine for girls called *The Girl's Own Paper* was started. Carpenter and Prichard note: "its format and price was the same, though its tone was predictably less robust" (207). They also note a very interesting fact while contrasting the two papers: in *The Boy's Own Paper*, the age limit for entrants in contests was 16 years whereas in *The Girl's Own Paper*, it was 25 years! Such historical facts, among other information, add to a re-examination of the notion of girlhood.

The focus of *The Girl's Own Paper*, from a glance at the contents of the first volume of the magazine, was to transform all girls into Victorian 'help-meets'. Not only were there articles about etiquette and general knowledge but also about household management and home-based skill development. Fiction written specifically with girl readers in mind too had a similar focus. However, the first volume does not indicate that a clear decision had been made on the specific age group for which the magazine was published. The style and design of the magazine allowed for a range of articles from 'How to Dress a Doll' to reports on study and career options for women. The very first volume of the magazine also included a report delineating the wondrous traits and pitiful lives of the 'Hindu Women'. Along with reiterating the confusion regarding the age until which a female can be thought of as a girl – with the upper age limit for subscription being set at 25 – the range of topics that were made available to females across age groups within one volume of the magazine seems to suggest that there was a bunching together of the female sex as a group that could and would access this magazine in the world of women. This fluidity of perception of girlhood and womanhood makes one wonder whether even late 19th-century Britain made distinctions among separate phases of female life experiences and thereby truly recognised girlhood or simply thought of girls as 'little women' (Alcott, 1868) and perceived some adult women to be grown-up girls.

In *A Critical History of Children's Literature* (1953), Cornelia Meigs lists a set of writers she labels the 'Little Female Academy' (after Fielding's 1749 book) and describes this set as devotedly working to create conscientious, obedient, disciplined, pious little 'angels' as models for Victorian children to emulate. Although very few children in the 20th and 21st centuries would be aware of these books, the immense popularity of these books at that time led to their influencing the creation of ideals of girlhood in the 19th century. Some of the writers of the 'Little Female Academy' such as Charlotte Yonge, Juliana Horatia Ewing, and Mrs Molesworth are read even now by scholars of children's literature, even though contemporary children may not find them accessible. In Charlotte Yonge's *Heartsease* (1854), a virtuous girl patiently braves an incredible amount of trouble to be rewarded with a good husband at the end of the story. In the same author's *The Daisy Chain* (1856), Ethel May gives up her pursuit of Greek and Latin to make herself a 'comfort to papa' after her mother's death and becomes a little caretaker for her numerous sisters and brothers[1] (Spacks, Patricia Meyer. *The Adolescent Idea: Myths of Youth and the Adult Imagination*. 213). Claudia Nelson quotes Yonge's nonfiction to show that there was a suppressed guilt, emerging from religious beliefs, underlying her injunctions to young girls, for Yonge wrote in *Womankind* in 1877: "I have no hesitation in declaring my full belief in the inferiority of woman, not that she brought it upon herself when Eve's weakness led to humankind's expulsion from Eden" (2007, 115). J. S. Bratton also states that "Charlotte Yonge regarded repression as perfectly natural, and leading only to good effects" and quotes her as remarking "the kindest thing to be done by a child is to teach it self-restraint" (1981, 180–181). Girls were encouraged to emulate the self-sacrificing 'sunbeams' in such stories and all those who did not conform to the stereotype were criticised as 'hoydens'. John Rowe Townsend (1983) calls such writing 'domestic dramas' and quotes Edward Salmon's description of it, given in *Juvenile Literature As It Is* (1888) as saying,

> [it] enables girls to read something above mere baby-tales and yet keeps them from the influence of novels of a sort that should be read only by persons capable of discreet judgement .... While it advances beyond the nursery, it stops short of the full blaze of the drawing-room.
>
> (76)

Some of these 'domestic dramas', according to Townsend, are *The Wide Wide World* (1850) and *Queechy* (1853), both by Elizabeth Wetherell; *The Lamplighter* (1854) by Maria Cummings; Martha Finley's Elsie series, which began with *Elsie Dinsmore* in 1857 and culminated in *Grandmother Elsie*; and the even now immensely popular American series by Louisa May Alcott commencing with *Little Women* in 1868 and culminating in 1886 with *Jo's Boys*. A similar series, which was popular among schoolgirls in India even in the last few decades of the 20th century, is Susan Coolidge's *What Katy Did* (1872) and the rest of the stories till Katy grows up and gets married.[2] Such girl characters, with similar growing-up stories, are evident even in the 20th century – one of the early 20th-century examples being Rebecca from *Rebecca of Sunnybrook Farm* (1903) by Kate Douglas Wiggin.

Townsend also mentions Juliana Horatia Ewing (1841–1885) and Louisa Stewart (1839–1921) – the latter wrote under the pseudonym of Mrs Molesworth – as important writers of the late-Victorian and early-Edwardian period. However, he believes that Frances Hodgson Burnett was more important than most of the writers of this period as a few of her novels are in circulation and being read by even 21st-century children.[3] Townsend mentions three of Burnett's books – *Little Lord Fauntleroy* (1886), *A Little Princess* (1905), and *The Secret Garden* (1911) – as remaining popular even in the late 20th century. These novels by Burnett will be studied in detail later in this chapter.

While there are interminable debates among adults about the appropriate kind of knowledge that can be made available for children, children manage to internalise all knowledge they are exposed to and sometimes present it in new and creative forms. A playground chant was noted by Peter and Iona Opie and recognised as a distortion of some Latin the children had to learn in school. Alison Lurie quoted from Iona Opie's notes made while observing British schoolchildren play in a school playground in *Boys and Girls Forever: Reflection on Children's Classics* (2003). Here is the chant and the original Latin piece:

Latin learnt in school:-	Playful cockney chant of the same:-
Brutus adsum jam forte,	Brutus 'ad some jam for tea
Caesar aderat.	Caesar 'ad a rat.
Brutus sic inomnibus,	Brutus sick in omnibus,
Caesar sicinat	Caesar sick in 'at.

The playful distortion of the inaccessible Latin is emancipatory in its appropriation of knowledge gathered in the civilising context of the schoolroom. While the playground and interactions with peers also have civilising effects on children, the social dynamics of the playground would be very different from situations of interactions between adults and children. Although a playground is far from a utopian world of equality, most children learn to successfully navigate through a world of peers with their interactions in this space. This quality of the playground and of play is attractive to educators, child therapists, social workers, and many other professionals who work with children. However, the presence of the adult in contexts such as the ones listed above changes the nature of play by affecting the playful element of play. Children's literature is among a few spaces where the play of children can be fictitiously recreated while foregrounding the playful element and retaining the essential aspect of the world of play as that of children, even with a marginal presence of adults in the narratives. One of the authors who made play and the playful the central aspect of her writing in her books for children was Frances Hodgson Burnett. While a detailed analysis of two of her novels – *A Little Princess* (1905) and *The Secret Garden* (1911) – will be undertaken in this chapter, there will be a brief examination of her most popular book *Little Lord Fauntleroy* (1886) and her autobiographical book *The One I Knew Best of All* (1892).

Frances Hodgson Burnett, too, like Henry James, had homes both in Britain and America during the turn of the 20th century. Although Burnett was born in Manchester in Britain, her family migrated to America when she was a very young child. However, she lived for many years in Europe and in Britain as a young woman. She continued to travel between Britain and America, fairly frequently, throughout her life. While Henry James became a British citizen towards the end of his life, Burnett retained her American citizenship and stayed in England for long periods of her life. She also wrote many of her famous books while she lived in England as a middle-aged woman. There is evidence that Henry James and Frances Hodgson Burnett were aware of each other's work. Humphrey Carpenter and Mari Prichard have mentioned in *The Oxford Companion to Children's Literature* (1984) that Burnett wrote several novels under the influence of Henry James and that James reviewed the London production of one of her plays. While James's work was influencing Burnett, there is also some evidence that James, in turn, was aware of Sigmund Freud's work. From the Norton critical edition of *The Turn of the Screw* (1889) we know that Henry James's sister was undergoing psychoanalytic treatment during the time James wrote this story. There are instances in Burnett's *The Secret Garden* (1911) that indicate her awareness of literature about mental health issues and the then contemporary treatments.

While this chapter argues that Burnett's work makes space for children to play out their fantasies, it is useful to acknowledge that an adult telling a tale of childhood is also recreating a fantasy of childhood. Peter Brooks states that the adventure tale is the perfect space for adults to play out their fantasies. The very nature of the genre demands that there is overt action in the narrative and the protagonist eventually triumphs over the challenges s/he has to face. Brooks goes on to speculate:

> If this is so, could we not, reflecting on such books as *Treasure Island*, *The Mysterious Island*, or even Frances Hodgson Burnett's *The Mysterious* [*sic*] *Garden*, consider that the child's adventure story is a perfect example of Freud's description of the "familiar" become the "uncanny", the *Heimlich* become the *unheimlich*? "The *unheimlich*," says Freud, "is what was once *heimisch* [*sic*], home-like, familiar; the prefix 'un' is the token of repression." Through the play of repression, the adult writing for children consciously or unconsciously, possibly because he is unwilling or unable to assume the burden of adult sexuality, metamorphoses the erotic quest for adventure which takes the hero far from the *heimisch* [*sic*], into a world where Woman and Mother are only implicit presences, to do battle with monsters, enigmas, and cataclysms, through his victory

to find triumphant peace. Does the child reader unconsciously decode the story, respond to the adventure because he interiorizes the *unheimisch* [sic] and feels its relevance to the *heimisch* [sic]? ("Towards Supreme Fictions", Yale French Studies, 43, 1969, 10)

Although the thrust of this project is different from Brooks' argument on the adult writer as being 'unwilling or unable to assume the burden of adult sexuality' and using a children's story to sublimate desires, Brooks' fore-grounding the Freudian idea of the uncanny as being integral to the adventure tale brings out the inherent complexity in the act of an adult recreating childhood through a tale.

Frances Hodgson Burnett's project on childhood is evident in her autobiography *The One I Knew The Best of All* (1892). In her autobiography, Burnett has not given any specific dates and Frances's age when some significant incidents occurred in her childhood is rarely mentioned. This work of Burnett reads more like a work of fiction than like an autobiography, but for the purpose of this project we will read it as an autobiography as she explicitly mentions that she is writing about her own childhood. Burnett starts her autobiography with the declaration that she began the work to gain access to the thoughts of a child. She says:

> I have so often wished that I could see the minds of young things with a sight stronger than that of very interested eyes, which can only see from the outside. There must be so many thoughts for which child courage and child language have not the exact words. So, remembering that there was one child of whom I could write from the inside point of view, and with certain knowledge, I began to make a sketch of the one I knew best of all.
>
> (vii–viii)

Burnett was recreating her childhood to project an image of girlhood that connected Britain and America in the second half of the 19th century. When Burnett wrote this account of her girlhood in Britain and America, she was a resident of America, married to an American citizen and a mother who had lost her first-born child. Although these biographical details show that Burnett was presumably fulfilling all the conventional roles of womanhood, the text reveals that she had not really distanced herself from her girlhood. As the revealing title shows, the child Frances, the one the author knew best, is similar to the other girl protagonists created by Burnett.

The child Frances, whom she rather exasperatingly calls 'The Small Person' throughout the narrative, fits into the acceptable stereotype of the 'good' girl in both the countries she lives in. As a very young child in England, Frances is an obedient, modest, intelligent, loving, and adorable child who escapes being the very image of Miss Goody Two Shoes due to a healthy dose of imagination. This imagination, coupled with a love of reading, spurs her into creating fantastic games for herself, which she executes with the help of her doll. Burnett writes:

> When I recall the adventures through which the Dolls of the Small Person passed, the tragedies of emotion, the scenes of battle, murder, and sudden death, I do not wonder that at times the sawdust burst forth from their calico cuticle in streams, and the Nursery floor was deluged with it. Was it a thing to cause surprise that they wore out and only lasted from one birthday to another? Their span of life was short, but they could not complain that their existence had not been full for them .... While the two little sisters of the Small Person arranged their doll's house prettily and had tea-parties out of miniature cups and saucers, and visited each other's corners of the Nursery, in *her* corner the Small Person entertained herself with wildly-thrilling histories, which she related to herself in an undertone, while she acted them with the assistance of her Doll.
>
> (46–47)

Later, as a schoolgirl, her imagination and a talent for storytelling make her one of the popular girls in school. After her family migrates to America due to strained economic circumstances, the adolescent Frances spends many blissful hours chasing birds and collecting flowers in the wilderness surrounding her house. The image created by Burnett of this phase of her girlhood is not only pastoral but is also akin to the depictions of the leisure activities of some of the early settlers in the New England colonies. Burnett's reference to the stories of James Fenimore Cooper reiterates the apparent similarity in their perception of America. She mentions that during their early days in America, Frances expected to meet Indians like the ones described in Cooper's novels and her description of the woods around her house is uncannily similar to the idyllic settings of the New World described in the works of fiction that were written in the early 19th century in America. Burnett titles the chapter describing their early days in America 'The Dryad Days' in her autobiography. While the physical setting of Frances's adolescent years was pastoral New England, the activities she reports to have spent her leisure periods in the afternoons is reminiscent of Maggie Tulliver, in George Eliot's *The Mill on the Floss* (1860). It is clear that her description of her everyday activities are more like those of English girls in the fiction of that period than the American girl one comes across in the fiction of American authors like Louisa May Alcott who was very popular around the time Burnett's family migrated to America. However, there are some resonances with incidents in Alcott's *Little Women* (1868). For instance, Burnett mentions that the strenuous financial situation of the household emboldened Frances into taking some measures to sell her stories to a magazine without consulting the men in her household. The modest British child thus transforms into the independent and enterprising American girl. Through the narrative, Frances acclimatises herself, apparently painlessly, to life in America. Although both her famous fictional girls – Sara Crewe (first in 1887 and then in 1905) and Mary Lennox (in 1911) – are children of English parents sent from colonial India to be brought up as English girls, Burnett has built on her memories of girlhood in the later part of the first half of the 19th century in England and America in these novels published in the early years of the 20th century. The intensity of Sara Crewe's 'pretending' with her doll is rather similar to Frances's involved imaginative play with her doll, and Mary Lennox's blossoming in the secret garden in an English manor is very similar to Frances revelling in the pristine air of America after 12 years of life in sooty Manchester. Frances, as can be seen in *The One I Knew the Best of All*, was an amalgam of an English and an American girl. By creating two immensely popular English 'sunbeams' in the characters of Sara and Mary, Burnett contributed to perpetuating the Victorian stereotype of the 'good' girl. Moreover, these novels also indicate the sociocultural implications of the colonial enterprise on childhood in England and vice versa.[4]

In Frances Hodgson Burnett's *A Little Princess* (1905), Sara Crewe and her father set out on a search for a doll on the eve of Sara's admission to a seminary for young girls. Her father works in British India and decides to leave his daughter in England after his wife dies in India, so that the girl would be brought up to be an English lady. There is an uncanny similarity between the way Sara thinks about the yet-to-be-bought doll and the way young women supposedly think about their yet-to-be-born babies. Sara has a name and a personality for the doll before she and her father set out to look for it. A direct analogy from Freud's theory of the resolution of the Oedipus complex can be drawn at this point by stating that Sara is prepared to accept a doll from her father rather than the fantasised baby. However, in the seminary, Sara actually takes up a younger girl to bestow her maternal feelings on. At the same time, the doll, Emily, still remains her link with her absent parent. In its significance as a link to a protected past with her father, the doll Emily can be likened to the Transitional Object defined by D. W. Winnicott. However, there are some moments in the narrative when Sara projects her feelings onto the doll and acts out her emotions on it almost as if the doll were a substitute for her, as was suggested by Freud in his three essays on female sexuality discussed in some detail in previous chapters of this work.

Before leaving her at the seminary, Sara's father provides her with things that were in excess of the needs of a very young girl in a boarding house. Although he overspends on fine things for her, he does not overtly engage with their emotions at being separated from each other, presumably for years. When she resignedly accepts the inevitable separation from him with mature remarks, he simply thinks she is quaint. While Sara's father provides for her as if she were a princess, Burnett, who called Sara Crewe a little princess in the title of her story, describes Sara as if she were a doll. One such instance is a description of Sara in one of her dancing frocks. The narrator says that Sara's maid was requested to "make her as diaphanous and fine as possible" (38). The narrative continues: "Today a frock the colour of a rose had been *put* on her" (Emphasis added, 38). The implied passivity of Sara about her physical appearance might lead the reader to believe that a doll or a mannequin was being described instead of a nearly 11-year-old girl. On Sara's 11th birthday, the head of the seminary, Miss Minchin receives news that Sara's father had died bankrupt in India. Sara is promptly reduced to the state of an unpaid servant from being the most favoured pupil of the seminary. She has to give up her doll-girl status with the news of her father's death. Miss Minchin informs Sara that she will have to work in the seminary to continue living there. Burnett's description of the situation is telling. Miss Minchin announces her intention with:

> "Don't put on grand airs", she said. "The time for that sort of thing is past. You are not a princess any longer. Your carriage and your pony will be sent away—your maid will be dismissed. You will wear your oldest and plainest clothes—your extravagant ones are no longer suited to your station. You are like Becky—you must work for your living".
>
> To her surprise, *a faint gleam of light came into the child's eyes— a shade of relief.*
>
> "Can I work?" she said. "If I can work it will not matter so much. What can I do?"
>
> (Emphasis added, 66)

Sara is relieved as Miss Minchin's plan provided her with a new role, that of a servant in the seminary. Although this was a drastic, sudden, and seemingly cruel shift in the fate of Sara Crewe, this announcement by Miss Minchin liberates her from a state of limbo. With news of her father's death, Sara had become aware that she could not retain her former doll-girl role but did not know any other role for herself. Sara starts living her new role with the same resignation she had shown at being separated from her father. During her hard times, Sara spends many lonely evenings in the attic talking to her doll. She is completely aware that it is 'pretend play' when she behaves as if Emily can understand her. It is play but it is very serious play. After a particularly bad experience as a servant of the seminary, Sara talks to Emily and actually gets distressed that Emily cannot respond. She flings the doll across the room saying, "You are nothing but a *doll* .... Nothing but a doll—doll—doll! You care for nothing. You are stuffed with sawdust. You never had a heart. Nothing could ever make you feel. You are a *doll*!" (94). Afterwards, she picks up the doll and forgives it with, "You can't help being a doll .... Perhaps you do your sawdust best" (94). The doll does not reappear in the entire story after this incident. With the violent rejection of the plaything, her doll, Sara indicates that she is no longer using it as an object to project her feelings or as a Winnicottian transition object, signalling an end of an emotional phase of her childhood.

Although the doll was chosen by Sara as the object that would help her live away from her father and the close association she made with doll is highlighted by her bringing it swathed in black to Miss Minchin's office when she was summoned there to discuss her future after her father's death, her violent rejection of her doll signifies her acceptance of her changed cir-cumstances. By throwing her chief plaything across the room, Sara com-pletely accepts her transformation from the doll-girl she was perceived as to a working-class child. While living as a servant in the academy, Sara's chief form of entertainment is her ability to pretend. She pretends many fantastical things about her life and that of Becky, a scullery maid whom she had befriended while she was the favourite pupil of the seminary. Due to all these 'pretends', Sara braves the cold attic, the hunger, and the fatigue from overwork without letting her bad experiences affect her personality in any negative manner. Sara and Becky subsist morally and emotionally only on a heavy diet of Sara's pretend stories. The two girls are rescued from the brink of insanity – gaining emotional sustenance solely through their 'pretend play' and facing the danger of getting lost in their pretence – by the appearance of Sara's father's business partner. This man had moved to England after retiring from business in India. One of his intentions while moving to England was to search for Sara and take care of her as his friend. Once again, Sara becomes a rich girl with doll-like clothes. This time, Sara's doll-girl image helps in soothing the conscience of her father's friend. This girl created by Burnett is a perfect 'good' girl who remains one through very trying times and grows into a miniature Perfect Lady by the end of the narrative.

While Sara's sessions of 'pretend play' with Becky come closest to day-dreaming as we understand it, Freud posits a useful distinction between a child's play and fantasy in 'The Creative Writer and Daydreaming' (1907) with the following words:

> The opposite of play is not seriousness—it is reality. For all the emotion it is charged with, the child is well able to distinguish his world of play from reality and likes to connect the objects and situ-ations he imagines to palpable and visible things in the real world. This link alone distinguishes the child's play from fantasizing.
>
> (2003, 26)

Freud continues his argument by drawing a contrast between reality and play to explain the need to and circumstances under which a person would fantasise in the following manner:

> When the child has grown up and ceased to play, after putting years of mental effort into understanding the realities of life, together with all the seriousness they call for, he may one day find himself in a frame of mind in which the opposition between play and reality is once more suspended.
>
> (2003, 26)

Furthermore, he goes on to describe the situation of an adolescent who has had to give up playing to prove that play is replaced by fantasy, which is also a form of day-dream in the following passage:

> The adolescent, then, gives up playing and seemingly forgoes the bonus of pleasure he once derived from it. But anyone familiar with the human mind knows that scarcely anything is so hard to forgo as a pleasure one has known. The truth is that we cannot forgo anything, but merely exchange one thing for another; what seems like a renunciation is in fact the invention of a substitute, a surrogate. And so the adolescent too, when he ceases to play, gives up nothing but the link with real objects. Instead of playing, he now fantasizes, building castles in the air and fashioning what are called day-dreams. Most people, I believe, construct fantasises at certain times in their lives.
>
> (26–27)

Sara's 'pretends' are her moments of day-dreaming or fantasising for her to cope with her traumatising change in circumstances. Her choice of day-dreaming to escape into a fantasy world instead of playing, as a child would have done, also signal a growing up into adolescence during the years she spends as an all-purpose maid at Miss Minchin's academy. Her eventual rescue from the life of a maid facilitates her regaining a place in the social class her father hoped her to stay in, and by the end of the narrative the descriptions of her dress, demeanour and her actions show that she is quite the little woman girls of her age and class were expected to be in that period.

A few years later, Frances Hodgson Burnett wrote another novel about the making of a British 'sunbeam' who, it is suggested, would become the lady of the manor of a mansion on the moors of Yorkshire. Burnett's *The Secret Garden* (1911) is the story of Mary Lennox who is sent to England after she loses her parents in India. Mary Lennox, presumably, has the least flattering of introductions for the protagonist of a novel for children. At the very beginning, the reader is told, "by the time she was six years old she was as tyrannical and selfish a little pig as ever lived" (11). Mary's parents die of cholera in an Indian town and she is forgotten in the colonial quarters of her parents. She calls out to get the attention of some soldiers who are checking a deserted bungalow for survivors after the outburst of an epidemic. She is then sent to an English clergyman's house where the clergyman's son renames her as 'Mistress Mary Quite Contrary' (17). Mary is accustomed to playing alone. While she had been living with her parents, she was left to be taken care of by servants as her pretty mother, whom Mary thought of as 'the memsahib' (12), busily partied with young British officers of the imperial services and her father was equally busy at work in the imperial enterprise of Britain. For the first nine years of her life, Mary had entertained herself and was left to lord it over servants. On being sent to live as a 'rescued' child in a British household in India, she preferred to play at gardening alone than to play with the clergyman's children and resisted their friendly advances. The children tease her with her new nickname and the clergyman's wife tells one of her friends that she agrees with the children that Mary is a contrary child.

In England, Mary is received by her Uncle Craven's housekeeper, Mrs Medlock, who promptly declares that Mary is the most disagreeable child she has ever seen. The girl is taken to her uncle's manor and then again left to her own devices. This time, though, the servant who is assigned the task of helping her out is a spirited young girl called Martha. She has 12 younger siblings and does not take any orders from a child who is younger than many of her younger siblings. Moreover, she openly laughs at Mary's inability to dress herself and firmly clamps down Mary's expectations that Martha would do all the tasks Mary's ayah in India did for her. Mary is quite surprised by Martha's behaviour with her. She learns more about the manor and the surroundings from Martha. Martha's mother, Susan Sowerby, extends her motherly gaze to this child as well. She sends her a skipping rope and talks to her guardian, Mr Craven. She requests Mr Craven to meet the child before leaving the manor for one of his tours. In that meeting, Mr Craven asks Mary if she wants toys, books, or dolls and the child requests a "bit of earth .... To plant seeds in – to make things grow – to see them come alive" (94). Left to entertain herself in a manor with hundreds of rooms and having heard about a garden that was locked up ten years back, Mary sets out to explore the house as well as the garden. She discovers the secret garden and, having indirectly sought permission from the owner of the garden to play in it, Mary sets out to transform it. With the help of Martha's brother Dickon, who had also found the garden on his own, Mary works towards transforming it from an almost dead garden to the beautiful garden it was before it was locked up ten years ago. Mary also accidentally finds out that there is another child in the manor – her cousin Colin, who is the heir to the estate.

Colin is considered an invalid by everybody, including himself, till Mary refuses to indulge him. She is not cowed down by his tantrums. On the contrary, she declares that his fits of illness are 'hysterics' (135) after having heard the word for the first time from Colin's nurse. The scene where Mary contradicts Colin reveals knowledge of the work of Freud on the part of the author although it does not indicate much allegiance with Freud's theories. Mary shouts at Colin asking him to stop screaming and crying, and the following scene ensues:

"I can't stop!" he gasped, and sobbed. "I can't—I can't!"

"You can!" shouted Mary. "Half that ails you is hysterics and temper—just hysterics—hysterics—hysterics!" and she stamped each time she said it.

"I felt the lump—I felt it," choked out Colin. "I knew I should. I shall have a hunch on my back and then I shall die," and he began to writhe again and turned on his face and sobbed and wailed, but he didn't scream.

"You didn't feel a lump!" contradicted Mary fiercely. "If you did it was only a hysterical lump. Hysterics makes lumps. There's nothing the matter with your horrid back—nothing but hysterics! Turn over and let me look at it!"

She liked the word "hysterics", and felt somehow as if it had an effect on him.

(135)

The two children are facing similar circumstances of being left to confront their fears of accosting the unknown and the unfamiliar without parental protection in a secluded manor at the edge of a moor. They eventually form a bond of friendship. Mary also includes Dickon in this circle of friends. The three children experience some carefree moments of playing while also navigating the difficult terrain of childhood amidst hired domestic staff of the large estates of a secluded English manor.

Colin's father, Mr Craven, leaves him tucked in a bed in a plush suite of room of the large manor, while he travelled the world to escape from the tragic memoires his estates invoke in him. Mr Craven has been mourning the death of his wife for ten years – in effect, all of Colin's life. All the people around Colin always felt that the boy would not live to be an adult. The hired workers in the manor sometimes discuss this in front of the boy. Colin too believes he will die soon and had thought for ten years of his life that he is too weak to walk. He spends his days as an invalid, lying on a bed and entertaining himself with picture books his father brings back from his travels. Of the residents of the village, only the servants of the household and the village doctor had ever seen the boy. The rest of the village just knows of him as the invalid in the manor. Mary, who was not told of his existence, accidentally meets him when she sets out to find the source of a wailing sound that had woken her up in the middle of the night. They become friends. Eventually, with Dickon's help, Mary smuggles the wheelchair-bound Colin to the garden. While the garden is coming alive, Mary is turning into a pretty English girl and Colin is gaining health. Dickon's mother, Susan Sowerby, helps the children's secret endeavour of transforming themselves by supplying them with food and wisdom. Simultaneously, Ben Weatherstaff, an old gardener who could not let the garden die out and had snuck in every few years to tend to it, discovers the children in the garden. They rope him into their project of bringing the garden back to life. By believing in the children and helping them in achieving their dreams, Susan Sowerby and Ben Weatherstaff are welcomed into the children's utopia. The other adults in the narrative, who were dismissive about the children's capacities, are despised and kept out of it. However, Mr Craven, the adult whose presence in the secret garden was most desired by Colin, is eventually directed towards the children's utopia because of a dream. Moreover, a letter from Susan Sowerby imploring him to return home acts a catalyst to his decision to return to his manor and to his son. When he finally enters the garden, about a decade after ordering that it be shut down, he sees that a 'sunbeam' has replaced his 'contrary' niece and that his invalid son is running towards him. That huge toy, the garden, transforms two contrary children into socially acceptable children. Unlike the static toy doll that has to be rejected for the child to outgrow a fantasy and accept her reality in *A Little Princess* (1905), in this later work, Burnett's use of a more dynamic toy highlights the significance of play and of the toy in the development of children into the roles chalked out for them. In choosing a skipping rope as a gift for the child, Susan Sowerby introduces a toy that would bring Mary out into the fresh air of the moor. This was in contrast to the confined lives that women of Mary's class were expected to lead but it was in keeping with the newly emerging theories about the need for fresh air and exercise for girls to grow into healthy women. Mary too displays a clear preference for activities that involve being outside the house. She literally skips her way to the garden that becomes the site of her transformation. Through a rigorous investment in play, Mary gets transformed into a 'sunbeam' from a sullen child and Colin changes from a sulking invalid to a healthy boy. The narrative ends with all the children in the story moving into their socially acceptable roles: the young lord of the manor (Colin), the self-effacing girl (Mary) who could eventually grow into the true helpmeet – the image that had gained traction in late-Victorian realist fiction as the ideal role for the middle- and upper-class woman – to the growing heir-apparent of the manor, the moor boy (Dickon) who might evolve into the perfect wood-keeper for the estates, and the working girl (Martha) who is already an apprentice to become an efficient housekeeper.

Apart from the very obvious presence of child protagonists who find ways to brave the adult world, these two novels of Burnett's have other significant similarities. In both stories, the child's ability to play is seen as therapeutic. Sara's play is based mostly on her ability to pretend and Mary's play is more physical. While Sara has a doll to play with, Mary actually hopes that the gift box sent by her guardian does not have a doll, as she would not have known what to do with it. Mary's toy is the garden that she discovers and resolves to bring back to life. In both these works, the protagonists needed a toy each to come to terms with change thereby reiterating that a toy of some sort is a necessary prop of childhood. Furthermore, the two girls are also 'dollified' in the narratives. Sara is a doll-girl when the story begins. For a brief while in the course of the narrative, she has to give up that persona. She copes with the change due to her constant fantasising in her 'pretend play' that she remained a doll-girl. Eventually, she resumes her persona of a doll-girl and is on the path to become a Perfect Lady. On the other hand, Mary starts out as the opposite of the doll-girl. She is declared to be a 'contrary' child and discussed among the adults around her as having "unattractive ways" (18). Unlike Sara, she is described as a plain child of a very pretty mother. While Sara was her father's 'Best Beloved', Mary had the feeling that she did not belong to anybody and that she had, in fact, never belonged to anybody. Her experiences of abandonment include waking up in a deserted bungalow after her parents' death, calling out for help, being sent to live with strangers, being called contrary by children of her age group and an unattractive child by the adults around her. While the clergyman's children in India tease her, and leave her to her own devices, she's taken up by the Sowerbys to gently initiate her into an apprenticeship for her eventual role of the Perfect Lady of a country manor in England. Mary becomes a stronger, healthier, and happier child in Misselthwaite Manor but she also becomes a self-effacing, dependent relative in a manor that belongs to her uncle and her cousin. The Mary Lennox who is sent from India to England is not liked by any of the adults in the novel, including the narrator of the story, as she is not the 'sunbeam' girls of that social class were supposed to be. All the adults in the novel, including the narrator, work towards socialising Mary into the doll-girl she has to be to grow up into a Perfect Lady.

The two girl protagonists of Burnett's most famous works are English victims of British colonialism. In *A Little Princess* (1905), Sara Crewe is sent to England by her single father for her to be moulded into the aspired Perfect Lady of Victorian England. She seems to have already perfected the ideal of the British 'sunbeam' during her brief childhood in colonial India. In her depiction of Sara's persona, Burnett does not dwell upon her upbringing. The readers do not know whether Sara was brought up into English ways with the focused attention of an English mother and the help of Indian servants in colonial India. On the other hand, Mary in *The Secret Garden* (1911) is sent to a large Gothic manor at the edge of a huge moor to live mostly with English servants after facing abandonment and alienation as an orphan in British India. The narrative faults the climate of India for Mary's physical health and the practices of the families of the English officers of the imperial services in India for her personality. It is suggested that after Mary reaches England, the weather and the 'English' ways of the servants of the manor serve as catalysts in turning Mary into the 'sunbeam' that will help roses to bloom in the abandoned rose garden of the estate. She also takes on the task of coaxing the abandoned young heir out of his invalid state to put in some serious work to grow up into his destined role as English nobility. Throughout the narrative, Mary displays the knowledge and skills she had acquired as a child growing up in British India to be critical of the feudal high-handedness of the 'young Rajah' who had, in fact, never displayed any initiative or interest in life until Mary 'discovered' him. When she finds him wailing about an imaginary lump on his back, she assures him that he is as 'normal' as any English ten-year-old boy. Whereas the English servants, who had continuously tolerated the boy's infantile tantrums, often point out to Mary that she has brought her inappropriate 'Indian' upbringing into the English manor and that the moor air and their firm civilising methods will rehabilitate her into her 'true' role as an English 'sunbeam'. Through these two child victims of British colonialism, Burnett seems to be covertly critical of the English imperial enterprise and tangentially addressed its repercussions on English children. However, by laying the blame on the perceived dangerousness of the Indian climate for the 'dysfunctionality' of the precocious Sara and the sullen Mary at the beginning of both the narratives, Burnett reiterates colonial English myths about the 'dangers' that befell the English while executing the white man's burden. With her rehabilitation of Sara and Mary into English 'sunbeams', Burnett perpetuates the stereotype and misses the opportunity to engage with the effects of British colonial enterprise on British children.

While these two narratives turn two English girls from unacceptable models of girlhood to the ideal of 19th-century English girlhood, Burnett's first novel with a child protagonist, *Little Lord Fauntleroy* (1886), transports an American boy to Britain to begin his apprenticeship to go to the House of Lords. Cedric Errol is the son of an American widow of an English captain who had to settle down in Britain. The captain's father had cut ties with him for making a bad marriage. Although Cedric is shown to be the child of a happy marriage, the narrative begins with his realising that his father is dead. Moreover, the 7-year-old boy begins believing that it is his responsibility to protect his mother. Throughout the narrative, he never addresses her as mother or any formal equivalent of that address. She is called "Dearest" by him. They seem to be a rather affectionate and self-contained mother–son pair until duty's call separates them. Not only does he have to relocate to England, to eventually inherit an earldom, but it is also expected of this young child that he will live without his mother in his grandfather's huge manor. The curmudgeonly grandfather needs an heir to his earldom and requires Cedric's presence in his estates. However, he does not want to accept his estranged son's widow into his family. While the young American mother is pensioned off to live alone in a dowager cottage on the outskirts of the estate, the Earl oversees the training of the boy to ensure that he grows into a befitting heir to an English earldom. Many incidents during the course of the narrative make the Earl realise the importance of the mother for his grandson's happiness. Eventually, he also understands that her presence improves his earldom. The narrative ends with the mother and son once again living under the same roof.

In the process of socialising the boy into the ideal of aspirational British masculinity, a 7-year-old boy's emotional need for the presence of his mother is deliberately overlooked. The boy is expected to be brave through a rapid succession of extremely traumatic incidents. He is suddenly removed from his life as middle-class boy growing up in New York to relocate to a manor in England, which takes him away from all his friends. He is then told that his mother will live in a separate house. Furthermore, he is told that he has to shift his allegiance from his strong faith in the presidential democracy of America to the parliamentary monarchy of Britain. However, his notions of a welfare-state model of running an estate come in handy in gaining the affections of the people of his grandfather's feudal estates. Cedric seems to bring his American upbringing and ideas into Britain to revive the fortunes of a decaying feudal structure. Amidst all this hectic activity in Cedric's life and the rapid pace of changes within the narrative, it is easy to forget that he is a 7-year-old boy. The big party at the end of the narrative to mark his eighth birthday and also to celebrate the consolidation of his position as the legitimate inheritor of the earldom come as a shock to a reader who would have noted many moments in the narrative where the boy displayed immense emotional maturity.

Many aspects of the narrative build this confusion about Cedric Errol's fictional life. To begin with, he is a 7-year-old boy who sports a hairstyle of shoulder-length hair that ends in curls, wears lace collars, knickers, and red stockings.[5] Even after his English grandfather takes charge of his life, Cedric's styling is not changed to a more masculine one. However, he is no longer called Cedric. The people of the estates and the adjoining village address him as Little Lord Fauntleroy. His grandfather addresses him with the formal address of Fauntleroy, whereas his mother continues to call him Ceddie. Although Cedric is so young that he can barely dress on his own, he discusses politics and business with adult men. He also needs to know that his mother will keep a light burning all night in one of the rooms of her cottage for him to be able to spot it from the window of his bedroom but will not allow himself to express his anguish at the separation from his mother. Although he is excited about a room full of toys, he willingly chooses to postpone meeting his new pony because he knows that his mother would be waiting to meet him. With a remarkably developed ability to postpone gratification, Cedric faces many sudden and strange changes in his life to gain a father figure in the form of his grandfather and to eventually reunite with his mother.

While Burnett's child protagonists in all the three novels are extremely successful in growing up into their destined roles through play, pretence and postponement of gratification, the children are toyed with in many ways. They are abandoned or their desires are overlooked in the process of moulding them into predestined roles for them in their families. Although the narratives seem to centre the trope of childhood such as play or the toy or the fantasy of regaining the lost protection of a father figure, all these established aspects of childhood are used to fit these children into roles assigned to them by their culture.

Many other stories written for children have also used the toy as a significant prop to socialise children into culturally acceptable behaviour. The writers of the 'Little Female Academy' were among the earliest who recognised the utility of toys in literature in inculcating morals in children. For example, in *Secret Gardens: A Study of the Golden Age of Children's Literature* (1987), Humphrey Carpenter mentions G. E. Farrow's *The Wallypug of Why* (1895), the story of a girl called Girlie whose doll takes her to "the land of Why, where all the questions and answers come from". As late as 1966, the doll was still being used to instil discipline and awaken sensitivity in the child characters of Richard Hughes' *Gertrude's Child*.

Not only do toys help in making life easier for the child but also make the child feel powerful and in control of her life in some cases. This is very well illustrated in one of the short stories in a late 20th-century anthology of stories in which the child–toy bond is central. This anthology is *The Silent Playmate: A Collection of Doll Stories* (1979) by Naomi Lewis. In one of the stories in this collection, Laurence Housman's story 'Rocking-Horse Land', Freedling, a five-year-old prince, is given a rocking-horse on his fifth birthday. The boy falls in love with this toy and plays with it throughout the day. At night, the rocking-horse comes to him and requests to be freed so that it could go back to its family in Rocking-Horse land. It tells the boy that he will find a white hair in its mane and that he should wind it around his little finger. It assures the boy that as long as the hair is on his finger it will come to him whenever it is called. The boy sets it free each night and calls it back at dawn. On getting a real pony as a gift on his sixth birthday, he frees it forever as he realises that he has outgrown the rocking-horse. The theme of the 'artificial' or 'dead' being replaced by the 'natural' and 'live' is a common thread through many of these stories, similar to the 'Secret Garden' in Burnett's eponymous novel.

Another story in the collection that has the theme of weaving a fantasy around a doll is Australian writer Ruth Ainsworth's 'Rag Bag'. Rag Bag is a doll that belongs to a girl called Carol. Her only playmates are her dolls – Rag Bag, Saucy Sally, and Jolly Roger. This story is different in many ways from the usual stories for children, as here Carol encounters a Fairy Child who is cruel, mean, selfish, and scary unlike fairies in conventional stories for children. The Fairy Child is jealous of Carol's ability to play with dolls. She wants Carol to give her a doll. With the help of her elder sister, Carol makes a doll out of a clothes peg for the Fairy Child. The Fairy Child comes back twice, demanding accessories for her doll – a handbag and a pair of earrings. She is again dissatisfied and tells Carol that she has thrown 'that wooden peg creature' (87) into the dustbin and demands Carol to give her one of her dolls as they can speak. Carol is quite amazed at the Fairy Child. She tries to explain to the Fairy Child, "But don't you understand …. It is all pretending. I speak in a high voice for Sally and a gruff one for Roger. It all seems real but I'm only playing. Only pretending" (88). Carol knows that she is pretending that her dolls have human abilities, but when she is actually threatened with the possibility of losing Rag Bag she believes that the doll can save herself from the Fairy Child and will come back to her. In this story, the doll that is threatened by separation from her owner is believed to have human powers of speech and action by the owner and it was a doll that belonged to her mother and grandmother before her. An argument can be made that this heirloom doll gifted by her protectors comes with the power of protecting Carol from the loss of a loved object. The doll stands for the mother and grandmother who will protect Carol from grief. Although Carol knows that she is pretending about her dolls, she has to create the fantasy of supernatural powers in her doll to protect herself from fear of loss.

A turn of the 21st-century anthology that mirrors the recognition of the complexities and pluralities of contemporary childhood is *The Faber Book of Contemporary Stories about Childhood* edited by Lorrie Moore in 1997. Moore has brought together stories by child narrators and memoirs of childhood that bring out the diversity of childhood. Moore's anthology challenges the perception of childhood as a classless, homogenous, conflict-free zone. While the child protagonist of Glenda Adams's *Lies* is trying to understand the complexities of the sexual game among the adults in her immediate intimate circle, the narrator of Kirsty Gunn's *Tinsel Bright* is grappling, in retrospect, with her puzzlement about her father's sexuality. Most of the stories are children's accounts of watching their parents cracking up or getting disillusioned or making drastic changes in their lifestyles and beliefs in the aftermath of World War II. The most poignant story of the anthology is Sandra Cisneros' *Barbie-Q*, published in 1991, in which two girls go to the market to pick up 'good bargains' after they hear that a toy store had caught fire. They settle for two slightly mutilated Barbie dolls because they know they cannot afford unblemished new dolls. While the story deals with the desire of these two girls to possess the much glamourised Barbie doll, it also shows an acceptance of reality by the two girls who settle for less-than-perfect dolls. These two girls have just one Barbie doll each and one extra doll dress, which they had fashioned out of an old sock and share between them. They pick up two damp and sooty-smelling Barbies and a few partially damaged accessories for the dolls from vendors who are selling these for throwaway prices. These dolls are among the toys salvaged from a huge fire in a large store. As argued earlier in this work, the doll is supposed to be perfect and a representation of the aspired ideal in most cultures. The doll is believed to be the Best Beloved. Furthermore, the Barbie is considered the epitome of fashion and glamour by people in the toy business and is a highly coveted possession or an extremely wished-for doll for most children. Sandra Cisneros' story makes a powerful impact as it challenges the notion of the doll being a representation of the ideal by deglamourising the most glamorous doll. Moreover, it also interrogates some 'givens' of childhood. The two girls in her story do not have any perfect dolls. They are ready to buy discarded or damaged Barbies and are excited about them just as much as children who buy these expensive toys from big stores are likely to be. Although the children in this story are happy to have dolls, they are also aware that they can afford only a few kinds of toys and have to buy their dolls carefully. In this story, childhood definitely does not seem the carefree and blissful period that it is usually purported to be.

An earlier novel that challenges the idea of childhood as being a homogenous period of bliss is Russell Hoban's *The Mouse and His Child* (1967). Hoban's novel is written for children but Carpenter and Prichard point out that it contains a parody of Samuel Beckett's later plays. This shows that while writing for children, Hoban also expected adults to read this book and get the literary allusions. In this novel, a toy mouse and his child together constitute a clockwork toy. The mouse and his child dance when wound up. This toy is a Christmas decoration till it breaks and is thrown in the bin. The dumped toy is picked up by a tramp who repairs the toys and leaves them to "[b]e tramps" (11). After a series of misadventures that the father–son duo battle together, they manage to create a comfortable world for themselves. This novel is an instance of children's literature where the entrenched notion of childhood as a period of bliss across sociocultural differences is challenged. However, children's literature for close to two centuries perpetuated such ideas and was routinely a tool to propagate stereotypical notions of childhood across many cultures.

Children's literature is not only rife with stereotypes, it is also a very powerful pedantic tool to incorporate these stereotypes in children's minds. This use of children's literature has been noticed across cultures and through many centuries. As noted earlier in this chapter, the earliest books written for children were primers and for a while they were the only kinds of books published for children. Later, when stories were written for children, the story itself started being used, and continues to be used, as an important educational toy.

While in 1699 Cotton Mather warned the children of New England that acts of disobedience have grave consequences, the importance of following rules is reiterated in 20th-century best-selling children's books too. Around three centuries after the Puritan preacher's grave warnings, J. K. Rowling shows the children of the post-globalised world, through her trend-setting Harry Potter series, that disobedience can lead children into potentially fatal situations. Most of the time in this series, all the children at the Hogwarts School of Witchcraft and Wizardry – including the much-threatened Harry – are safe as long as they obey the rules of the school. Any kind of transgression jeopardises their safety. For instance, in *The Order of the Phoenix* (2003), Harry and his friends are under the strictest security for the greater part of the novel. They are warned right at the beginning that they have to abide by all the school rules and a few more rules are added specifically for the three friends to abide by. The explanation they are given is that they will put their lives in danger if they transgress. In spite of warnings by their teachers, the children go on to disobey the rules many times. A series of transgressions leads them into a situation where the Principal of their school, Prof Dumbledore, has to intervene to ensure that they do not get killed. Although the Harry Potter series continuously reiterates the injunction that children should obey the rules laid out by the people in charge of the children's well-being, the children eventually triumph through many well-meaning transgressions of rules; thereby undermining the credibility of these rules for the child readers of these books. In fact, the best of children's literature has always had the dual function of reinforcing authority as well as showcasing children triumphing over tyrannical authority figures.

Children's stories with subtle but firm 'civilising' messages were always encouraged by parents, teachers, educators, and, sometimes, even by scholars of children's literature. However, children have always liked stories in which the child protagonists get away with much harmless mischief. One of the early writers of this kind of fiction was Enid Blyton. Her first book appeared in 1922 and the last one in the late 1960s. In a literary career spanning more than four decades, Blyton was equally loved and criticised. Children have been reading her work from the early decades of the 20th century to now in spite of serious disapproval of her work by many parents and educators. One of the reasons for discouraging late 20th-century children from reading Blyton's work is the accusation of racism Blyton had to face on account of her depictions of Golliwogs in her Noddy series. In one of the Noddy stories – *Here Comes Noddy* – three Golliwogs attack Noddy. While Carpenter and Prichard carefully state that "it has been suggested that a scene in *Here Comes Noddy*, in which Noddy is set upon in a dark wood by three Golliwogs, is really a story about a racial mugging" (69) the explicit naming of one of the Golliwogs as Nigger foregrounds the racism in the narrative. In another novel, *The Little Black Doll*, Enid Blyton has narrated the story of a black doll whose blackness gets washed away by magic rain. The other factor about her writing that educators and parents find discouraging is that she used very limited vocabulary in her writing. Furthermore, Blyton has also been accused of sexism due to her portrayal of stereotyped female roles. While propagation of racism and sexism, in any form and through any medium, should be unequivocally condemned, the conflict of opinion between her target audience and the people responsible for their welfare makes a crucial point. While children read for pleasure, the adults around them want children to read for instruction. Adults tend to continue the process of educating and civilising the child even through leisure activities. Not only books but toys have also acquired the role of instructors. Most toy stores stock educational toys that are enthusiastically bought by parents and other adults for their children. These toys supposedly make learning more interesting as children can receive instruction through objects they cherish and play with. However, some thought needs to be given to the harmful effects of corrupting the very nature of play. Development psychologists like Jean Piaget and Erik Erikson have shown that play contributes a lot to the mental, social, and physical development of a child. One should also remember that playing is a very important aspect of the emotional life of a child. James Higgins declares, "playing, as children, means playing is the most serious thing in the world" (*Beyond Words: Mystical Fancy in Children's Literature*, 1970, 78). While the temptation to 'civilise' the child by incorporating education into play has become an established pedagogic practice, the practice removes the playful aspect of play, thereby affecting its efficacy for a child's emotional growth. Also, turning play into a learning activity makes dents on a child's agency by intruding into the leisure moments of the child.

Stories with toys as one of the focal points of the story also seem to be favourites in trying to inculcate morals in young people. As mentioned earlier in this chapter, the doll was used to instil discipline and awaken sensitivity in the child characters of Richard Hughes's *Gertrude's Child* (1966). In Hughes's story, Gertrude is a rather dissatisfied doll. She runs away from the girl she belongs to. On her way, she meets an old man who asks her if she would like to own a little girl. The old man reveals that he keeps a shop where he sells little girls and/or boys to dolls. Gertrude gets a girl from him. She names her Annie and proceeds to treat her exactly the way she was treated by the girl she ran away from. After neglecting and ill-treating Annie quite a bit, Gertrude is saved by Annie from being eaten by a lion. Gertrude then realises her folly and the story ends on the wise note of the child and the doll deciding to get rid of the power structure of 'owner and owned' with Gertrude remarking, "Listen. I think it's a stupid idea, dolls *having* to belong to children or children to dolls. Why can't they just be friends?" (Lewis, Naomi. Ed. *The Silent Playmate*, 1979, 176).

In marked contrast to stories written for children, the fiction of childhood written for adults almost never presents the toy as a pedantic tool. As discussed in the previous chapter, many novels with the child in focus show evidence of one or more child character(s) in the novel being treated as a 'toy', thereby constructing a lasting fiction about childhood as the ideal period for the moulding of a human being into a predetermined role in sociocultural institutions such as families. An unusual novel where such rei-fication is reciprocated is Harper Lee's *To Kill a Mockingbird* (1960). In this novel, the favourite game of two children, the narrator Scot and her older brother Jem, is to provoke their reclusive neighbour Arthur Radley to come out of the unusual life of confinement he seems to lead. Arthur Radley is rumoured to be insane and is kept in isolation by his ageing parents after having been in some undisclosed trouble with the law as a teenager. Due to Arthur's complete absence from social life and the rumours in their small town, the children too believe him to be insane. Jem and Scot christen him Boo Radley and spend an entire summer trying to bring him out of his seclu-sion. They realise that Arthur notices their efforts when he leaves a gift for them in the hollow of a tree that stands between the two houses. Arthur's use of the tree as a secret hiding place to communicate with the two chil-dren reveals his remarkable closeness to the world of children. His gift is a set of 'dolls' carved out of soap bars to roughly resemble the silhouettes of a boy and a girl. A close reading of the circumstances of the 'gift-giving' illuminates the fact that while the children have converted Boo Radley into a 'toy' of sorts, to Arthur they are like two dolls. There is a clear similarity in the perceptions of Arthur and the children towards each other. While the children find the allegedly invalid Boo Radley a vulnerable adult who can be converted to a 'toy', to the isolated, but probably mentally and emotion-ally adult, Arthur the two children come across as 'innocent' and harmless children.

The toy–child link continues through literature and the toy, quite often, plays the dual role of being the transition object and the projection of a self in many narratives of childhood. However, the child in literature – whether it is written for adults or for children – is no longer just a reified 'toy-like' presence in contemporary literature. Nevertheless, the resonances of a long period of reification of childhood were seen even in late 20th-century Anglo-American literature, with some changes in the perception of childhood after the two world wars. However, 19th-century notions of childhood travelled into colonial India and its repercussions are seen even in late 20th-century Indian literature in English. The next chapter will deal with some of these resonances and repercussions.

Notes

1 Ethel May's story is very similar to the biographical detail about the childhood and youth of Elizabeth Barrett Browning whose *Aurora Leigh* was published in 1856.
2 There were local variations of such series depicting the growing up of girls in other English-speaking Commonwealth countries. While L. M. Montgomery introduced such a girl character in Canada with *Anne of Green Gables* as late as 1908 and went on to create a very successful series of books that begin with her being adopted as a foster child and end with Anne as a trained teacher who gives

up her job to get married and start her own family, Ethel Turner had already created 'sunbeam' children in Australia in *Seven Little Australians* (1894).

3 During the early years of this research, conversations with Indian women who studied in schools in which English was the medium of instruction revealed that almost all of them recalled borrowing Burnett's books from their school libraries even as late as the last decade of the 20th century and placed those books among their favourites of the books they read as children.

4 It would not be out of place to note in this work that Frances Hodgson Burnett never travelled to India and did not have any sort of close connection with the British colonies in India, whereas she frequently moved between Britain and the United States of America throughout her life; had homes in both nations; her children were American citizens; and both her husbands were American and British citizens respectively. It can be safely stated that she had no first-hand experience of colonial life in British India.

5 There is much academic work on the coverage by the then popular press on the styling trend for small boys started by the illustrations in the first edition of this book. Cedric's clothes and hairstyle were considered more feminine than the then accepted image of the British boy. Gretchen Holbrook Gerzina suggests in her introduction to the *Annotated Secret Garden* (2007) that it was not Burnett's intention to depict a feminine styling although she had shared a photograph of her younger son Vivian with curly blonde locks and a lace collar with the publishers of the book.

5

RESONANCES AND REPERCUSSIONS

> Let me tell you that this Solanka's whole room, and remem-
> ber we're talking here about a fellow of King's College,
> Cambridge, England, was crawling with dolls, and I do mean
> dolls. Once I noticed that, I couldn't leave fast enough. God
> forbid he should mistake me for a dolly and poke me in the
> stomach till I said *Ma-ma*.
>
> Salman Rushdie. *Fury*. 2001. 174

The preceding four chapters discuss the diverse ways in which the toy–child
bond worked in the construction of childhood and gender in the late 19th
and early 20th centuries. This chapter will focus on the repercussions of the
reification of childhood and its resonances in Indian literature in English. It
will, however, begin with a discussion of a few changes in the perceptions of
childhood in the Anglo-American world after the two world wars brought
about sweeping changes across the two continents.

In the early decades of the 20th century, the fiction of childhood registered
a few changes in the 'norms' of childhood. Some of the changes occurred as
an aftermath of the two world wars. The First World War significantly challenged the then contemporary worldview. With the large-scale recruitment
of men into the armed forces through most of Europe and later in the United
States of America too, women had to enter the workforce. The role of the
woman as a homemaker that had become firmly established among a large
section of the population of Britain and America had to be re-examined
due to the war. The by then entrenched demarcation between the separate
spheres of the Home and the World nearly collapsed. Deirdre Beddoe, in
Discovering Women's History (1983) argues that the change was a welcome
one for women "who felt themselves suffocated by the [Perfect Lady] stereotype" (27). With significant changes in the domestic sphere, often leading to
lasting changes in the family structure, children had to rapidly adapt to the
new ways of living in many households. In effect, this meant that they had
to 'grow up' early due to the happenings around them. There is evidence

DOI: 10.4324/9781003093275-5

of this change in the perception of childhood in novels set in the period between the two world wars.

The fiction of childhood that was written for adults first showed signs of awareness of this shift in perspectives on childhood. Rumer Godden's *An Episode of Sparrows* (1955) depicts the effect of the war on the children of a London neighbourhood, including their having to adapt to the remarkable changes in the urban landscape of their part of the metropolis. Lovejoy Mason is a homeless child who is being cared for by the owner of a failing restaurant. Lovejoy, like Mary in *The Secret Garden* (1911), wants a bit of earth. While the early-Edwardian child Mary got an entire garden to bring to life, Lovejoy and the street urchins she befriends get into trouble when they 'borrow' a few buckets of earth from a private garden to grow some flowers on a bombed-out patch of land in the public square. Olivia, one of the adults in the narrative, secretly supports the children's endeavour. Godden shows the effect of the war on the life of children while trying to reiterate the notion that children are innocent people and childhood needs to be 'preserved' as it was perceived to be in the pre-war years.

However, there are many instances of the fiction of childhood written after the Second World War that record drastic changes to the former notions of childhood in Europe and America. David Lodge firmly but gently heralds the beginning of the loss of the 'innocence' of childhood immediately after the Second World War in *Out of the Shelter* (1970). Timothy is a young British boy when the war is declared. He spends most nights hiding in the shelter built to prevent people from being harmed by bomb attacks. His sister Kath goes to work in the Salvation Army during the war. Immediately after the war, 16-year-old Timothy is sent by his parents to 'spy' on his sister. Kath is posted in Heidelberg, Germany, with the Allied Forces working in the post-war rehabilitation efforts in Europe. During the vacation, Timothy grows up to realise that he can build a life that does not include his parents. He makes friends; has his first sexual experience; understands his sister better; and becomes close to her during that short vacation.

An earlier short story from Ireland that deals with the adjustments a very young child had to make due to the changes in his family is Frank O Connor's 'My Oedipus Complex' (1950). The story presents the point of view of a very young boy, Larry, whose father has gone to serve in the army during the First World War. The first-person narrative is a mildly amused recollection by an adult narrator, who recalls his attachment to his mother and hostility towards the mostly absent father. Although the story's title and contents suggest that it was an adult's recollection of experiencing the Oedipus complex, the story narrates a very young boy's rapid adaptation to domestic changes necessitated by the war. Around the age noted by Freud as the period during which a child would experience Oedipal feelings, Larry's father is at war and makes very short visits home. The father's presence is felt as an intrusion by Larry because of the close emotional bond he shared with his mother. After the war ends and the father returns home, the father and son are openly, and sometimes aggressively, hostile towards each other. However, the birth of a younger sibling and the mother's attention getting drawn by the new-born unite the father and son into forming a masculine bond through a shared interest in toys such as automobiles and locomotives, toys that are still considered typically masculine. The story, from the title onwards, portrays not only a seemingly clean illustration of the Oedipus complex but also a dubiously neat resolution to it. However, the lucid recollection of childhood emotions by an adult narrator belies the resolution of the complex at the age suggested in the narrative. The mock humourous presentation of it lends the story to being interpreted as an act of sublimation through creative writing instead of it being a documentation of a clean resolution of the Oedipus complex. Nevertheless, it is an instance of an acknowledgement within the fiction of childhood that children have sexual feelings and learn to process them in the course of growing up, which was a serious divergence from the established reification of the child as an innocent asexual being.

Another novel that looks at childhood significantly differently from the usual notions of 'innocence' is Muriel Spark's *The Prime of Miss Jean Brodie* (1961). Miss Jean Brodie is a teacher in a conventional school for girls in Britain during the 1930s. Her boyfriend is killed in the First World War and she chooses to remain single. She tells her students things that were considered unsuitable for children. For instance, she talks about her romance with her boyfriend to her students. She also encourages them to think against the grain. She chooses a few girls, all of them striking for their traits, and forms a coterie, which she calls the Brodie Set. The headmistress and the other teachers have serious issues with Jean Brodie's unusual methods in interacting with the girls in the class or with her coterie after school hours. Eventually, one of the girls from the Brodie Set betrays her by telling the school authorities that she teaches them 'fascist ideas'. Although the novel ends with a schoolgirl reporting on her mentor to the school authorities, its treatment of the relationship between the teacher and her posse significantly challenges the ensconced notions of good behaviour and bad behaviour for school girls, reiterated over a couple of centuries of fiction of childhood. The girls in the novel, not just those in the Brodie Set, are not treated as innocent, sexually ignorant, pre-teens with whom matters such as love, loss of love, betrayal in love, were typically not discussed.

A significant movement, which partly evolved as an aftermath of the two wars, led to a momentous shift in the perception of childhood and crucially changed the perception of childhood in literature and culture. This was the Children's Rights Movement. The impact of the Children's Rights Movement started being seen in literature in Britain and America in the 1970s. Writers for children began to address issues such as poverty, disability, and dysfunctional families. However, Carpenter and Prichard state that

117

these issues "became fashionable in the 1970s" (1984, 427) in children's literature. They also quote Nina Bawden who remarks that these issues should be addressed only if they are relevant to the plot of a novel and not as statutory inclusions to keep up with the trend. Although children's literature was not actively presenting the changes in childhood after the war, the work of activists led to a social acceptance of the heterogeneity of childhood. In 1974, John Holt published *Escape from Childhood: The Needs and Rights of Children* with 11 explicitly stated rights of children. While some of these rights may have universal acceptance – like the right to be treated no worse than an adult by the law – there are some that would lead to heated debates, such as the right to live away from home and choose/make one's own home and the right to work for money (15). Even though some of the rights suggested by Holt would be completely unacceptable in some societies and would be considered fantastical in many others, these rights buttress the recognition of childhood as a significant phenomenon by itself, in contradistinction to the historical perception of childhood as a formative stage in human life. In *The Children's Rights Movement: A History of Advocacy and Protection* (1991), Joseph M. Hawes traces the history of Children's Rights in the United States of America from its colonial times as New England. He quotes the laws passed by the Pilgrim Fathers that recognise a child's right to defend itself by retaliation when facing cruelty in the form of extreme physical harm by parents. The law could intervene in such situations. Hawes gives a list of legislations ranging from the adoption by the state of Massachusetts of the *Body of Liberties* in 1641, which brought in a progressive change by allowing children to defend themselves against abuse while also shockingly prescribing capital punishment for rebellious children over 16, to the passing of the Juvenile Delinquency Prevention and Control Act passed by the US Congress in 1968. However, Hawes states that the Children's Rights Movement came of age only in the 1960s in the USA. Thus, the debate on the Rights of the Child in Britain and America from the late 1960s onwards renewed the focus on childhood.

In 1971, Shulamith Firestone declared the abolition of childhood in *The Dialectic of Sex*, by arguing that the segregation of children from the rest of society retards their growth (87). Firestone has also pointed out that perpetually linking women with children is detrimental to both of them. She states:

> the nature of this bond is no more than shared oppression … moreover this oppression is intertwined and mutually reinforced in such complex ways that we will be unable to speak of the liberation of women without also discussing the liberation of children, and vice versa. The heart of woman's oppression is her childbearing and childrearing roles. And in turn children are defined in relation to this role and are psychologically formed by it; what they become as

adults and the sorts of relationships they are able to form determine the society they will ultimately build.

(72)

The works of Nancy Chodrow and others who work on motherhood and maternal dynamics also bear testimony to the fact that there is a diversity of opinion about the effects of mothering on women. However, Firestone's argument had a powerful impact on some women in the 1970s, and thereby on a few children who were traditionally expected to be nurtured by these women. In 1983, Valerie Polakov made a strong case for the de-institution-alisation of childhood in *The Erosion of Childhood*. However, the United Nations entered the debate only in 1989 when the General Assembly adopted the Convention of the Rights of the Child on 20 November that year.

The Preamble of the Convention starts with the declaration that the States Parties of the Convention have agreed on 54 articles after having considered that

in accordance with the principles proclaimed in the Charter of the United Nations, recognition of the inherent dignity and of the equal and inalienable rights of *all members* of the human family is the foundation of freedom, justice and peace in the world.

(Emphasis added, 39)

The Convention also states that

the child should be fully prepared *to live an individual life* in society, and brought up in the spirit of the ideals proclaimed in the Charter of the United Nations, and in particular in the spirit of peace, dignity, tolerance, freedom, equality and solidarity.

(Emphasis added, 40)

Most of the 54 articles assure basic facilities like sanitation, health, and education but Articles 12 to 15 assure more than that. Some of these articles assure the right to form and express one's opinions about matters that affect their life; freedom to seek, receive, and impart information across frontiers; freedom of thought and choice of religion; right to freely assemble and the right to privacy even within their homes. Article 37, which recognises "the right of the child to rest and leisure, to engage in play and recreational activities appropriate to the age of the child and to participate freely in cultural life and the arts" (57), shows that the Convention recognises the fact that some children are deprived of these things which are commonly believed to be 'givens' of childhood.

119

While the States Parties have agreed to ensure that these 54 articles not only provide the rights of children but also help in formulating policies for children, the Plan of Action for Implementing the World Declaration on the Survival, Protection and Development of Children in the 1990s, that was agreed upon at the World Summit for Children on 30 September 1990, focuses primarily on providing the basic needs of children. Other rights like freedom of expression, freedom to seek and impart information, freedom of thought, conscience and religion, and the right to not be subjected to an intrusion of privacy have been completely ignored. The Plan, which was agreed by the States Parties on 30 September 1990, addresses the issue of development of children as part of the larger scheme of development of the nation. Some of the statistics revealed by the plan are quite shocking. It mentions that 40,000 children die every day and that 100 million die every year. Out of this 100 million, 14 million die of preventable and/or treatable diseases. This Plan also realises that:

> Effective implementation of this Plan of action will require concerted national action and international co-operation. As affirmed in the declaration, such action and co-operation must be guided by the principle of a "first call for children"—a principle that the essential needs of children should be given high priority in the allocation of resources, in bad times as well as in good times, at national and international as well as at family levels.
>
> (24)

Although the Plan is well-intentioned, it does not live up to the essence of the Convention's agreements. While the Convention recognises the child as an individual, the Plan treats the child as a vulnerable and helpless being that needs to be protected and saved.

India is one of the States Parties of the Convention of the Rights of the Child adopted by the United Nations General Assembly on 20 November 1989. India's commitment to the Convention arises from Article 39 of the Directive Principles of State Policy in the Constitution of India. The Article declares that the State shall direct its policy towards securing that the health and strength of children will not be abused and that the citizens of the nation are not forced by economic necessity to enter vocations that are unsuited for their age or strength. It also declares that the State should direct its policy towards giving opportunities and facilities to children to develop healthily in an atmosphere of freedom and dignity while working towards protecting children and youth from exploitation and decadence. A decade after the Plan was agreed upon, the Department of Women and Child Development brought out the India Report on the World Summit for Children. While India has recorded a marked improvement in providing health care to children, lowering infant mortality rates, immunising children from preventable diseases, and increasing literacy levels, many other rights of children stated by the Convention are still not addressed. However, some civil society organisations are working towards securing the rights of child labourers in India. Nandana Reddy has recorded the work of a non-governmental organisation called the Concerned for Working Children (CWC) that has been working closely with child labourers from 1977 onwards. Reddy recounts that the organisation germinated when child workers in an industrial estate attended a meeting that was to be addressed by trade union leaders. None of these children could imagine a situation where they might survive without having to work for their living. Reddy makes a very pertinent distinction between labour and work and also points out that neither is every kind of education necessarily good nor is all monetised work bad in every kind of context. Banning children from working for a living can be harmful to them, in some situations. She says,

> [T]he legal environment provided no visibility for working children. By banning their work in the formal sector and providing no protection in the others, it was virtually ignoring this group of young workers, denying them their rights as children, even their right to survival through work. It was literally sweeping the issue under the carpet and hoping that it would somehow go away.
>
> (2005, 105)

The children on the other hand, were fully aware that they had to work to survive and asked for "protection from harmful or hazardous work, equal wages for equal work, a medical insurance that was simple, access to education and vocational training, and a career development fund that would mature when they turned 18 years [old] instead of a provident fund" (105). After facing hostility from the trade unions that viewed child labourers as competitors to adults, the children decided to form their own unions. The children also recognised that their concerns differed slightly from that of adult workers. They launched an organisation called Bhima Sangha in 1989 and declared 30th April as Child Labour Day. This initiative eventually expanded into a network of organisations of working children and is supported by the International Movement for Working Children. This network is an independent subset of the trade union movement. It has its own newspapers and community radio/ audio news programmes, and does documentation work. The Bhima Sangha gained enough credibility to negotiate with state governments and worked towards improving health care for street children, making access to the government ration shops easier, demanding schools and daycare centres, and growing forests. In 1995, the Toofan Programme was launched which led to the formation of children's councils that interact with local governments.

However, this movement has suffered a setback due to governmental policies. The Indian government usually deals with child labour by 'rescuing' child workers after 'raiding' their work-spaces and 'rehabilitating' them by enrolling them in 'educational institutions' that are often under-equipped to optimally educate children who enter the system much later than their peers who enter the schooling system at the age of 5 or 6. More often than not these children drop out of the schools to which they have been assigned and join the unorganised work-sector to avoid being 'rescued' and to eke out a living. Reddy says, "[I]n order to hear the voice of children, as also other marginalized groups, we need to struggle for a *humane development model* and not *development with a human face*" (109). A more recent book that emerged from interviews of children who live outside of their homes and have to work for their livelihood is Lara Shankar's *Midway Station: Real Life Stories of Homeless Children* (2006). In this work, Shankar records her conversation with 11 children living in shelters in Delhi in the first few years of this century. Although the book records a diversity of experiences across gender and age ranges, each one of them told Shankar that they would never advise any other child to leave their home, whatever their circumstances may be. This shows that the world outside the home is still not a space that a child can navigate without experiencing situations that are worse than abusive homes.

However, there has been dedicated work for more than a century to ensure that children in India have a right to dignity of life, which presupposes a right to access food, health, safety, and the hope for a good future. One way to ensure that children can hope to have a life of dignity was believed to be education and to that effect the Right to Education Act was passed in 2009. Sarada Balagopalan begins her 2014 study on children, labour, and schooling with the remark that "India continues to have the dubious distinction of the world's highest number of working children" (2) and mentions the passing of the Right to Education Act (2009) as a signal by the Indian state that it is committed towards ensuring "each child receives quality schooling" (2). In the course of explaining the history of education policies in India, Balagopalan goes back to colonial education policies and remarks that "colonial schooling practices beginning from the mid-nineteenth century worked with a 'schizophrenic' agenda where efforts to expand schooling coexisted with a deliberate restraining of the aspirations of children who enrolled" (60). To attempt to understand the complexities underlying colonial policies on schooling Indian children, one needs to read Macaulay's Minutes of 1835. The underlying intention of the commission and its minutes are clear in Point 30 of the minutes, which reads: "It would be manifestly absurd to educate the rising generation with a view to a state of things which we mean to alter before they reach manhood" (11). It can be inferred that the members who wrote and ratified the Minutes had clearly stated hopes of bringing about cultural changes of the nature where knowledge of old cultural practices would become redundant by the time school boys grew up to become cultural influencers. The Indian

Educational Policy of 1913 records the measures taken by the British government in India to facilitate the spread of English-medium schools in India. This Policy begins with an excerpt of King George V's speech at Calcutta University on 6 January 1912, in which he wishes that there would be a network of schools and colleges across India and that the education imparted in these institutions would bring enlightenment into the homes of his Indian subjects. Although it would be difficult to find fault with someone who wishes and hopes for universal education, the policies the British government formulated to fulfil the King's wishes – based on Macaulay's minutes and reports from the 1813 charter to the 1913 Indian Education Policy – cleverly and carefully 'proved' that Indian children have to be taught British literature and culture for the formation of a good character. The 'civilising' mission of the British education policy in the late 19th and early 20th centuries worked with an explicit agenda of promoting British thought and culture through schools in India. However, as Sarada Balagopalan points out, the policies and curricula devised and propagated by the British in the early 20th century also retained some traditional inequities of Indian culture. She states that:

> colonial disciplinary projects like the industrial, half-time and factory schools ... helped institutionalize a parallel apparatus of schooling for children who were either already engaged in labour or were viewed within a future of manual work.... More significantly, the State managed to advance this agenda—of reproducing caste and class hierarchies through schooling—by deploying a language of liberal benevolence, which was their sympathetic identification with what they perceived as native adult 'preference' for children's continued immersion in labour.
>
> (61)

While Balagopalan was describing the skewed schooling received by native children who were being trained to aspire to British ideals as they continued to work and were expected to either become manual labourers or lower-level intellectual labour in the imperial government, Anglo-Indian orphans were also trained for specific kinds of work in the British government. This becomes evident in the training of Kim in Rudyard Kipling's eponymous novel of 1901.

Through this significant work Rudyard Kipling depicts a colonial childhood of a British boy in late 19th-century India. Though Kipling wrote *Kim* many years after leaving India and after a brief but significant stay in America, the protagonist resonates with Kipling's familiarity of India of his childhood and young adult days. Unlike the orphan Kim who grew up in the bazaars of Lahore, Kipling was born in Bombay (now Mumbai) and spent the first five years of his life in India as a much adored English child whose primary caregivers were Indian servants. Kipling and his younger sister were sent to England, to live with an English family that had advertised its willingness to take in boarders. Kipling calls the boarding house the House of Desolation in his posthumously published autobiography *Something of Myself* (1938). As mentioned by Sandra Kemp in *Kipling's Hidden Narratives* (1988), though his mother 'rescued' Rudyard from that house on receiving a letter from her sister, in which the latter mentioned Rudyard's troubles with his eyesight, Kipling's sister continued to live with that family for another three years. Kemp suggests that Mrs Holloway, the woman who ran the establishment and was called 'Aunty Rosa' by the two Kipling children could not have been "the cruel stepmother depicted in these imaginative children's tales" (52) if their mother chose to leave her younger child for three more years with her. However, Jose Harris, describing the fairly common practice of British families in colonial India of sending their children to England, notes in a footnote that Kipling's "account of the 'house of desolation' was no mere fictional extravaganza" (82) and that his findings from his research into the family of William Beveridge lead him to realise that "the experience of the young Beveridges, left for two years with English guardians while their parents were in India, closely resembled that of Kipling" (82). Moreover, the detrimental effect this decision had on the child is evident from the recurrence of the trauma of separation and feelings of being a misfit in many works of Kipling among which are 'Baa Baa Black Sheep' (1888), *The Light that Failed* (1890), 'The Potted Princess' (1893), *The Jungle Book* (1894), *The Second Jungle Book* (1895), *Kim* (1901), and finally stated clearly in his memoir *Something of Myself* (1938). While these stories helped Kipling in sublimating the affect of the early separation from his affectionate parents and in coming to terms with the loss of the adoration of the servants he experienced during his early childhood in India, *Kim* is the story of a British boy who never goes to England but grows up on the streets of India. Lynda Prescott states that Kipling had mentioned that one of his reasons for writing was "to tell the English something about the world outside England and *Kim* can be seen, among other things, as a vehicle for transmitting knowledge about India to the British and American reading public" (2000, 74). While that could have been one of Kipling's motives, it also seems like the 'day dream' of a boy who did not have to leave India to go to live in the House of Desolation. The term 'day dream' is being used here in the way Freud suggested in his essay 'Creative Writers and Day-Dreaming'. Other than Freud's frequent use of literary and cultural narratives to theorise on human behaviour, as has been mentioned at many points in this work, many literary works too seem to lend themselves to quite interesting psychoanalytic readings. Freud's 'Creative Writers and Day-dreaming' is one of the earliest essays that connects psychoanalysis to literature. Here, Freud draws an analogy between literature and daydreams. Freud gave his first theory on the structure of literature in this essay. He argues that literature satisfies unfulfilled or partially acceptable wishes. These wishes are disguised unconscious wishes. Therefore literature, like a dream, is full of symbols and psychoanalysis can decode the meaning of these symbols. Furthermore, Freud also speculated on the reasons behind aesthetic pleasure. According to Freud, the writer creates scope for the unabashed enjoyment of unacceptable fantasies of the readers by disguising them in the text. Meredith Skura says, "Freud virtually equated fantasy with text. He certainly equated fantasy with the crude daydream text, and he implied that the fantasy had similarly intimate connection with the more artful manifest story in a literary text" (59). Therefore, the writer, as well as the reader, derives pleasure from the text. Even if Kipling wrote to inform his British and American readers about 19th-century colonial India, the text itself narrated the life of a boy who had the freedom to travel the length and breadth of the Grand Trunk Road in India in a land which did not seem alien to him in the course of his training for his vocation. The vocation, though, was that of joining the Great Game of the British Empire in the Indian colony. Kipling's uncritical support of British imperialism, evident in many of his works, was criticised even by his contemporaries such as George Orwell. Later, many postcolonial Indian scholars put *Kim* under the postcolonial lens in path-breaking studies from the second half of the 20th century onwards. Ashis Nandy calls Kipling a "tormented, internally split writer" (261) and points out that Edmund Wilson remarked on the wasted potential of Kim's exposure to India in his "ultimately [deciding] to become a servitor of the Raj" (1995, 261). However, the depiction of the Irish orphan growing up on the Grand Trunk Road is worth examining as a work that falls under the rubric of the fiction of childhood emerging from colonial India.

Although the novel opens with the boy sitting astride a canon in the middle of a busy marketplace in Lahore, very soon the reader becomes aware of the underlying vulnerability of the orphan who is growing up as a 'bazaar-boy'. Kim's Irish father leaves him with the 'legacy' of an Irish name and his draft papers for an Irish regiment in India. The latter is rolled up into an amulet and worn around Kim's neck, while the orphaned boy is growing up on the streets of Lahore largely dependent on the kindness of the townspeople. He integrates so much into Indian life that the bazaar letter writer, with whom he is negotiating the price of a letter he is getting written for one of his many money-making mysterious jobs, remarks on his bargaining prowess and his illiteracy. The letter writer exclaims, "Once more, what manner of white boy art thou?" (103) indicating that white boys were not expected to be unlettered and in frequent need of the services of a letter writer. Kim learns varied skills through the many father-figures in his life among whom are an English curator of a museum in Lahore,[1] an Arab horse trader, an Anglicised Bengali spy working for the British Empire, an Anglo-Indian detective also working for the British imperial services, the colonel of his father's Irish regiment, and the Catholic priest of the regiment. In addition to all these people, Kim chooses to become the chela of a lama who is looking for a river in the land of the Buddha. All these father-figures contribute in many direct or indirect ways to pull Kim out of his Huckleberry Finn like attempts of escaping the 'sivilizing' ways of adults and push him into becoming a cog in the Great Game of the British Empire in India. Prescott mentions in her criticism of the "thriller element" (72) in *Kim* that:

> The phrase [the Great Game] was not Kipling's invention: it was coined by a cavalry officer named Arthur Conolly in the mid-nineteenth century in relation to Anglo-Russian conflicts in Asia, and is generally thought to allude to chess-like diplomatic manoeuvres (a compliment to Russian prowess at this game); however, since Conolly had been a schoolboy at Rugby in the 1820s, when the new version of football evolved, he might have had a much more physical game in mind. Certainly, Kipling's treatment of the Great Game as sport evokes images of India as a playing-field rather than a chessboard.
>
> (72)

Prescott goes on to mention that "the border-disputes involving Russia, India and Afghanistan were settled by the mid-1890s" (72) and that its centrality in the plot serves as "a means of displacing Indian politics as an issue in the novel" (72). While it is true that Kim travels across the then breadth of the Indian subcontinent on the Grand Trunk Road in the 1890s without any serious discussion of British colonisation of the subcontinent or Indian resistance to it, it cannot be overlooked that Kim is a boy who is being toyed with through the narrative to eventually integrate him into the British imperial services. This Irish orphan boy is appropriated by his dead father's regiment; sent to a boarding school where he feels like a misfit; and is eventually pulled into espionage. Throughout this process, Kim does not realise that he is being groomed to join forces with the oppressors of people he considered as his own – the Indians among whom he grew up and learned to identify with. Throughout the narrative, the boy is depicted as one who believes that life is a series of interesting adventures but he is getting pulled into various colonial manoeuvres at great risk to his life without his knowledge. Kim becomes a unique illustration of the possible life of a British orphan in colonial India.

Along with *Kim*, Rudyard Kipling's large body of work also depicts childhood in India in many of his short stories and some of his novels. It can be argued that Kipling's sharp gaze at India was mostly through the lens of childhood (Mudiganti, 2021). However, a more contemporary representation of the British orphan growing up in the early years of postcolonial India can be seen in the many autobiographical works of Ruskin Bond. Beginning with *The Room on the Roof* (1955) when he was a young adult of 21 and culminating in *A Song of India* (2020) written as an 85-year-old man, Bond presents a more nuanced view of India. Unlike Kipling who struggled with "[s]eparate sides" (133) to his head, Bond's autobiographical works reveal a struggle to be identified as an Indian belonging to India.

While Ruskin Bond's autobiographical works depict the travails of a boy of English parentage growing up as an Indian in postcolonial India, R. K. Narayan captured the experience of Indian middle-class boyhood in a small town in colonised India in *Swami and Friends* (1935). Although Swaminathan's father is an advocate practising in the courts governed by British laws in a small town in South India and chooses to send his son to an English-medium school run by British missionaries, there are many instances in the narrative when the 10-year-old boy puts up a spirited resistance to the domineering ways of the coloniser. He challenges his Scripture teacher's interpretation of the Gita and finds himself in trouble at school due to his father's terse letter to the headmaster of the school, in which the father protests against the covert proselytising attempted by the teacher. Furthermore, he gets sucked into the nationalist struggle when he attends a political rally with his friend. He gets almost beaten by the police and nearly loses his cherished friendship with the son of the Deputy Superintendent of Police. He, then, goes on to rebel in such a way against the violent corporal punishment meted out at his missionary school for his 'political' actions that his father had to take him out of the school. Swaminathan is sent to the only other school in the town although it is believed to offer a markedly lower standard of education. Narayan's seemingly simply tales of boyhood in the 1930s in India are also revelatory of the Indian intellectual's and writer's response to colonialism and its effects on Indian childhood. Although it is not an outright protest against colonial education methods, Swaminathan's father puts up a spirited, albeit Anglicised, response to British ways and tacitly encourages the boy's resistance to colonisation. However, the culture of the British enters into their lives through recreations such as cricket and tennis that seeped into Indian cultural consciousness to become the cherished pastime of school boys even in very small towns across India. The resonances of British ideals of appropriate behaviour for school boys are also seen in the expectations of actions and choices made by Swaminathan and his friends among themselves just as much as it is expected by the school authorities. Their families, though, seem to amalgamate Indian ways with the British education process they chose for their boys. The boys, therefore, are products of two kinds of cultural systems. Although they would not be expected to grow up into ideals of British masculinity, as would have been the expectation of boys in British public schools of that period, the school curriculum set by the British school board was most likely to create Anglicised Indian boys. The influence of British social systems is seen even in the organising of the household space, for Swaminathan and his father share a study room, which was fit into a traditionally built Indian household. However, the lives of the women in their household and the brief glimpses of the other women in Malgudi show that women in upper-class, upper-caste households too were firmly rooted in traditional Indian ways. Although Indian girls from diverse sections of Indian society were also getting exposed to British education as early as the second half of the 19th century, thereby learning about British ideals of femininity, the resonances of girl-hoods geared towards emulating a British ideal can be felt in Indian English fiction written only in the second half of the 20th century. Sunita Peacock argues that despite the introduction of Christian education in the mission-ary schools started in the 1850s in Bengal, educated Bengali women were expected to behave like a 'Bhardramahila' and that she could not behave like a "memsahib". Peacock elaborates this in the following manner:

> A 'memsahib' was an Englishwoman who of course followed a western style of living, eating, drinking and smoking and keeping company of men. An educated Indian/ Bengali woman could not do these things because by doing so she would not only lose her identity but the identity of her country. The women of India were the holders of their country's culture.
>
> (3)

Ruby Lal's work on the books written in Urdu, Hindi, and Hindustanti specifically to train girls into good conduct shows that the Indian girl was trained in ways that amalgamated the traditional values inculcated by older women within families with new skills and knowledge expected of the mod-ern educated girl in the late 19th and early 20th centuries. Lal uses the phrase "girl-child/woman" (2013, 46) to mention the Indian woman, high-lighting the lack of clear categorisations of life stages and specific training based on different life stages. Additionally, she also explains the need to create this composite label in the following way:

> One needs also to underline the diachrony implicit in the figure of the girl-child/woman. Since education and improvement were hailed as the signs of the time, and these had built into them the possibility, indeed the inescapability, of change, growth and maturity (improve-ment), the girl-child/woman could not just be the self-same, con-stant compound person. Such a figure was always liable to overflow the boundaries of the construction of girl-child, woman, or both.
>
> (46)

Lal's formulation and elaboration reiterate that girlhood as a distinct cate-gory from womanhood was not clearly noticeable in the literature written with a targeted readership among the female sex in the late 19th and early

20th centuries in India. In their two-volume anthology, *Women Writing in India* (1991), Susie Tharu and K. Lalita have collected little-known works by women in India from the 6th century BC to the present day – written in quite a few Indian languages – and have given a rather comprehensive history of the formation of the image of the Ideal Indian Woman but have neither made specific mentions of the period of women's lives that would be recognised as girlhood in our contemporary society nor have they traced its historical perceptions in Indian society. This lacuna cannot be held against their unique and landmark work but it can be read as revelatory of the oversight of girlhood as a phenomenon by itself, in Indian society.

A brief consideration of the depictions of girlhood in English literature written in the 20th century by Indians leads to the realisation that the reification of the girl into a type – either the 'good' angel in the house or the 'bad' hoyden – led to insensitivity towards her in the cultural context of 20th-century India. The insensitivity towards the rights to selfhood of a girl coupled with some traditional practices can be seen as catalysts to grave societal violence like female foeticide, female infanticide, and dowry death. Sudhir Kakar mentions that women's folksongs in India reveal the "painful awareness of inferiority" (1981, 58) apparent in "the celebration of sons and the mere tolerance of daughters" (58). Based on his clinical work with urban Indian women across class, caste, and religious barriers who sought treatment for mental health issues, Kakar posits that:

> girls and women in a dramatically patriarchal society will turn the aggression against themselves and transform the cultural devaluation into feelings of worthlessness and inferiority. There is scattered evidence that such a propensity indeed exists among many communities of Indian women, that hostility towards men and potential aggression against male infants are often turned inward, subsumed in a diffuse hostility against oneself, in a conversion of outrage into self-deprecation. At least among the upper middle class women who today seek psychotherapy, the buried feeling, "I am a girl and thus worthless and 'bad'", is often encountered below the surface of an active, emancipated femininity.
>
> (59)

Although the official statistics on the welfare of girls and women in India are quite dismal, the spate of literature in English by women in the late 20th century gives some cause for optimism, for it voices the lives of historically marginalised people such as women and children who were largely confined to the private sphere of the domestic space. Owing to the work of Indian feminist scholars in the last two decades of the 20th century, there is now a substantial body of work depicting girlhood in India, both pre-independence and post-independence, within access of the academic and non-academic reader.

The earliest post-independence Indian English novel that depicted girlhood at some length is Kamala Markandaya's *Nectar in a Sieve* published in 1955. This novel has a rural setting and describes the turmoil of landless peasants in South India. The lives led by Rukumani, the narrator and her daughter, Irawaddy are quite unlike the ones led by women and girls in urban India in the same period. Attia Hosain's *Sunlight on a Broken Column* (1961) describes the childhood and adolescence of Laila, a girl from a progressive and westernised Muslim zamindari family in the early 1950s. Muriel Wasi's *Too High for Rivalry* (1967) is set in an English-medium school for girls in the early 1960s and deals quite a bit with the then contemporary practices of girls' education and the discussions on the appropriate curriculum for upper-class Indian girls. *Fire on the Mountain* (1977), by Anita Desai is the story of Nanda Kaul, a reclusive old lady, who is forced to disrupt her life of much-awaited solitude to accommodate her great-granddaughter Raka. Nanda Kaul had spent a life of self-effacement as a daughter, wife, mother, and grandmother and wished to be 'discharged' of her duties in her old age. Rama Mehta's *Inside the Haveli* (1977) deals with the cloistered lives of the women of the erstwhile rulers of a small principality in postcolonial newly demo-cratic India. Shashi Deshpande's *The Dark Holds No Terrors* (1980) is the story of a doctor who comes back to her father's house, in order to escape her husband, although her return revokes bitter memories of the gender-based discrimination she had faced as a child in her urban middle-class household. Bapsi Sidhwa's *Ice-Candy Man* (1988) is narrated by Lenny Sethi who recalls her childhood in Lahore and her bewilderment at the changes taking place among the people around her during the incredibly violent partition of the country into two independent nations. Although Sidhwa is a Pakistani writer, this work has been considered because it depicts a very important part of Indian history and gives the point of view of a child from a community (the Parsi community) that was not directly involved in the bloodshed that fol-lowed the decision of dividing the country along communal lines into India and Pakistan. Manorama Mathai's *Mulligatawny Soup* (1993) is a narration by an English teenaged girl of the girlhood in the India of the late 1940s of her middle-aged neighbour Elsie Nora Ronby, who is an Anglo-Indian immi-grant to England. Arundhati Roy's *The God of Small Things* (1997) is set in a small town in Kerala but the narrator Rahel belongs to a highly western-ised, Syrian Christian, upper-middle-class family. In Manju Kapur's *Difficult Daughters* (1998) the narrator is trying to trace the girlhood experiences of her mother, in rural Punjab of the early 1940s, so that she could come to terms with her uneasy relationship with her mother and the void she feels on her death. Anjana Appachana's *Listening Now* (1998) is set in the emerging metropolis of Delhi of the 1950s and depicts the lives of the women and girls of the educated and salaried middle classes in newly independent India.

Although all these novels are unique in their own ways, one common element can be traced through all of them. Covertly or overtly, they all deal with the 'growing up' experiences of a girl; each girl is trying to assert herself and find a space of her own, with various degrees of success in the face of different levels of 'civilising' attempts. Rukumani wants the best of everything for her daughter Irawaddy in *Nectar in a Seive* (1955) and therefore tries to prevent her from doing anything she considers risky. Laila in *Sunlight on a Broken Column* (1961) and Geeta in *Inside the Haveli* (1977) are gently groomed by the family members and the servants in the household to demurely accept their 'roles' in their large patriarchal households. Lenny Sethi in *Ice-Candy Man* (1988) is exasperated that she is perpetually expected to perform the 'good' girl, whereas she would like some freedom to explore the world around her and learn to process the complex emotions the older people around her exude. Raka in *Fire on the Mountain* (1977) finds her stay at her great-grandmother's place very comfortable as she is largely left alone by the retiring old lady while her parents had been unsuccessfully forcing her to attend social gatherings to make her behave like the children of their friends. Raka stands out among all the girls listed here in being firmly indifferent to all civilising mores and can be read as Desai's depiction of the young Indian girl who could violently resist the trajectory of life set through decades of colonial ideas of the ideal Indian girlhood. Sarita in *The Dark Holds No Terrors* (1980) never gets over the trauma of being blamed for the death of her younger brother in a freak accident while they were playing together but walks out of her sexually violent marriage and finds emotional sustenance in her career as a doctor. Elsie Nora in *Mulligatawny Soup* (1993) is an Anglo-Indian girl who is made to believe by her family that she is superior to her classmates as she is a descendant of the 'rulers', i.e., the British and that Britain is 'Home', but when she reaches Britain as an adult she is a misfit there. Rahel in *The God of Small Things* (1997) craves to be accepted by Ammu despite all her 'faults'. Ira in *Difficult Daughters* (1998) tries to find out why she was a 'difficult daughter' for her parents and realises that her mother too was a 'difficult daughter' to her parents as the expectations of the parents from their children almost never matches the children's desires for themselves. Malavika does not need to struggle for such attention from the women in her life in *Listening Now* (1998). Malavika is growing up in a predominantly female world and gets much empathetic attention without having to seek it. Her quest, though, is for her father whom she has never met. She realises, quite poignantly, that the matriarchy she has been experiencing through her life protects her from the repercussions of the grave emotional hurt that her absentee father and his patriarchal family caused her mother. Each one of these novels written in the second half of the 20th century by Indian women depicts girlhood in

India and the unique ways in which the girls come to terms with stereotypical sociocultural expectations to carve a successful life for themselves.

Apart from fiction, Indian literature boasts quite a few autobiographies by women. In *Voices from Within: Early Personal Narratives of Bengali Women* (1991), Malavika Karlekar studies quite a few autobiographies of women written in late 19th-century Bengal. Most of these were written in Bengali but Karlekar also mentions a work written in English. One can locate translations of autobiographies and biographies of quite a few women of the pre-independence period. One such is the biography of the first Indian woman to get a medical degree. Written in Marathi by S. J. Joshi and translated into English in 1992 by Asha Damle, the biography is titled *Anandi Gopal* and is the story of Anandibai Joshi's marriage to Gopal Joshi who sent her to the United States of America in the late 19th century to study medicine. Other personal narrations of girlhood in the 1940s and 1950s, which could be located, are Urmila Haksar's *The Future That Was* (1972) and Whabiz Merchant's *Home on a Hill: A Bombay Girlhood* (1991). There are many new late 20th-century and 21st-century biographies, autobiographies, and life narratives of Indian women, written in English or other Indian languages, which depict girlhood memories of attempts to emulate an ideal image of girlhood. Some of these narratives also record training by older women to grow these girls up into the then contemporary ideals of Indian womanhood.

This substantial body of postcolonial Indian English novels of female *bildungsroman* and life narratives illuminate the contemporary sociocultural 'norms' of girlhood in Indian society. All the girls in these novels are struggling with the pressure of being 'good' girls. The 'virtues' expected in them are more or less similar to the ones expected among the 'good' girls in the fiction written during the Victorian and early-Edwardian times in England, with minor variations, such as in the training and practice of cultural traditions followed by their families. India's experience as a colony of Britain for nearly 100 years has thus had a significant impact on some sociocultural aspects in India. With the passing of Macaulay's Minutes on Education in February 1835, there was governmental support to schools that used English as the medium of instruction in India. By the late 19th and early 20th centuries, the English-educated classes in India read English literature as part of their studies as well as for leisure. The dominant ideas of that period penetrated into the cultural consciousness of India largely through this class of people and the educational policies passed by the British for India. Indians who went to England to study or work were influenced by the dominant ideas of English society in that period and in turn brought about changes in their families. The influence of English ideas on Indian men penetrated into Indian families and eventually affected the 'norms' of childhood in India. In 'Relating Histories: Definitions of Literacy, Literature, Gender in Early Nineteenth Century Calcutta and England' Kumkum Sangari delineates the creation of the Modern Indian

Woman in India before Independence. Sangari posits that the "reforming colonial ventures" (1991, 40) crucially contributed to the formation of the Modern Indian Woman. Sangari argues that this image was created to simplify the heterogeneity of traditional womanhood in India into a stereotype that can easily be subjugated eventually. This Modern Indian Woman was created to emulate the asexual, home-based, 'helpmeet' of the late Victorian man, i.e., a later version of The Perfect Lady. Since childhood was mostly considered a formative period, girls were supposed to hone themselves to eventually grow up into the ideal woman – the Modern Indian Woman. The 'virtues' encouraged in girls were similar to those encouraged in young Victorian girls. Therefore, Irawaddy, Laila, Geeta, Lenny, Raka, Sarita, Elsie Nora, Ira, and Rahel have to struggle to be 'Angels in the House' much against their inclination to do so. The fictional genealogy of the postcolonial girl reveals that the colonial experience left a significant impact in the formation of 'norms' of childhood in 20th-century India. These fictional accounts of girlhood in India record reverberations of India's colonial encounter even in the 1990s, showing the traces of the cultural impact of colonialism even in contemporary India.

While these girls struggle against reification, Mila in Salman Rushdie's *fin-de-siècle*, *Fury* (2001), deliberately fashions herself in the image of a doll called Little Brain created by a scientist called Malik Solanka and popularised by an English TV show. In this complex novel, Rushdie weaves in history, psychoanalytic references, incest, and existential issues. Solanka migrates from India to England, teaches English in one of the best colleges in England, learns from his first wife's PhD thesis that women were reified in Shakespeare's plays, makes dolls as a hobby, and then has a sexual relationship with Mila who has not only modelled herself to be like the most famous of his dolls but has also had a sexual relationship with her father till he died. Mila dresses and behaves like the animated and televised version of Solanka's doll, Little Brain, and also confronts a disturbed Solanka with "Professor, you're the one who's sick. I'm telling you again. What we did wasn't wrong. It was play. Serious play, dangerous play, maybe, but play" (173). Solanka had already justified his actions, which he knew to be inappropriate, after a minimal foray into ethics. The narrator records:

> At first he told himself it would be wrong to do this to Mila, to dollify her thus, but then—he argued back against himself—had she not done it to herself, had she not by her own admission made early-period Little Brain her model and inspiration? Was she not quite plainly presenting herself to him in the role of the True One he had lost?
>
> (124)

Mila also consoles herself and Solanka with: "Everybody needs a doll to play with" (131). Although Mila accepts that she is being used after having been reified, she refuses to be considered a victim. Moreover, she manages to create a rather forceful, self-reflexive personality for herself through this reification.

Rushdie's novel makes clear and multiple statements that the reification of a girl into a 'doll' can lead to the use of the girl as an object of sexual pleasure. Unlike Mila in Rushdie's novel, the protagonist of Kamala Das's "A Doll for the Child-Prostitute" (1977) does not have the scope to reflect on the abuse she suffered. In this story, a 12-year-old girl, who is sold to a brothel-keeper by her poverty-ridden mother, asks her client – a middle-aged policeman – for a doll after her only playmate in the brothel dies. Her friend had died due to a shoddily performed abortion executed in-house by an ill-equipped midwife. After gifting the doll, the girl's client continues to visit her and regularly pays the brothel-keeper but abstains from sexual relations with the girl. The girl's childhood is seemingly 'recovered' by the gift of the doll by her client. The implications of the gift as well as the sudden change in the relationship of the girl and her client due to the gift of the doll reiterate that the toy is a significant prop in sustaining the 'myth' of the innocence of childhood. However, examining the story in the light of Freud's theories on infantile sexuality and female sexuality bring out the darker aspects of the story. The indulgent gift of a doll by her much older client seems like an attempt within the narrative to recover the lost 'innocence' of the child prostitute, especially because the policeman is seemingly protecting the girl from other clients by continuing to be her benefactor. While the girl is probably temporarily safe from other immediate threats of sexual abuse, her abuser turning into her protector after indulging her wish to be infantilised does not leave much scope for her to cognitively process the abuse she had already experienced. Her client's support of the girl's regression to a pre-sexualised state she is experiencing due to the trauma of her friend's death is a well-meaning but potentially harmful gesture. This kindness from her abuser might normalise his abusive behaviour for the girl and exonerate him of the guilt of sexual abuse of a child. While he might believe that he has expiated for his actions, the girl might learn to accept abusive behaviour by this adult as normal and acceptable. Moreover, as argued by Freud in 'Note on the "Magic Notepad"' (1925), the traces of the traumatic experience, although seemingly invisible, would remain in the consciousness. The gift of a doll and abstinence by her benefactor could temporarily assuage the girl's emotional pain but the abuse suffered by her will have left lasting traces on her consciousness. An encouragement into regression is hardly likely to help her process her experiences for her to overcome her trauma.

An older American novel that addresses the serious repercussions of facing sexual abuse in childhood is Toni Morrison's *The Bluest Eye* (1970). In this much-examined novel, Pecola Breedlove slowly sinks into insanity after her father rapes her, while the narrator, Claudia, a playmate of Pecola, develops an intense hatred towards blue-eyed, blond dolls and expresses a desire to physically harm girls with blue eyes and blonde hair. Claudia's dislike for White girls stems from her observation that they receive deferential treatment from the adults around her, whereas she and her friends face abuse from those very adults. While Morrison's novel foregrounds the differential treatment faced by girls from Black or White racial origins even in 20th-century America, it also deals with one of the gravest consequences, across cultures and epochs, of this idealisation of children leading to the reification of the child into an asexual creature. The novel shows that the conflation of the child with a doll, which was meant to be a representation of a love object, may lead to the abuse of children by adults for sexual pleasure. Although there were some path-breaking studies on child sexual abuse in the last few decades of the 20th century in Britain and the United States of America, Pinki Virani's *Bitter Chocolate* (2000) stands out as one of the earliest studies of child sexual abuse in India. Virani records the narratives of survivors of child sexual abuse and highlights the vulnerability of a child who is a victim or a survivor of sexual abuse in India. However, most of these narratives are either narrated by an adult survivor or are fictional accounts written by adults.

Among the many issues that constrain the study of childhood is the lack of material that can generate readings of childhood from a child's perspective. Due to inevitable reasons, in many genres of literature, the child is almost always constructed by someone who is not a child. The writer of the fiction of childhood is almost always an adult, at least biologically and legally. This quite often leads to the study of childhood, at least at present, only through its representations by people who no longer experience it. However, there is some scope for a study of childhood through the writings of children, albeit very scarce, in these contemporary times of self-publishing on the Internet. Moreover, there has always been some creative writing by children that has reached a wider audience through sporadic instances of publication of juvenilia. Children do write compositions as part of school curricula, write fiction to amuse themselves and their playmates and sometimes maintain journals. The fiction written by the four Bronte children to create games for themselves is well-documented. The juvenilia written for internal circulation by a few members of the Dodgson family was resurrected by researchers of Lewis Carroll's life and works. Frances Hodgson Burnett also mentioned in her memoir that she used to make stories to amuse her schoolmates. *The Diary of a Young Girl* (1947) is a widely known translated and edited version of the journal of Anne Frank, a young Jewish girl, who wrote it while hiding from the Nazis during the German Holocaust in the mid-20th century. These accounts are still part of the 'pre-history' from the 19th and early 20th centuries of a detailed history of 'childhood by children'. In this context, Nandana Reddy's declaration: "[w]hat is needed is to enable children to write their own history and reshape society closer to their vision of a better world" (109) becomes extremely pertinent. Although this work could not study constructions of childhood by children, it has attempted to establish that childhood is a construction by depicting the creation and reiteration of the cultural stereotypes of childhood with the hope that childhood studies would bring in a greater acceptance of the complex pluralities of childhood.

Note

1 Jan Montefiore, among others, records that the curator of the Lahore museum was modeled on Kipling's father John Lockwood Kipling who actually worked for a while as the curator of the art museum in Lahore. This assignment of the senior Kipling coincided with Kipling's return to India to work as a journalist after completing his schooling in a school started expressly with the purpose of training boys to join the British imperial services.

BIBLIOGRAPHY

Alcott, Louisa May. *Little Women*. (1868). New York: Modern Promotions, 1982.
_____ . *Jo's Boys*. (1886). London: Penguin, 1994.
Altick, Richard D. "The Social Background". *Backgrounds to Victorian Literature*. San Francisco: Chandler Publishing Company, 1967.
Appachana, Anjana. *Listening Now*. New Delhi: India Ink, 1998.
Aries, Phillipe. *Centuries of Childhood: A Social History of Family Life*. Trans. Robert Baldick. New York: Vintage Books, Random House Inc., 1960.
Armstrong, Nancy. *Desire and Domestic Fiction*. Oxford: OUP, 1987.
Arnold, Arnold. *The World Book of Children's Games*. London: Macmillan, 1975.
Auerbach, Nina. "Magi and Maidens: The Romance of the Victorian Freud". *Critical Inquiry*. 8:2, Winter 1981, 281–300.
Avery, Gillian. *Behold The Child: American Children and Their Books 1621 - 1922*. Baltimore, Maryland: The Johns Hopkins UP, 1994.
Avery, Gillian and Julia Briggs, ed. *Children and their Books: A Celebration of the Work of Iona and Peter Opie*. Oxford: OUP, 1989.
Balagopalan, Sarada. *Inhabiting 'Childhood': Children, Labour and Schooling in Postcolonial India*. New Delhi: Palgrave Macmillan, 2014.
Barthes, Roland. "Toys". *Mythologies*. (1957). London: Jonathan Cape, 1972.
Barrie, J. M. *Peter Pan*. (1911). Mahwah, New Jersey: Watermill Press, 1987.
Baudry, Francis. "Literature and Psychoanalysis". *International Encyclopeida of Psychiatry, Psychology, Psychoanalysis and Neurology*. Ed. Benjamin B. Wolman. 6 vols. New York: Aesculapius Publishers, 1997.
Beales, Ross W. Jr. "In Search of the Historical Child: Miniature Adulthood and Youth in Colonial New England". Hiner and Harves, 8–24.
Beddoe, Deirdre. *Discovering Women's History: A Practical Manual*. (1983). London: Pandora Press, 1987.
Bernheimer, Charles and Claire Kahane, eds. *In Dora's Case: Freud – Hysteria – Feminism*. New York: Columbia U P, 1985.
Bell, Millicent. "Class, Sex, and the Victorian Governess: James's *The Turn of the Screw*". *New Essays on Daisy Miller and The Turn of the Screw*. Ed. Vivian R. Polak. Cambridge: CUP, 1993. 91–119.
Bellamy, Joan. "Barriers of Silence: Women in Victorian Fiction". *In Search of Victorian Values: Aspects of Nineteenth Century Thought and Society*. Ed. Eric M. Sigsworth. Manchester: Manchester U P, 1988.

Bettelheim, Bruno. *Uses Of Enchantment: The Meaning and Importance of Fairy Tales*. New York: Alfred A. Knopf, 1976.

Bharat, Meenakshi. *The Ultimate Colony: The Child in Postcolonial Fiction*. New Delhi: Allied Publishers, 2003.

Bond, Ruskin. *The Room on the Roof*. (1954). Gurgaon, Haryana: Penguin, 2014.

_____ . *A Song of India*. Gurgaon, Haryana: Penguin, 2020.

Boose, Lynda E. and Betty S. Flowers, eds. *Daughters and Fathers*. Baltimore, Maryland, USA: The Johns Hopkins U P, 1989.

Bowlby, Rachel. "Introduction." *Studies in Hysteria*. Eds. Sigmund Freud and Josef Breuer. London: Penguin, 2004. vii–xxxiii.

Branca, Patricia. *Silent Sisterhood: Middle-Class Women in the Victorian Home*. London: Croom Helm, 1975.

Bratton, J. S. *The Impact of Victorian Children's Fiction*. London: Croom Helm, 1981.

Brooks, Peter. "Towards Supreme Fictions". *Yale French Studies*. 43, 1969, 5–14.

Bronte, Charlotte. *Jane Eyre*. (1847). Madras: Macmillan India Limited, 1988.

Bronte, Emily. *Wuthering Heights*. (1847). New York: Tom Doherty Associates, 1988.

Browning, Elizabeth Barrett. *Aurora Leigh*. (1856). London: J. Miller, 1864.

Burnett, Frances Hodgson. *A Little Princess*. (1905). Middlesex: Puffin, 1984.

_____ . *Little Lord Fauntleroy*. New York: Charles Scribner & Sons, 1886.

_____ . *The One I Knew the Best of All*. London: Frederick Warne and Co, 1892.

_____ . *The Secret Garden*. (1911). Hertfordshire: Wordsworth Editions Ltd., 1993.

Butler, Samuel. *The Way of All Flesh*. (1903). London: Jonathan Cape, 1921.

Carpenter, Humphrey and Mari Prichard. *The Oxford Companion to Children's Literature*. (1984). Oxford: OUP, 1999.

Carpenter, Humphrey. *Secret Gardens: A Study of the Golden Age of Children's Literature*. London: Unwin Hyman, 1987.

Cargill, Oscar. "*The Turn of the Screw* and Alice James". Kimbrough. 145–159.

Carroll, Lewis. *Alice's Adventures in Wonderland*. (1865). Hertfordshire: Wordsworth Editions Ltd., 1993.

_____ . *Through the Looking Glass*. (1878). Hertfordshire: Wordsworth, 1993.

Cisneros, Sandra. *Barbie-Q*. Lorrie Moore. 73–74.

Coolidge, Susan. *What Katy Did*. (1872). Middlesex: Puffin, 1982.

_____ . *What Katy Did Next*. (1886). Middlesex: Puffin, 1983.

Chapman, Raymond. *Forms of Speech in Victorian Fiction*. London: Longman, 1994.

_____ . *The Victorian Debate*. London: Weiderfled & Nicolson, 1970.

Coveney, Peter. *Poor Monkey: The Child in Literature*. London: Rockliff, 1957.

Cruse, Amy. *The Victorians and their Books*. London: George Allen & Unwin, 1935.

Dalsimer, Katherine. *Female Adolescence: Psychoanalytic Reflections of Works of Literature*. New Haven: Yale UP, 1986.

Darton, Harvey F. J. *Children's Books in England*. (1932). 3rd ed. Cambridge: CUP, 1982.

Das, Kamala. "A Doll for the Child Prostitute". (1977). *Padmavati, The Harlot and Other Stories*. Bangalore: Sterling Publishers, 1992.

Davidson, Cathy N. and E. M. Broner. eds. *The Lost Tradition: Mothers and Daughters In Literature*. New York: Frederick Ungar Publishing Co., 1980.

de Beauvoir, Simone. *The Second Sex*. (1949). Ed. and Trans. H. M. Parshley. London: Vintage, 1997.

deMause, Lloyd. Ed. *The History of Childhood*. (1974). A Jason Aronson Book. Maryland: Rowman Littlefield, 2006.

Degler, Carl N. "What ought to Be and What was; Women's Sexuality in the Nineteenth Century". *The American Historical Review*. 79, 1974, 1467–1490.

Delamont, Sara and Lorna Duffin, eds. *The Nineteenth Century Woman: Her Cultural And Physical World*. London: Croom Helm, 1978.

Desai, Anita. *Fire on the Mountain*. (1977). Bombay, Allied Publishers, 1997.

Deshpande, Shashi. *The Dark Holds No Terrors*. (1980). New Delhi: Penguin, 1990.

Dexter, Catherine. *The Oracle Doll*. New York: Dell Publishing, 1985.

Dickens, Charles. *Bleak House*. (1853). Hertfordshire: Wordsworth Classics, 1993.

_____. *Dombey and Son*. (1848). Harmondsworth: Penguin, 1980.

_____. *Hard Times*. (1854). New Delhi: Rupa & Co., 1981.

_____. *David Copperfield*. (1850). Oxford: OUP, 1981.

_____. *Great Expectations*. (1861). New York: Airmont Publishing Company Inc., 1965.

_____. *Little Dorrit*. (1857). Hertfordshire: Wordsworth Editions, 1996.

Dyhouse, Carol. *Girls Growing Up in Late Victorian and Edwardian England*. London: Routledge & Kegan Paul, 1981.

Edel, Leon. "The Point of View". Kimbrough. 228–234.

Eliot, George. *Silas Marner*. (1861). Mahwah; New Jersey: Watermill Press, 1983.

_____. *The Mill on the Floss*. (1860). Hertfordshire: Wordsworth Editions, 1995.

Everett, Barbara. "Henry James's Children". Avery and Briggs. 317–335.

Erikson, H. Erik. *Toys and Reasons: Stages in the Ritualization of Experience*. New York: W. W. Norton & Company, 1977.

Felman, Shoshana. "Turning the Screw of Interpretation". Vice. 106–114.

Fiedler, Leslie A. *The Collected Works of Leslie Fiedler*. Vol. 1. New York: Stein and Day, 1971.

Firestone, Shulamith. *The Dialectic of Sex*. New York: Bantam Books, 1971.

Flint, Kate. *The Victorian Novelist: Social Problems and Social Change*. London: Croom Helm, 1987.

Foucault, Michel. *The History of Sexuality: Vol I: An Introduction*. Trans. Robert Hurley. New York: Vintage Books; Random House Inc., 1990.

Fowler, Virginia C. *Henry James' American Girl: The Embroidery on the Canvas*. Wisconsin: The U of Wisconsin P, 1984.

Fox, George et al, ed. *Writers, Critics and Children*. New York: Agathon Press, 1976.

Frank, Anne. *The Diary of a Young Girl*. (1947). Trans. B. M. Mooyaart-Doubleday, New York: Bantam, 1993.

Freiwald, Bina. "Of Selfsame Desire: Patmore's The Angel in the House". *Texas Studies in Literature and Language*. 30:4, Winter 1998, 538–561. JSTOR. http://www.jstor.org/stable/40754874.

Freud, Anna. *Introduction to Psychoanalysis: Lectures for Child Analysts and Teachers 1922–1935*. London: The Hogarth Press, 1974.

Freud, Sigmund. "'Civilzed' Sexual Morality and Modern Nervous Illness". (1905). *Civilization, Society, and Religion*. London: Penguin, 1991. 29–25.

_____. "Female Sexuality". *On Sexuality*. Vol. 7. London: Penguin, 1991. 369–392.

_____. "Femaleness". (1933). *Introductory Lectures on Psychoanalysis: New Series.* The New Penguin Freud Series. Trans. Helena Ragg-Kirkby. London: Penguin, 2003.

_____. *Five Lectures on Psychoanalysis, Leonardo da Vinci and Other Works.* (1910). The Standard Edition of the Complete Works of Sigmund Freud. Vol. 11. Trans. James Strachey. London: The Hogarth Press and the Institute of Psychoanalysis, 1957.

_____. "Formulations on the Two Principles of Mental Functioning". (1911). *On Metapsychology.* London: Penguin, 1991.

_____. "Fragment of an Analysis of a Case of Hysteria". (1905). *A Case of Hysteria. Three Essays on Sexuality and Other Works.* The Standard Edition of the Complete Works of Sigmund Freud. Vol. 7. Trans. James Strachey. London: Vintage, 2001.

_____. "Note on the 'Magic Notepad'". (1925). *The Penguin Freud Reader.* Ed. Adam Phillips. London: Penguin, 2006. 101–105.

_____. "On Narcissism: An Introduction". (1911). *On Metapsychology.* London: Penguin, 1991.

_____. *On Psychopathology: Inhibitions, Symptoms and Anxiety and Other Works.* Vol. 10. The Pelican Freud Library. London: Penguin, 1979.

_____. "Some Psychical Consequences of the Anatomical Distinction Between the Sexes". (1925). *On Sexuality.* Vol. 7. London: Penguin, 1991.

_____ and Josef Breuer. *Studies in Hysteria.* (1895). London: Penguin, 2004.

_____. *Three Essays on the Theory of Sexuality.* (1905). Trans & Ed. James Strachey. The Standard Edition of the Complete Works of Sigmund Freud. Vol. 7. London: Vintage, 2001. 125–243.

_____. *Two Short Accounts of Psychoanalysis: Five Lectures on Psycho-Analysis and the Question of Lay Analysis.* Trans & Ed. James Strachey. London: Penguin, 1991.

_____. "The Creative Writer and Daydreaming". *The Uncanny.* The New Penguin Freud Library. Ed. Adam Phillips. Trans. David McLintock. London: Penguin, 2003. 23 – 34.

_____. "The Uncanny". *The Uncanny.* The New Penguin Freud Library. Ed. Adam Phillips. Trans. David McLintock. London: Penguin, 2003. 121 – 162.

Fritzsch, Karlewald and Manfred Bachmann. *An Illustrated History of German Toys.* New York: Hastings House Publishers, 1978.

Frosh, Stephen. *The Politics of Psychoanalysis: An Introduction to Freudian and Post-Freudian Theory.* London: Macmillan, 1987.

Gard, Roger, ed. *Henry James: The Critical Heritage.* London: Routledge, 1968.

Garvey, Catherine. *Play.* Cambridge, Massachusetts: Harvard U P, 1977.

Gavin, Adrienne E. Intro and Ed. *The Child in British Literature: Literary Constructions of Childhood, Medieval to Contemporary.* Basingstoke, Hampshire: Palgrave Macmillan, 2012.

Gay, Peter. *Freud: A Life for Our Time.* New York: W. W. Norton & Company, 1988.

Gerzina, Gretchen Holbrook. *The Annotated Secret Garden.* Ed. Frances Hodgson Burnett. New York: W. W. Norton & Company, 2007.

Gibbs, Nancy. "The Real Magic of Harry Potter". *Time.* June 2003, 41–47.

Gilbert, Sandra and Susan Gubar, eds. *The Madwoman in the Attic: The Woman Writer and the Nineteenth Century Literary Imagination*. New Haven: Yale UP, 1979.

Goddard, Harold C. "A Pre-Freudian Reading of *The Turn of the Screw*". (1957). Kimbrough, 181–209.

Godden, Rumer. *An Episode of Sparrows*. London: The Reprint Society, 1956.

Gorham, Deborah. *The Victorian Girl and the Feminine Ideal*. Bloomington: Indiana UP, 1982.

Goswami, Supriya. *Colonial India in Children's Literature*. New York: Routledge, 2012.

Grahame, Kenneth. *The Golden Age*. (1895). Hertfordshire: Wordsworth, 1993.

Green, Roger Lancelyn. "The Golden Age of Children's Books". *Essays and Studies*. 1962. New Series, 1967, 59–73.

Grylls, David. *Guardians and Angels – Parents and Children in Nineteenth Century Literature*. London: Faber and Faber, 1978.

Haksar, Urmila. *The Future That Was*. Bombay: Allied Publishers, 1972.

Harris, Jose. *Private Lives and Public Spirit: A Social History of Britain 1870-1914*. Oxford: OUP, 1993.

Hawes, Joseph M. *The Children's Rights Movement: A History of Advocacy and Protection*. Woodbridge, US: Twayne Publishers Inc., 1991.

Higgins, James E. *Beyond Words: Mystical Fancy in Children's Literature*. New York: Teachers College Press, 1970.

Hiner, N. Ray and Joseph M. Harves, eds. *Growing Up in America: Children in Historical Perspective*. Chicago: University of Illinois Press, 1985.

Holt, John. *Escape from Childhood: The Needs and Rights of Children*. Harmondsworth: Penguin, 1975.

Hoban, Russell. *The Mouse and His Child*. London: Faber and Faber, 1969.

Hosain, Attia. *Sunlight on a Broken Column*. (1961). New Delhi: Penguin, 1990.

Houghton, Walter E. "Character of the Age". *Backgrounds to Victorian Literature*. Ed. Richard Levine. San Francisco: Chandler Publishing Company, 1967.

Housman, Lawrence. "Rocking-Horse Land". Naomi Lewis. 95–107.

Hughes, Richard. "Gertrude's Child". Naomi Lewis. 155–176.

Huizinga, J. *Homo Ludens: A Study of the Play-element in Culture*. Boston: Beacon Press, 1955.

Humphries, Jane. *Chidhood and Child Labour in the British Industrial Revolution*. Cambridge: Cambridge University Press, 2010.

Hunt, Peter. *Children's Literature: The Development of Criticism*. London: Routledge, 1990.

_____. *Criticism, Theory, and Children's Literature*. Oxford: Basil Blackwell, 1991.

_____. "Winnie-the-Pooh and Domestic Fantasy". *Stories and Society*. Ed. Dennis Butts. London: Macmillan, 1992.

James, Henry. *Daisy Miller*. (1878). London: Penguin Classics, 1986.

_____. "Preface". *The Novels and Tales of Henry James*. New York Edition. Vol 11. Fairfield, New Jersey: Augustus M. Kelley Publishers, 1979.

_____. *The Turn of the Screw*. (1898). London: Penguin, 1994.

_____. *What Maisie Knew*. (1897). London: Penguin, 1985.

_____. *Watch and Ward*. (1871). Gloucestershire: Sutton Publishing Ltd., 1997.

Jenks, Chris, ed. *The Sociology of Childhood*. London: Batsford Academic and Educational Ltd, 1982.

Joshi, S. J. *Anandi Gopal*. Trans. Asha Damle. Calcutta: Stree, 1992.

Kakar, Sudhir. *The Inner World: A Psychoanalytic Study of Childhood in India*. (1978). New Delhi: Oxford India Paperbacks, Oxford University Press, 1982.

Kapur, Manju. *Difficult Daughters*. New Delhi: Penguin, 1992.

Karlekar, Malavika. *Voices From Within: Early Personal Narratives of Bengali Women*. (1991). Delhi: Oxford University Press, 1993.

Kemp, Sandra and Lisa Lewis. *Kipling's Hidden Narratives*. Oxford: Basil Blackwell, 1988.

Kenton, Edna. "Henry James to the Ruminant Reader: The Turn of the Screw". Kimbrough. 209–211.

Kessen, William. *The Child*. New York: John Walay & Sons, 1965.

Kimbrough, Robert, ed. *Norton Critical Edition of The Turn of The Screw by Henry James*. New York: W. W. Norton & Company, 1966.

Kipling, Rudyard. "Baa Baa, Black Sheep". (1888) *Best Short Stories of Rudyard Kipling*. Ed. Jeffrey Meyers. New York: Signet; New American Library, 1987.

_____ . *Kim*. (1901). Ed. Harish Trivedi. London: Penguin, 2011.

_____ . *Something of Myself*. (1938). Intro. Jan Montefiore. Hertfordshire: Wordsworth Editions, 2008.

_____ . *The Jungle Book* (1894) and *The Second Jungle Book* (1895). Hertfordshire: Wordsworth Editions, 2007.

_____. *The Light that Failed*. (1890). Harmondsworth: Penguin, 1970.

_____ . "The Potted Princess" (1893). http://www.kiplingsociety.co.uk/potted.htm

Kilne, Daniel T. "'That child may doon to fadres reverence': Children and Childhood in Middle English Literature". Adrienne E. Gavin. 2012. 21–37.

Kuhn, Reinhard. *Corruption in Paradise: The Child in Western Literature*. Hanover: University Press of New England, 1982.

Kuznets, Lois R. *When Toys Come Alive*. New Haven: Yale University Press, 1994.

Lal, Ruby. *In Pursuit of Playfulness*. (2013) Delhi: Primus, 2019.

Landau, Elliot, Sherrie Landau Epstein and Ann Plaat Stone, eds. *Child Development Through Literature*. New Jersey: Prentice-Hall, Inc., 1972.

Lee, Harper. *To Kill a Mocking Bird*. (1960). London: Arrow, 1997.

Lewis, Jane. *Women in England: 1870 – 1950*. Sussex: Wheatsheaf Books, 1984.

Lewis, Noami. *The Silent Playmate: A Collection of Doll Stories*. London: Victor Gollanz Ltd, 1979.

Lodge, David. *Out of the Shelter*. (1970). Harmondsworth: Penguin, 1985.

Lurie, Alison. *Boys and Girls Forever: Reflections on Children's Classics*. London: Chatto & Windus, 2003.

Markandaya, Kamala. *Nectar in a Sieve*. Bombay: Jaico, 1955.

Marten, James. *The History of Childhood*. A Very Short Introduction Series. London: OUP, 2018.

Mathai, Manorama. *Mulligatawny Soup*. New Delhi: Penguin, 1993.

Meigs, Cornelia et al. *A Critical History of Children's Literature*. New York: The Macmillan Company, 1953.

Mehta, Rama. *Inside the Haveli*. (1977). New Delhi: Arnold-Heinman, 1997.

Merchant, W. D. *Home on a Hill: A Bombay Girlhood*. Washington D.C.: Three Continents Press, 1991.

Milne, A.A. *The House at Pooh Corner*. (1927). London: Methuen, 1968.

_____. *Now We are Six*. (1927). New York: Dell, 1970.

_____. *Winnie-the-Pooh*. (1926). London: Methuen, 1968.

Ministry of Human Resource Development. *India Report on the World Summit for Children*. New Delhi: Department of Women and Child Development, Ministry of Human Resource Development and UNICEF, 2000.

_____. *The Rights of the Child*. New Delhi: Department of Women and Child Development, Ministry of Human Resource Development and UNICEF, 1990.

_____, ed. *The Selected Melanie Klein*. London: Penguin, 1991.

Mollinger, Robert N. *Psychoanalysis and Literature: An Introduction*. Chicago: Nelson-Hall, 1981.

Moore, Lorrie, ed. *The Faber Book of Contemporary Stories about Childhood*. London: Faber and Faber, 1997.

Montgomery, L. M. *Anne of Green Gables*. Toronto: McGraw-Hill Ryerson, 1942.

Morrison, Toni. *The Bluest Eye*. (1970). London: Vintage, 1999.

Montefiore, Jan. *Rudyard Kipling*. Northcote: Tavistock, Devon, 2007.

Mudiganti, Usha. "Through the lens of Childhood: Kipling's Claim to India". *Kipling in India: India in Kipling*. Eds. Harish Trivedi and Jan Montefiore. Abindon: Routledge, 2021. 132–144.

Nandy, Ashis. "Reconstructing Childhood: A Critique of the Ideology of Adulthood". *Traditions, Tyranny and Utopias*. Delhi: OUP, 1992.

_____. *The Intimate Enemy: Loss and Recovery of Self under Colonialism*. (1983). 2nd Edition, Delhi: OUP, 2014.

_____. *The Savage Freud and other essays on possible and retrievable selves*. Delhi: OUP, 1995.

Narayan, R. K. *Swami and Friends*. (1935). Chennai: India Thought Publications, 2011.

Nelson, Claudia. *Family Ties in Victorian England*. Westport, Connecticut: Praeger, 2007.

Nesbit, E. *The Railway Children*. (1905). Hertfordshire: Wordsworth, 1993.

O' Connor, Frank. "My Oedipus Complex". (1953). *The Genius and Other Stories*. London: Penguin, 1995. 23–43.

Patmore, Coventry. *The Angel in the House*. (1858). London and Cambridge: Macmillan and Co, 1863.

Peacock, Sunita. "The Education of the Indian Woman against the Backdrop of the Education Woman in the Nineteenth Century". *Forum on Public Policy*, 2009, 1–9.

Phillips, Adam. *Winnicott*. Fontana Modern Masters, Series Editor: Frank Kermode. London: Fontana Press, 1988.

_____. "Introduction". *The Penguin Freud Reader*. London: Penguin, 2006. vii–xv.

Polakov, Valerie. *The Erosion of Childhood*. Chicago: The University of Chicago Press, 1992.

Poplawski, Paul. *English Literature in Context*. Delhi: Cambridge University Press, 2008.

Powling, Chris. "On the Permanence of Pooh". *The Best of Books for Keeps*. Ed. Chris Powling. London: The Bodley Head, 1994.

143

Prescott, Lynda. "The White Man's Burden: *Kim*". *Literature and Nation: Britain and India 1800–1990*. Eds. Richard Allen and Harish Trivedi. London: Routledge, 2000. 67–77.

Price, Danielle E. "Cultivating Mary: The Victorian *Secret Garden*". *Children's Literature Association Quarterly*. 26:1, Spring 2001, 4–14.

Reddy, Nandana. "Working with Children". *Seminar*. 545, January 2005, 104–109.

Reynolds, Kimberley. *Children's Literature: in the 1890s and the 1990s*. Plymouth: Northcote House Publishers, 1994.

Richards, Angela. Introduction and Editor. *On Sexuality*. Sigmund Freud. Penguin Freud Library. Vol. 7. London: Penguin, 1991.

Rodgers, Daniel T. "Socializing Middle-Class Children: Institutions, Fables, and Work Values in Nineteenth-Century America". Hiner and Harves. 119–132.

Rose, Jacqueline. *The Case of Peter Pan or the Impossibility of Children's Fiction*. London: Macmillan, 1984.

_____. "Feminine Sexuality: An Introduction". Vice. 130–135.

Roth, Michael S. *Psycho-Analysis as History: Negation and Freedom in Freud*. (1987). Delhi: OUP, 1997.

Rousseau, Jean-Jacques, "The Child in Nature". *The Child*. Ed. William Kessen New York: John Wiley & Sons Inc., 1965.

Rowling, J. K. *Harry Potter and the Order of the Phoenix*. London: Bloomsbury, 2003.

Roy, Arundhati. *The God of Small Things*. New Delhi: India Ink, 1997.

Rushdie, Salman. *Fury*. London: Jonathan Cape, 2001.

Sangari, Kumkum. "Relating histories: Definitions of Literacy, Literature, Gender in Early Nineteenth Century Calcutta and England". *Rethinking English*. Ed. Svati Joshi. New Delhi: Triank, 1991.

Sen, Satadru. *Colonial Childhoods: The Juvenile Periphery of India 1850 – 1945*. London: Anthem Press, 2005.

Shankar, Lara. *Midway Station: Real-Life Stories of Homeless Children*. New Delhi: Penguin Books, 2006.

Sharpe, Sue. *Just Like a Girl: How Girls Learn to be Women*. Harmondsworth: Penguin, 1976.

_____. *Just Like a Girl: How Girls Learn to be Women: From The Seventies to the Nineties*. London: Penguin, 1994.

Shattock, Joanne. *The Cambridge Companion to English Literature: 1830 – 1914*. Cambridge: CUP, 2010.

Shirwadkar, Meena. *Image of the Woman in the Indo-Anglian Novel*. New Delhi: Sterling Publishers, 1979.

Showalter, Elaine. "Family Secrets and Domestic Subversion: Rebellion in the Novels of the 1860s". *The Victorian Family: Structure and Stresses*. Ed. Anthony S. Wohl, London: Croom Helm, 1978.

Sidhwa, Bapsi. *Ice-Candy Man*. (1988). New Delhi: Penguin, 1989.

Sigsworth, Eric M. *In Search of Victorian Values: Aspects of Nineteenth Century Thought and Society*. Manchester: Manchester University Press, 1988.

Skura, Meredith Anne. *The Literary Use of the Psychoanalytic Process*. New Haven: Yale UP, 1981.

Slaughter, Martina. "Edmund Wilson and *The Turn of the Screw*. Kimbrough. 211–214.

Spacks, Patricia Meyer. *The Adolescent Idea: Myths of Youth and the Adult Imagination*. New York: Basic Books, Inc., 1981.

Spark, Muriel. *The Prime of Miss Jean Brodie*. (1961). Harmondsworth: Penguin, 1969.

Spilka, Mark. "Turning the Freudian Screw: How Not to Do It". Kimbrough, 245–251.

Solomon, Eric. "The Return of the Screw". Kimbrough. 237–245.

Stage, Sarah J. "Out of the Attic: Studies of Victorian Sexuality". *American Quarterly*. 27:4, Oct. 1975, 480–485.

Stein, Sara. *Girls and Boys: The Limits of Non-Sexist Childrearing*. London: Chatto & Windus, 1984.

Sutton-Smith, Brian. *Toys as Culture*. New York: Gardner Press Inc., 1986.

The Girl's Own Paper. Volume 1, January 1880, https://www.victorianvoices.net/magazines/GOP/GOP1880.shtml. Date of access: 06.06.2021.

Tharu, Susie and K. Lalita, eds. *Women Writing in India*. (1991). 1&2, Delhi: Oxford University Press, 2012.

Thorold, D. J. "Introduction". *Hard Times* (1854). Charles Dickens. Hertfordshire: Wordsworth Editions, 2000. ix–xxi.

Townsend, John Rowe. *Written for Children: An Outline of English Language Children's Literature*. (1965). 2nd Rev. ed. Harmondsworth: Penguin, 1983.

_____. *Written for Children: An Outline of English Language Children's Literature*. 5th ed. London: The Bodley Head Press, 1990.

Trites, Roberta Seelinger. "Psychoanalytic Approaches to Children's Literature: Landmarks, Signposts, Maps". *Children's Literature Association Quarterly*. 25:2, Summer 2000, 66–67.

Tucker, Nicholas. *The Child and the Books: A Psychological and Literary Exploration*. Cambridge: Cambridge University Press, 1981.

Twain, Mark. *The Adventures of Huckleberry Finn*. (1885). New York: Book Esentials Promotions, Inc. 1994.

Veblen, Thorstein. *The Theory of the Leisure Class*. (1899). New Brunswick: Transaction Publishers, 1992.

Viswanathan, Gauri. *Masks of Conquest: Literary Study of British Rule in India*. New York: Columbia University Press, 2015.

Vice, Sue. *Psychoanalytic Criticism: A Reader*. Cambridge: Ploty Press, 1996.

Vicinus, Martha. *Independent Women: Work and Community for Single Women 1825–1950*. Women in Culture and Society Series. Chicago: The University of Chicago Press, 1985.

Virani, Pinki. *Bitter Chocolate: Child Sexual Abuse in India*. New Delhi: Penguin, 2000.

Wallace, Jo-Ann. "De-scribing The Water-Babies: 'The child' in Post-colonial Theory". *De-Scribing Empire: Post-colonialism and Textuality*. Eds. Chris Tiffin and Alan Lawson. London: Routledge. 171–184.

Wasi, Muriel. *Too High for Rivlary*. Bombay: Kuttub Popular Press, 1967.

Waterson, Bill. *The Calvin and Hobbes Tenth Anniversary Book*. London: Warner, 1995.

Wilson, Edmund. "The Ambiguity of Henry James". Vice. 100–106.

Woolf, Virginia. *A Room of One's Own* (1929). London: The Hogarth Press, 1959.

_____. "Henry James's Ghosts". Kimbrough. 179–180.

_____. "Professions for Women". (1931). *Collected Essays*, Vol. 2. London: The Hogarth Press, 1972.

Young, Robert M. *Oedipus Complex*. Ideas in Psychoanalysis Series. Cambridge: Icon Books, 2001.

Zipes, Jack. *Don't Bet on the Prince: Contemporary Feminist Fairy Tales in North America and England*. (1986). New York: Routledge, 1989.

INDEX

Note: page numbers followed by n refer to notes.

INDEX

For Product Safety Concerns and Information please contact our EU
representative GPSR@taylorandfrancis.com
Taylor & Francis Verlag GmbH, Kaufingerstraße 24, 80331 München, Germany

www.ingramcontent.com/pod-product-compliance
Lightning Source LLC
Chambersburg PA
CBHW071121100726
47908CB00008B/2455

* 9 7 8 0 3 6 7 5 5 3 8 9 0 *